"West has an eerie way with words, an uncanny ability to conjure the perfect image. *Last Things* is at once poetic and urgent, evocative and authentic, everything I love in a book."
—Victoria Schwab,
author of the #1 *New York Times* bestseller *This Savage Song*

## WITHDRAWN

I take the path straight through the woods. The trees lean back as I pass. They whisper and hiss. They know what I am. They know what I know.

My own house isn't far away, on a mossy dead-end road deep in the oaks and pines. I'll pass Anders's house first. Take one more look. Make sure he's inside. Watch his windows. Wait until he shuts off the lights. Maybe.

Maybe I'll wait even longer than that. Maybe I'll watch all night.

# LAST THINGS

# JACQUELINE WEST

Greenwillow Books
*An Imprint of* HarperCollins*Publishers*

Last Things
Copyright © 2019 by Jacqueline West
First published in hardcover in 2019 by Greenwillow Books;
first paperback edition, 2020.

The text of this book is set in 12-point Granjon.
Book design by Paul Zakris

Library of Congress Cataloging-in-Publication Data

Names: West, Jacqueline, author.
Title: Last things / by Jacqueline West.
Description: First edition. | New York, NY : Greenwillow Books, an imprint of HarperCollinsPublishers, [2019] | Summary: "Anders Thorson, front man of his metal band, Last Things, is unusually gifted for a teenager, but strange things in the Minnesota woods near his hometown are threatening him. Thea, the new girl in town, says she's there to protect him, but is that the whole truth?"—Provided by publisher.
Identifiers: LCCN 2018045967 | ISBN 9780062875075 (pbk. ed.)
Subjects: | CYAC: Bands (Music)—Fiction. | Heavy metal (Music)—Fiction. | Supernatural—Fiction. | Demonology—Fiction.
Classification: LCC PZ7.W51776 Las 2019 | DDC [Fic]—dc23
LC record available at https://lccn.loc.gov/2018045967

20 21 22 23 24 PC/LSCH 10 9 8 7 6 5 4 3 2 1
First Edition

**GREENWILLOW BOOKS**

For Ryan

**I like the edges.**

Places where things end. Fade out. Disappear. Where two things eat away at each other until neither of them really exists anymore. Sharp edges. Frayed edges. Places that are more than one thing, or nothing. It's more comfortable at the edge. No one really pays attention to you if that's where you live, or stand, or eat your lunch.

Most people don't even notice that you're watching them.

On Friday nights I go to the Crow's Nest. Everyone goes to the Crow's Nest. All the kids from high school, all the bored twentysomethings, all the coffee drinkers and scruffy artists and metal fans within a fifty-mile radius. Last Things plays on Friday nights. There's not much else to do in Greenwood, even on a Friday night. And Last Things is special. They'd be special anywhere.

In a town like Greenwood, they're legendary.

The Crow's Nest Coffeehouse is out of town, down a twisty road that leads back to the river, if you're not in a hurry to get there. The woods lean in around it. They lean farther and farther. They drop acorns and send out reaching suckers. They'll get this spot back eventually. They'll take everything.

The Crow's Nest is an old farmhouse with the innards ripped out. The interior is just one huge room, with a stage at the back and a coffee bar at the front. The walls are so coated with stickers and posters and ragged-edged artwork that there's no telling what they're made of, or what color they used to be. Part of one outer wall has been replaced by a row of glass doors, so the room leads straight out onto a weathered porch, and from there to an overgrown patio full of mismatched tables and junkyard statues and climbing vines and chipped bathtub planters full of dirt and whatever kinds of flowers survive on a decade of tough love.

On nights when Last Things plays, the place is packed.

Guys in T-shirts and leather, girls in black. A blur of tattoos on exposed skin. Piercings. Heavy boots. Thick makeup. Clumps of soft-faced freshmen, out past their usual curfews, whispering about music. Every table taken. The floor in front of the stage already occupied by rows of the most hard-core fans.

Sometimes I take a table at the edge of the patio. There's one behind a potted juniper that has a clear view of the stage. If that spot's taken, I pick a seat in back, at the very end of the coffee bar, where Ike and Janos are busy at the espresso grinder or drizzling sickly caramel syrup into the lattes the other girls order.

I order café au lait. Not sweet, but not bitter. Just on the edge.

And it's cheap.

Last fall, after I'd ordered café au lait for three weeks in a row, Janos started charging me for a regular coffee, which makes it even cheaper. Sometimes he hands the cup over with a friendly wink.

I come alone. I'm no trouble.

Not to him.

Then I take my spot, on the edge of the patio or at the end of the coffee bar, and I watch the half-ready stage, and I watch the crowd waiting, talking, shoving, texting, posting photos of their eyeliner or their perfect pouting lips, and I sip my coffee.

And, of course, I watch the woods. They're always closer than you think.

Someone lets out a whoop. Patrick, the drummer, and Jezz, the bassist, have stepped unobtrusively onto the stage. Jezz is lanky, with long sun-blond hair; Patrick has a buzz cut and burly shoulders and arms. Jezz looks like a surfer who got lost here in northern Minnesota. Patrick looks like he could rip a car apart with his bare hands and then put it correctly back together again.

They arrange mic stands, check amps. It takes ages. They're particular.

It's actually Anders who's particular. But he doesn't help with the setup. He doesn't appear until the very end. Because the moment he steps onto the stage, everything changes. The taste of the coffee. The lights. The air. It's an energy that can't be sustained, not while the band futzes around with plugs and strings and cords. It starts to feel dangerous. The simmer before an overflowing boil.

So Anders waits until everything is set.

Then he steps through a back door onto the little stage, holding his black electric guitar—I've heard he calls it "Yvonne"—and there's a shift in the air. People scream, as though half of them haven't sat across the aisle from him in math class.

And they haven't, really. Classroom Anders blends in.

He's medium height, with choppy brown hair and the kind of features you only start to notice the second or third time you look: well-shaped face, nice edges, sleepy-lidded eyes. You could pass him in a crowded school hallway and not look up.

But seeing him on stage is different. You wonder how you didn't see it all along. You wonder how you ever looked at anything else.

He seems taller, looming over the packed room. His face is harder. His hands, sliding into place on the black guitar, are long-fingered and rough. But the way they move isn't.

There's a beat. A blast of feedback.

The first song starts.

It's "Dead Girl." I recognize it immediately. I know all the songs by heart. Even the new ones, the ones they've only played in public once or twice. The ones they've never played in public at all.

Patrick hunches behind the drums, his arms a muscular blur. Jezz leans back like the bass in his hands is a counterweight.

And Anders. At the front of the stage. At the microphone. The black guitar in his hands. Anders.

Anders.

*My hands are always cold*
*she says, she says*
*I forgot my coat*
*she says, she says*

*Would you walk me home*
*Walk me home and I'll be warm*

I'm not the only one who knows all the words. Half
the crowd is screaming along.

*Just a little more*
*she says, she says*
*It's lonely underground*
*she says, she says*

*But we always leave the door—*
*We always leave the door open*

By the second song there's a pit forming in front of the
stage. Bodies are jumping, writhing, smashing into one
another. The music gets faster. Harder. The floor trembles.
Energy crashes off the raggedy walls. It shoves back at
the woods. It pushes out the emptiness.

I stay at the edge, sipping my coffee. But the music has gotten into my blood, too. My heart thumps in rhythm.

Finally, when the energy can't rise any higher, everything stops.

There's a hush. That floating feeling, after the ground disappears beneath you but before the fall.

Anders plans all of this. The order and number of songs, the moment when the hunger will peak. The pause.

He trades Yvonne for the acoustic guitar.

The roaring, thrashing crowd goes still. Patrick rubs a thick forearm over his face and rests his sticks in his lap. Takes a long drink of water. Jezz backs toward the wall, where the shadows erase him.

The song starts with a few instrumental lines. A melody moves up and down the lower strings.

The room has been sealed in glass. No one moves, or everything will shatter.

Anders starts to sing.

For most songs, he uses a growl, a mix of low tones and monster rasp. But this is his real voice. It's smooth and warm and softer than you'd expect.

The song is called "Deep Water."

I've heard it four times, because that's how many times he's played it. I'm at every show. At the edge. Keeping watch.

*Nothing you can do*
*She's got secrets, depths where you can't go*
*She's been here before*
*One day she'll carry you away*

Everyone keeps still. No whispers. No click of cups on tabletops.

The woods are listening, too. A soft, cold wind, a wind that has passed through the palms of ten thousand rustling leaves, moves across my ear like a breath. The woods are getting hungry. But they'll wait. For now.

The song holds us all. Metalheads. High school cliques. The things that wait in the woods.

Anders's fingers move over the strings. Slowly and softly enough that the strangeness is hidden now, wrapped up in the perfection of the song like one knot in a silver tapestry, one tiny bug in a dewy spiderweb. Most people are too caught up in the music to notice. But if you watch as closely as I watch, you see.

A final note soars and soars, holding everything still, until Anders silences it with the press of his fingers.

The end.

Before anyone can applaud, scream, clap, anything, Patrick and Jezz jump into the next song. It's

"Breakdown." Driving and hard and deafening. The audience, set free, loses its mind.

I finally pull my eyes from the stage.

It doesn't take long to find Frankie in the crowd.

It's only because Anders is onstage that everyone in the room isn't staring at her. Frankie has a force like gravity. Wherever she stands becomes the center of everything else. Elements arrange themselves around her. She's the opposite of everything I am.

Frankie has dark brown hair and full lips. She doesn't wear makeup. She looks like the heroine of a romantic French movie. I watch her watch Anders, which she only does part of the time. Now she's whispering to a friend. Getting another drink. Doodling something on a napkin, which she passes to someone else. Not what you would expect from the lead singer's girlfriend. Or maybe you would.

The band plays three more songs. The air in the room gets thicker. The woods creep closer. The sky is blackening like something scorched.

They end with "Superhero." Everybody—everybody—knows the words to this one.

*They came down from another world*
*bigger than ours, stronger than ours*

*Beautiful strangers*
*under a sun where there's nothing new at all*

*Look around at the mess we've made*
*bigger than us, better than us*
*Opportunities we waste*
*in a place that starts to seem too small*

*We need a caped crusader*
*We need a savior*

*It comes down to this*
*Red leather gloves and a long black list*
*We know we asked for this*
*X-ray vision and an iron fist*

*Someone to rescue us*
*bigger than us, smarter than us*
*Decide and think for us*
*when all we build is doomed to fall*

*Someone who'll protect us*
*bigger than us, stronger than us*

*Close and lock the doors on us*
*keep us safe behind the walls*

*Now bow down*
*I said GET DOWN*

*It comes down to this*
*Red leather gloves and a long black list*
*You know we asked for this*
*X-ray vision and an iron fist*

Anders breaks into a guitar solo.

Watching the show, no one would have thought he was holding back. But it's suddenly clear that he was.

His fingers on the neck of the guitar are a blur. The other hand, like a claw, tears at its strings. Fast. Fast. Impossibly fast.

No one should be able to play this fast.

Not so flawlessly. Not so young.

Outside, just beyond the wall of sound, the woods roar.

The crowd is too deep in the frenzy to notice.

Sometimes I think Ike catches it, leaning one big elbow on the counter, behind his gleaming espresso machine.

He owns the place. He's got thick skin and sharp gray eyes. There's not much that slips past him. But his face never gives anything away.

The solo tears to an end. The chorus blasts back one last time.

*You know we asked for this*
*X-ray vision and an iron fist*
*X-RAY VISION AND AN IRON FIST*

With the last line, the noise in the room is so loud—the screaming guitar, Anders's amplified voice, the voices of the crowd singing along—that it actually has weight. It presses down on me.

But then the song ends, and everything collapses into the hailstorm of applause.

Anders takes one quick little bow. He turns and walks off the stage.

Jezz and Patrick wave, hold up their sticks and their bass, soaking up a few more moments. Then they walk off, too.

The applause and screaming slowly, finally, die out. The crowd turns back into people. They look at one another. Laugh. Fracture into small groups to smoke a cigarette, make out, climb into cars. Frankie and her friends glimmer away.

I don't move.

Once the room is mostly clear, and Ike and Janos are wiping tables and putting up chairs, the band finally comes back out onstage. They wind cords, collapse stands. A few fans, headbanger guys and some giggling girls, press up to the stage. Some of the girls ask Anders for autographs. One of them asks him to sign the skin of her arm. Then she darts off, blushing, laughing, and floats out the door with her friends.

Another journalist is here tonight. He's recording on his cell phone, jotting notes in a tiny book now and then. He stands at the edge of the stage, leaning back in his peeling screen-printed concert T-shirt and battered black jacket. The room is quiet enough now that I can hear their conversation.

They're talking about Mastodon. Trivium. Alaya. The journalist scatters metal band names like confetti. Jezz and Patrick are only half listening. The journalist isn't really talking to them anyway. It's Anders he's speaking to. It's always Anders.

The band put their instruments in heavy black cases. They gather armloads of cords. Climb down from the stage. The journalist doesn't help, but he follows them out the side door to their cars, still talking.

I know, because I follow them, too.

It's dark now. A cool April night, with thick blue sky and tangled clouds shutting out the moon. The woods are still a little too close. They've quieted, though. I can feel them pulling back, a loosening in the air. Patrick and Jezz hoist their stuff into the bed of Patrick's black truck. Anders's trunk is open. He lays his guitars inside. There are blankets in the trunk, I notice, ready to cushion the cases. It looks like the scene of a cozy abduction.

The journalist finally stops talking. He shakes hands with the band, Anders last.

"Thanks again, guys. I'll be in touch when the piece is up."

"Cool. Thanks," says Jezz.

"Drive safe, man," says Patrick.

Anders doesn't say anything.

Patrick shuts the back of the truck. His eyes catch on me, lingering in the shadows, back by the overgrown porch. "Hey." He nudges Anders. "Look. Your stalker is here."

Anders finally looks in my direction. His face stays absolutely still. But his eyes meet mine for long enough that it's almost like a greeting. This is as much as I can ask for. I have to keep hidden everywhere else. But at The Crow's Nest, I'm just another fan. Another follower. Here, he thinks he's safe. Anders turns back to the car, closes the trunk. He murmurs something to Jezz and Patrick. They all laugh.

He doesn't give me another glance.

They climb into their cars, Jezz and Patrick into the truck, heading toward the east side of town, Jezz's house, Patrick's place, and Anders heading toward his house, not far away, here on the northwest, near the woods.

I wait until their taillights have winked out in the distance, down the cracked asphalt of the road.

I get my bicycle. I take the path straight through the woods. The trees lean back as I pass. They whisper and hiss. They know what I am. They know what I know.

My own house isn't far away, on a mossy dead-end road deep in the oaks and pines. I'll pass Anders's house first. Take one more look. Make sure he's inside. Watch his windows. Wait until he shuts off the lights. Maybe.

Maybe I'll wait even longer than that. Maybe I'll watch all night.

# ANDERS

When I get home, I take an epic shower. I do this after every show at the Crow's Nest. It's the start of my comedown. And I need to come down, or I'd still be buzzing from the energy of the show at four a.m. I'm sure Mom and Dad think I'm doing some embarrassing and perverted teenage guy thing in here. They'd be surprised to know I'm just standing with my back to the showerhead, my hands hanging at my sides, letting the spray pound the aching muscles in my back.

Not that I really want them to know this, either.

I keep the water right on the edge of blistering. Hot enough that when I climb out, the bathroom is one big cloud, and I'm just a shadow on the foggy mirror. Even when I wipe the fog away, I barely recognize myself. I grew three inches last year, long after I'd stopped expecting it. Free weights and push-ups have changed things, too. These days, my arms look less like something that could have been squeezed out of a toothpaste tube. Plus, Patrick's sister gives me free haircuts in exchange for letting her practice her cosmetology school techniques on me, so I don't look like the poster boy for the fifteen-dollar kids' cut at ValuClips anymore.

I look like—

I don't know.

I clear another stripe of mirror with my forearm. The guy staring back at me from that blurry stripe is taller, broader, choppier haired than the kid I still expect to see. I put on the rock-star face. Aloof, a little haughty. A little hard. The guy in the mirror almost pulls it off. He can fake it, anyway. Except for the eyes. His eyes still show what a complete and perpetual dork he is.

I drop the face and lean into the mirror, palms on the counter.

Tonight was good. Really good. Amazingly, mind-blowingly good. Jezz and Patrick and I know each other so well and have played together so long that it always feels like we're part of one electrical circuit. But tonight, like it has more and more often, the electricity laced out of us and ran through the entire room, all the heartbeats pounding in rhythm, the crowd giving back everything we gave to them.

That feeling, that connected, electrical feeling, is the best thing in the entire world. It's like a shot of adrenaline that goes on and on until your whole body is practically throwing off sparks, and you feel like you could run straight up the side of a building and dive up into the sky.

I hate that it ever has to end, even for those couple of seconds between songs. When I'm not playing, I'm just me. Standing there. Getting stared at by a hundred people who all know my name. That's why I always jump into the next song as fast as possible. It's why, even when I'm not onstage, I'd rather be playing than doing anything else.

I'd rather be the guy with the guitar.

The guy with the guitar might actually be worthy of people screaming his name. That guy would know how to deal with journalists and fans. He'd always be able to find clothes that say *rock star,* not *garage sale poser.* I'm pretty sure he'd tell any little metalhead complaining about the side effects of fame to suck it up, loser.

I mean, Last Things isn't *famous.* Not really. But we've got the bite-sized, backwoods version of fame. Okay, is it a little weird to have girls who've seen you in your school gym shorts asking for your autograph, and to start recognizing your very own stalkers, the ones who hang around until the very end of the night, staring at you but never saying anything at all? Yeah. Sure. But isn't it also worth it about a million times over?

Yes. Yes. Yes.

Plus, there's just one thing I have to remember to put everything back in perspective. They don't love *me*. Even the obsessive online fans who say they do. They don't know me. They don't know me at all. They just love the music.

I get that. I feel exactly the same way.

I lean toward my reflection again. I put on the rock-star face. My chin rises. My jaw goes tight. *Suck it up, loser.*

"Anders?" Mom's voice calls from outside the bathroom door.

If there's anything that can immediately make you feel *not* like a rock star, it's your mom calling to you through a bathroom door. I back away from the mirror. "Yeah?"

"How did it go tonight?"

"Fine," I shout back.

"Good crowd?"

"Yeah. It was pretty full."

"Did you play anything new?"

I guess this isn't going to be a short interview. And there's no point telling Mom I can't hear her. She'll just wait and follow me down to my bedroom. I tuck a frayed towel tight around my waist and open the door.

Mom stands in the hall, still dressed from a long day at the front desk of the Greenwood-Halmstad Hospital, in her blue sweater set and beaded necklace.

"A couple new things," I tell her. "Mostly old stuff."

"I'm sorry your dad and I couldn't be there," she says. "I had that staff meeting tonight, and it went late. *Really* late." Behind the glint of her glasses, Mom's eyes are tired. "But that should be the last one for a while."

Mom and Dad haven't come to a show at the Crow's Nest in . . . I can't remember how long, that's how long it's been. I know Dad hasn't been to a show since I announced I'd be taking a year after graduation to see where this music thing leads. For Mom, it's been almost as long. And that's fine. It's harder to keep up the rock-star face when your mom is in the audience, beaming up at you.

"That's okay. It's the Crow's Nest." I give her a half smile. "Not really your and Dad's scene."

Mom opens her mouth, mock offended. "You know we can headbang with the best of them." She pauses.

"That's what they call it, right? Headbang?"

Now I give a whole smile. "Yes, Mom. That's what they call it."

Mom smiles back. "Are you hungry? I could make you something."

"Nah, I ate. Thanks."

"Where did you eat?"

"Crow's Nest. They gave us sandwiches."

Mom's eyebrows tighten. I can tell her mind is already going to the wallet inside her old faux-leather purse, counting the cash. "Do you owe them for it?"

"No. Don't worry about it. Ike says it's payment."

"Well. That's nice." Mom looks at me for a minute. She smiles slightly, her head tilted to one side. She looks like she's staring at a painting, trying to figure out exactly what it's supposed to be a picture of.

"Well," she says again. "Good night then."

"'Night."

Mom reaches up and rubs my bare shoulder. I let her. Down the hall, I can hear the TV blaring the noise of a baseball game. There's a hiss and click as Dad opens a beer can. Then Mom's hand glides away. She turns and heads toward the living room.

When I was younger I had all these daydreams about

what I'd do for Mom and Dad when I became a huge rock star. I'd buy them a mansion and fancy cars and a speedboat and nice clothes, and they'd never have to worry about money again. Little-kid fantasies. Now I mostly think about how much money I'll save them just by taking care of myself. Then they won't have to pay for my guitar lessons, or the picks and strings and sheet music, or the car insurance that shot up when I got my first speeding ticket.

Mom tries to keep money stuff quiet. But Dad's not so subtle. I know things are tight. And I know that my spending every spare minute on music instead of washing dishes at some crappy local grease pit is making Dad's blood pressure climb even higher.

Sometimes I imagine handing him a huge check, back payment for everything he's had to pay for in my entire life. And then all the threads of guilt that tie me here will be snapped, and I'll get out of Greenwood for good.

I grab my clothes from the bathroom floor and head down the hall.

My room is at the opposite end of the house from Mom and Dad's. Dad designed the house himself, before I was born, and oversaw the crew that built it. He hasn't designed anything since. Over the last few years, he's done less of a lot of things. Nobody's building houses in Greenwood anymore. Our place is a long, low ranch house covered in rough wood shingles. It looks like a giant pine tree fell over and someone hollowed it out and moved in. The house is surrounded by other, actual pines. There's a carpet of moss and pine needles on the roof, in the yard, everywhere. My room faces the woods. You can see out the window into trees that go on and on.

I shut the bedroom door quietly behind me.

There's a growl-squeak from under my bed. A second later a little gray monster barrels out and runs into my ankles.

"Hey, Goblin." I bend down and rub the cat between his raggedy ears. Goblin is old and deaf, with bony shoulders and snaggleteeth and breath so bad it could wilt a houseplant. He might be my favorite creature on earth. He doesn't say *meow* anymore, I suppose because he can't hear himself. Instead he says *mirk* and *ackk* and *eeeooww,* and a bunch of other cat words he's invented to suit his cat moods. And he always waits under my bed for me to come home.

*Rrrurk,* says Goblin, butting his head against my foot. After I've rubbed him enough, he leaps heavily onto my bed and curls up in the blankets.

I throw the towel over the chair and pull on a fresh pair of boxer shorts. I don't turn on the light. I'd rather hide in the dark for a while. Even when I'm alone in my room, I swear, sometimes I feel the pressure of eyes on me. In this little town, there's always someone watching. There's enough glow from the night sky for me to make my way around the room anyway. I could do it with my eyes closed: Twin bed. Scarred dresser covered with stickers and metal band logos drawn by hand with black Sharpie. Desk and chair. Sound system pieced together from garage sales and Goodwill. And, beside my bed, the guitars. My first acoustic, cheap and light as balsa wood. My new acoustic, still in its case from the show. My old ninety-dollar Epiphone Les Paul Special. And the black Ibanez electric. The most valuable, most beautiful thing I own.

Yvonne.

I sit down on the end of the bed. I've already played for almost five hours today: two hours of practice, warm-up, sound check, the show. But I can't help myself. I unzip the case and pull Yvonne into my lap. I run my fingers down the strings, feeling the buzz of the wires against my fingertips.

As long as I'm playing, I can shut off the rest of my

brain. I can stop thinking about what my face is doing, and about how my autograph on some girl's arm looked like it was written by a six-year-old girl, and about all the people screaming for our set tonight, and about Dad not even looking up from the TV when I walked into the house, and about the much worse things—the things I can't tell anyone, that I barely confess to myself. There's nothing left but the music.

I don't plug into the amp. I just practice the pentatonic scale, as fast as I can, up and down the fretboard. Then I practice fingerwork. First finger to second, second finger to third, third to fourth, as fast as I can. Until the tendons are screaming.

Then I lay Yvonne on the bed, climb down onto the rough dark blue carpet, and do fifty push-ups on my knuckles. The skin on the backs of my hands burns. After fifty I stretch for a minute: neck, shoulders, hands. Then I pick up the guitar again. Scales, slightly faster this time.

I'll do this for a while. Until the last of the adrenaline from the show has finally drained away, and my whole body aches, but in a good way, like after a long run, and I can just pass out, without the rest of my brain ever turning itself back on. I'm just getting down on the floor for the next round of push-ups when there's a tap at the window.

I jerk up. My heart jumps.

Someone is outside.

At first all I can see is a shape. It looks human. It's small and short-haired, and it's pressed right up to the glass.

Then it lifts one hand in a little fingertip wave, and I realize that it's Frankie Lynde.

And I'm standing beside my bed, out of breath, my mouth hanging open, in nothing but my ratty boxer shorts.

Jesus Christ.

I grab a pair of jeans from the laundry pile, yanking them up over my damp skin as I stumble toward the window.

She's seen me like this before. Shirtless, out of breath. The memory makes my frozen heart start to thud again.

Rock-star face. Rock-star face.

I shake my hair out of my eyes and shove the window open. A rush of cool, damp air pours into the room.

*Mrk?* says Goblin from over my shoulder.

My window is just high enough that Frankie needed to stand on something to look inside. She's rolled a stump over from the firepit out back. In the moonlight her hair is sleek and her skin is silvery gold and perfect.

Everything about her is perfect.

"Hey," she says. She smiles.

My heart trips, but I keep my face still. "Hey."

"How's it going in there?"

"Fine. How's it going out there?"

"Also fine. Although Sasha spilled some iced green tea on Mason's phone, and now he might have to kill her. Or get a new phone. Whatever's easier."

In the background I can hear a shriek. "Stop it, Mason! That won't bring your phone back from the dead!" There's crunching, steps running through pine needles. Somebody laughs.

"Who else is out there?"

"Just me and Sasha and Mason and Gwynn. We might drive around for a while. The moon's so bright."

Of course Frankie isn't alone. She's never alone. That's the kind of girl Frankie is: the kind who's surrounded by people who love her every minute of every day.

Frankie is fun. She's cool. She's also the most beautiful human being I've ever seen in real life. If it weren't for the music, a girl like Frankie Lynde wouldn't even give me two seconds of her attention. She notices me for the same reason everybody else does, and I know it.

I'm not whining. I'm not. But I'm also not going to pretend something's real when I know that if my guitar suddenly disappeared, Frankie Lynde would disappear, too.

"We were all at the show," Frankie says. "Did you see us?"

Did I see them? I can't remember. While I play, I focus on one face after another until all of them melt into one blurry gray face, and nothing sticks in my mind at all.

"I don't know," I say.

"Well, we were there. And you were great." Frankie smiles again. "So. Want to come out with us?" She raises one eyebrow. "I suppose you'd have to put a shirt on."

I shift my weight so that a little more of my chest will be hidden behind the window frame, trying to look as casual as possible. Then I think about what she's asking. Driving around town with Frankie's friends, having to keep up the rock-star act all night. I can barely keep it up right now. I'd rather be alone with Yvonne and the music.

"I don't think so," I tell her. "I'm down for the night."

Frankie doesn't beg. She probably doesn't know how. She just gives a little sigh. It's as close as she ever gets to seeming disappointed. Her eyes flick to my bare chest, just for a second. I'm not sure if she's pleased, or if she's only less than disgusted, but she doesn't look disappointed anymore.

"Okay," she says. "Well—have a good night in there."

"Have a good night out there."

She hesitates for a second, like she's waiting for me to say something else, or to change my mind and climb out the window after her. But my feet might as well be glued to the worn blue carpet.

Another beat, and Frankie is jumping down from the stump, running off toward the trees, disappearing. I hear more footsteps in the pine needles. More laughter.

Frankie's laugh is like music.

It's a cliché, but I mean it. Her laugh is sound perfectly arranged in time. It's too perfect to be effortless, but it sounds effortless anyway.

Somewhere in the distance, there's an engine, and then the woods fade to quiet again.

I shut the window.

I sit back down on the end of the bed. Goblin crawls across the blankets and flops down next to me with a little grunt, his curving spine pressed against my back. I haven't even picked up Yvonne again when it hits me.

A chord. A line of melody. Another chord.

It comes like a punch, just like always. Air knocked

out of my lungs; thoughts scattered. There's nothing left but the spot where the fist struck.

I grab the notebook and pencil from the bedside table and get it all down as fast as I can.

*What are you waiting for?*
*I know you're listening*
*Why are you holding still*
*clenching that key in your hand*

*What are you hoping for?*
*All alone, one a.m.*
*Why are you here again*
*standing still until you can't stand it anymore*

*And you're not*
*the flying bullet*
*And you're not*
*the speeding car*
*And you're not*
*even the empty sky behind a falling star*

*What can you see?*
*The darkness closes*

*What does it mean*
*that every light is too light to hold you down*

*And you're not*
*the buried bullet*
*And you're not*
*the totaled car*
*And you're not*
*even the empty sky where there was a falling star*

When it's done, I feel hungover. I'm guessing this is what a hangover feels like, anyway. I've only been seriously drunk once in my life, and then I puked so much, I don't think there was enough of anything left in my system to give me one. But after the songs come, I feel exhausted and empty, just like I did then. Like my brain is out of my control. Like my stomach is a wrung-out sock and my mouth is carpeted with sour paste, and like I'm not sure what I was doing five seconds ago.

It's been this way for almost two years now. As long as I've been writing anything decent. A song comes: Everything else in my brain fizzes out. I've had to stop in the middle of a math test to scribble notes and lyrics under my desk. I've had to pretend I was sick and bolt from the dinner table. It's like when some big breaking news story comes on TV, and it's on every channel, interrupting every show, and everything else has to stop. Everything but the song.

And the songs always come in one finished piece. I can hear the bass line, the drums, the guitar intro, and solos. There's no voice, but there are always lyrics, playing in the tone where I'm supposed to sing or shout them. They fill up my skull, blasting at top volume again and again, louder and louder, until I release them all on paper.

It's exhausting, but it's exhilarating. It's a lot like the shows. I guess there's a reason people want to get drunk again and again.

It's gone on long enough, and I've gotten enough good songs out of it, that I guess this is just the way my songwriting works. Other composers have described feeling the same way. Beethoven even said, "Tones sound, and roar and storm about me until I have set them down in notes." Not that I'm Beethoven or anything. Just that what happens to me when a song comes isn't *that* strange.

This is what I tell myself.

And the way that I can play, the way my hands have gotten faster and faster, and how it sometimes feels like I'm not even the one controlling them—that's because

I've practiced like crazy for the last nine years.

This is what I tell myself, too.

Even though I'm less and less sure I believe it.

I put Yvonne gently back on her stand. I set the notebook and pencil in their place.

Then I stretch out on the bed, on top of the sheets. Goblin's stinky breath caresses my shin.

I don't fall asleep, not the way I used to. But eventually something shorts out. Things go dark. And I'm finally gone.

**There's a pine tree with a trunk so wide that three people could hide behind it,** about a hundred feet from the Thorsons' house. It's far from the road, so no one driving by will catch me in their headlights or spot my old blue bicycle buried in a patch of shrubs.

The bark of the pine is rough, jagged, gnawed like a sheet of rusted metal. Gluey sap trails from the knotholes. If I press against it, it will rip out strands of my long hair.

The tree doesn't want me here. It would like to scratch me, sting me. It would like me not to be so close. The woods want me gone.

I peer out from around the trunk.

There's enough moonlight pushing through the hazy sky that I can see everything. The woods. The lawn. The low, shingled house. I can see his bedroom window.

It's on the very end of the house, the only window in

the short stretch of wall. There are curtains, gray ones, but they're almost never closed. On quiet nights I can hear him practicing. Composing. Fractured bones of music tumbling through the window.

There's no music now.

First he'll shower. Sometimes he'll eat, if his mother talks him into it. Then he'll head to his room. He'll pet his cat. He doesn't always turn the lights on. But I know when he's there.

I shift my foot on the thick pine needles. Inch forward for a better view.

The woods watch us both.

A crunch of tires. Voices in the trees. Car doors slam.

Someone has parked on the shoulder of the road, out of sight of the Thorsons' house. I can hear them, two, three, four of them, their running feet on the pine needles as light as a family of deer.

Gold limbs and sleek brown hair flashing past me. Frankie. Her friends scamper in the trees to my right. One of them holds up a glass bottle, threatening to splash it. All of them laughing. The woods hold their breath.

I crouch beside the big pine. They don't notice me.

Frankie flits to the bedroom window. I watch her

climb onto a stump, tap at the glass. A second later the window rises.

Anders stands inside. I can see the outlines of his face, moon-blue planes and shadows.

I can't hear their words. They don't talk long.

*No,* I think. *Anders. Don't go. Don't go.*

Frankie leaps off the stump. She runs back into the trees, where someone else is shrieking, "Stop it, you lunatic!" and laughing.

"Let's go," says Frankie's voice. "I want to drive around for a while."

I take a breath. He's not leaving.

"What, am I just your chauffeur?" says a guy's voice.

"Not *just* my chauffeur," says Frankie. "Come on."

Someone else laughs. Voices evaporating. Slam of car doors. Tires whirring away, away, until the road is quiet and empty again, and the woods come back to life.

They lean closer now. They whisper to the long, low house. They stroke it with their shadows.

I keep my eyes fixed on the window.

Then it starts.

The music.

Nothing is born already finished. Already perfect. Nothing should be.

But this is. Every time.

I hold my breath.

They're here. The dark things.

No one is around to watch me, to notice what happens to my eyes when I let myself see. No one to notice how they burn.

I scan the woods.

Dark things are everywhere. In the shadows. In every trembling needle on every pine tree. Darkness slithers from their bodies, from their too-long, crooked limbs. They're right here.

But so am I.

I stand perfectly still. Until the music stops, and afterward. Half an hour. An hour. The moon combs through the branches above me, reaching down with tiny filaments of light.

The window stays shut. The light stays out.

At last I feel the woods shift. The weave unravels. The night sky sifts through. The trees lean back, silent again.

Anders is asleep.

He's safe for tonight.

For a sliver of a minute, I let myself imagine him in his bed, cotton sheets against his skin, his eyes shut, his lips relaxed, apart—

I shove myself away from the tree.

I yank my bike out of the bushes. It's a very used Schwinn, colored sky blue with matte house paint. Its wheels tick softly as I climb on. I pedal through the woods, weaving between trees, letting the branches touch but not catch me, letting the moonlight lead me back to the road.

The road is deserted. Still, I stick to the pavement's very edge, balancing the bike on the weedy shoulder. At County N, I turn.

Our road is narrower. Twistier. There's nothing on it, not for two more turns. Nothing but Aunt Mae's place.

Aunt Mae's place is an old farmhouse, although the woods have already taken back whatever fields once surrounded it. It's pale blue and very used, just like my bike. There are no lights on inside. I leave the bike on the porch and unlock the front door with my key.

Just down the short hallway, in the living room, the TV mumbles to itself. Faint pulses of blue light wash the walls. Aunt Mae leaves the TV on almost all the time. For company. She rarely has any other kind. Now and then someone will leave a bottle or some home baking in a bundle on the porch. Every once in a while, an old lady will drive out for a visit, the kind of old lady who carries a rosary and a bottle of holy water and saints' medals in her purse, whose eyes never quite focus, who asks Aunt Mae to sit and pray with her. And sometimes kids from town come out here, too. They smash pumpkins on the driveway. Toss toilet paper into the trees. Leave nylon witches' hats on the mailbox.

But now she has me.

I tiptoe far enough down the hall that I can make out the shape of Aunt Mae on the couch, her head on the armrest, her body covered in blankets. I watch until I see her eyelids flicker, her chest rise and fall. Then I head the other way, quietly, into the kitchen.

The kitchen smells of lemon balm and rust, with a light layer of mildew. I pull one of the empty jam jars from the cupboard and run the tap until the water is slightly less than warm. I drink. Wipe my mouth with the back of my hand. It was a long night.

It isn't quite over.

I climb the narrow staircase. My room is to the left, above the kitchen. The eaves are low. Slanted walls, two windows, iron-frame twin bed. On the dresser, a row of ten votive candles in little glass cups. I strike a match on a sandpaper strip and light them all.

On the wall above the candles hangs a picture. It's

smaller than a postcard, smaller than a photograph printed at a drugstore. It was posted on a metal music blog last fall, taken by someone with a decent camera. I printed it out at the public library.

In the photograph Anders is onstage. Lips parted. Eyes almost shut. The fluttering wicks turn his image to oily black and gold.

I close my eyes.

*Anders. Anders. Anders.*

I repeat his name like a chant. Like a song of my own.

*Anders. Anders. Anders.*

We've lasted one more night.

Around the house, the woods creak and whisper and groan.

But they are shut outside. Anders is asleep, in his own quiet house. And I am here.

I blow the candles out. I fold back the blue cotton quilt with its yarn knots and its fading flowers, untie and pull off my shoes. Then, at last, I climb into bed. The woods will whisper to me all night long.

**There's not much more pathetically lonely than a bowl of milk with just three** Cheerios floating in it.

I reach across the breakfast table and grab the yellow box. Now I run the risk of overcompensating, having to add more milk and then more cereal in a never-ending downward spiral, but I can't face those three drifting Cheerios any longer.

Dad watches me pour. His eyes are tired.

"You were up early today," he says.

I have a flash of those minutes sitting on the end of my bed, morning sun sieving through the pine needles, the guitar in my hands. Even the memory makes my heart lift. Suddenly I can't wait to be playing again, making the lines a little smoother, the notes even cleaner. God. I'm such an addict.

"Sorry," I say through a mouthful of Os. "I just played

the acoustic. I didn't think I'd wake you."

"I was already up," Dad says. "What was that? Pink Floyd?"

I shovel in another mass of cereal. "Yep."

Dad nods. He rubs his head with the flat of one hand. Dad's hands are like baseball mitts, broad and tough enough to grab a flying fastball or hoist a splintering beam without flinching. His face is permanently sun-burned. The bottoms of his feet are like cement. He is his own protective gear.

"Your mom said you had a good show last night," Dad goes on as Mom drifts back to the kitchen table with a fresh mug of coffee. Goblin twists through her ankles, begging for scratches.

"Yeah," I say, swallowing. "They want us to add a second night. Be the regular Friday and Saturday thing."

Dad's eyes don't exactly narrow, but I can see the eyelids around them tighten, like he's bracing for a blast of saw-dust. "And he's still not paying you? That Ike Lawrence?"

"He gives them dinner," Mom puts in. "Right, Anders? And free drinks."

"You draw crowds for him every week," Dad goes on. "Now two nights a week. And he still expects you to do it for free?"

The tendons along my neck go tight.

Ike has been offering to pay us for months. I remember him striding toward us across the Crow's Nest after a set last summer when we had completely packed the house. Ike could win a Henry Rollins look-alike contest any day of the week without even changing his clothes. He smiled his dry little hint of a smile. "With the way you're pulling people in, I think the time has come for me to start paying you." He looked around at the three of us. "You're not open mic material anymore. You're a draw. And I know it."

Ike had been there for us, given us a stage and support and free sandwiches ever since we *were* the sloppiest of open mic material. I didn't want to take more. Not from him.

"We want to keep things pure for now. You know?" I said. "Get in our ten thousand hours of practice before we make the jump to pro."

Behind me I heard Jezz suck in a breath.

But Ike just grinned. "So you're not ready to sell out yet." He folded his beefy arms. "Just make sure when you do that you do it for the right people. Or at least for the right money." Then he turned around and strode away.

*"Dude,"* Jezz had said, jabbing me in the side. Patrick had just stared.

We had a fight about it later, but at the end we all agreed that we wouldn't sign any contracts or take any official payments until we had graduated, just to make things clean and simple. I kept up the lie about wanting to keep Last Things pure for now. Because I couldn't tell them the truth: that I didn't really deserve any of this. That the way everyone saw me was based on a lie. I couldn't tell Ike Lawrence, and I couldn't tell my own band, and I sure as hell can't tell my dad.

I just shrug, looking down into my cereal bowl.

"You know, pretty soon, you're going to have to stand up for yourself. Declare that your time has value." Dad turns his coffee mug in a little circle. "You've made it clear that that's your plan." His voice gets harsher with each sentence. We've had this fight so many times, it's like one big patch of scar tissue. "If you're going to try to do this music stuff for a living, even as a side job, you're going to have to stop letting people talk you into giving it away."

I should defend Ike. But it's easier just to shrug again.

"You put it to him this way," Dad plows on. "You tell Ike Lawrence he can at least cover your expenses if he wants you three to be his unpaid house band."

I glance at Dad sideways. "Expenses?"

"Your equipment, for starters. Transportation. Music lessons. It all adds up."

There it is again. A familiar push on another familiar bruise. "Yeah," I say. "I know it does. This summer I'll mow lawns again, and—"

"Summer," Dad cuts me off. "Sure." He turns to Mom, his tone shifting. "Did you say you were heading to Halmstad today?"

Mom nods, happy to have things moving into a lighter key. "I have to return those shoes to Petersons. They just weren't—*Anders.*" Mom stops me before I can push my chair back and walk away from the table. "What happened to your hand?"

"Oh." I hide the carpet-burned knuckles against my side. "I scraped it on the stage when we were loading up last night. No big deal."

"You look tired," says Mom. "Did you get enough sleep last night?"

I look past her at the old cuckoo clock with the pinecone pendulums that hangs on the kitchen wall. It's almost nine-thirty. "Yeah. I'm fine."

"You don't think two shows a week will be too much for you?"

"No. I'm fine. Really." I set my bowl in the sink. "I'm going over to Jezz's before my lesson. That article is supposed to get posted this morning. We said we'd read it together."

Mom's face goes from worried to bright again. "Which article?"

"The one in *Urban Planner*. That arts magazine."

Dad's eyes are on his plate. "How are you going to get there?"

" . . . My car."

"*Your* car? You mean the Nissan?" Dad says pointedly. "Your mom needs it for errands. I'm going to be changing the oil in the wagon today. It's overdue. And it's been awhile since you've filled the tank, by the way."

There's no use asking to take the truck. Dad's let me drive his pickup twice in my life, always with him in the passenger seat, his work boots pressing phantom brake pedals the whole time.

"Fine," I say from the kitchen doorway. "I'll see if someone can pick me up."

Mom says something to Dad as I leave the room, but I'm heading down the hall so fast that I can't hear it.

Patrick pulls into the driveway half an hour later. The thing he drives and the thing my dad drives are both called trucks, but in the same way a champion German shepherd and a twenty-pound junkyard mutt are both called dogs. Patrick's truck is mostly rust, with some black paint in between. Its prickly fabric seats are exploding with split seams and cigarette burns. The interior smells like oil, old coffee, cut grass, and feet.

"Thanks for driving all the way out here." I lift Yvonne's case into the cab. No way I'd let her slide around back there in the bed. "I'll pay you back."

"No problem," he says.

Even though I know it is kind of a problem. Even though Patrick with his job making pizzas at Papa Julio's doesn't have much more money for gas than I do.

Patrick turns up the radio, which just barely picks up the rock station from the Cities.

"FFDP," I groan. "God. They're *still* playing this song?"

"Only every twenty minutes," says Patrick.

"I need a Five Finger Death Punch in my ears."

"You're such a snob, man." Patrick is wearing his tiny half grin, which is how I know he doesn't really mean it. Everything Patrick does is so dry and understated, you have to look for little clues to decode what he's actually thinking. I know him well enough that I can usually catch the truth. "Sorry there's no Scandinavian death metal station we can pick up from here."

"Hey, I'm impressed that this thing has a working radio at all," I say. "What did it come with, an eight-track player?"

Patrick's half grin curls a tiny bit higher. "Phonograph."

I crack up.

We stream around a curve, past a riverbed, through a spread of thick old pines. A waft of air sweeps up over my leg. I glance down. There's a hole in the floor near Patrick's left foot. Through it, I can see straight down to the asphalt streaking below.

"Holy crap, dude," I say. "There's a hole in your floor."

"Yep." Patrick's face doesn't even change. "I was listening to System of a Down the other day and tapping my foot—"

"*Tapping* your foot?"

He shrugs with one shoulder. "Guess I tapped a little too hard."

"Guess you're driving the Flintstone mobile."

One corner of Patrick's mouth grins higher. He cranks up the Five Finger Death Punch.

Jezz is waiting for us in his room, which is half of his parents' entire basement. He even has his own bathroom down there. It's pretty sketchy, with a flimsy tin-walled shower and a utility sink with a mirror hung over it, but at least it's private. His actual bedroom is big enough that there's space for an old couch at one end. There's a long built-in desk in the corner, cluttered with cords and iPods and discs and empty Mountain Dew cans. Jezz is sitting at the desk when we come in. He does a slow twirl in the chair, grinning at us the whole time.

Patrick and I flop down on the couch, which is covered with so many layers of Jezz's clothes that you can't even tell what color it is.

"Is it up yet?" Patrick asks.

Jezz does another spin in the desk chair. A Slayer T-shirt flaps on the chair back like a flag. "Yep. Twenty minutes ago. Already two hundred thirty views and thirty-five comments."

"There's video?" I ask. "Which song?"

"'Superhero.'" Jezz's smile gets even wider. "It's good. The sound's decent. And you can see the crowd going nuts."

"You already read it?" says Patrick.

Jezz's eyebrows shoot up. "No. I waited. I said I would."

I feel that buzzing electric feeling, that mixture of nerves and adrenaline and dread and hunger that comes on before a show. Nothing to do but dive in. "Okay," I say. "Let's read it."

"I've got it up on my phone," says Patrick.

"I'll read it on mine," says Jezz, getting up. "Here. Anders. You take the computer."

The phone in my pocket is just a phone. The guys know this. They're nice about it, which makes it sting a little more.

We all shut up and read.

*At the end of a potholed road a few miles beyond the small town of Greenwood, somewhere deep in the Northwoods of Minnesota, you'll find the Crow's Nest Coffeehouse. And inside the Crow's Nest—on Friday nights, anyway—you'll find the future of American metal.*

My heartbeat switches to double time.

*On this Friday night in mid-April, just like every other Friday night for the past year, Last Things takes the stage. The crowd, which packs the coffeehouse from wall to wall, screams. The band launches into a blistering set of twenty original songs. Some are reminiscent of Tool's mathematically swirling rhythms, some hint at the beautiful melodic lines of Opeth, and some sound like nothing but themselves.*

There's the link to the video. "Superhero." In the still image, my head is bent, my left fist clamped around Yvonne's neck, my strumming hand an upward blur. The other guys aren't visible.

*From the driving, distorted pulse of "Breakdown," to heartbreaking, stripped-down solos like "Deep Water," Last Things has cultivated a sound that's drawing fans from as far off as Minneapolis.*

*The three-piece ensemble, featuring Jezz Smith (bass), Patrick Murray (drums), and Anders Thorson (lead guitar, vocals), has been playing together for four years. A deal with a major label is just around the corner.*

*. . . But first, they have to finish high school.*

*"We all agreed that we'd wait to sign anything until we had our diplomas," says drummer Murray, 18.*

*"We can't wait to sell out," laughs bassist Smith, also 18.*

*Smith and Murray are talented musicians, the foundation of a tight ensemble. But Thorson's skills as vocalist, guitarist, and composer push the band into another sphere.*

Oh, Jesus. It takes every single muscle in my body to keep the smile off my face.

*Onstage, Thorson is an engine of sharp, wordplay-heavy lyrics, a vocal range that goes from pitch-black growl to rich baritone, and guitar skills decades beyond his age. But as soon as he sets down the guitar, he's self-effacing. Almost shy.*

*When asked how he feels about being called a prodigy, his face clouds.*

*"I don't like that term," he says. "It's just years of lessons and practicing and sitting in your room alone. Just being an obsessive loser, basically."*

*He's even more reticent about his songwriting process.*

*"I don't really have a process. Ideas come to me. I write them down."*

*"That's what he's like," says Murray as Anders ducks away to pack up an amp. "He can't really talk about music. He just plays it."*

*What's it like working with someone like Thorson?*

*Smith grins. "You know how you'll be driving down some empty country road and some maniac passes you going insanely fast, and without even thinking about it, you're suddenly going ninety miles an hour, trying to catch up? Yeah. That's what it's like."*

Aw, Jezz. The gratitude and guilt both come so fast, I can feel my face turn red.

*Last Things will play the Crow's Nest every Friday and Saturday night between now and the end of August. Metal fans: Here's your chance to say you heard them before the rest of the world.*

*Because the rest of the world will hear.*

When I finish, it's quiet. I'm not sure if this is because the other guys are still reading, or what. My cheeks are flaming so hard, I don't want to turn around.

"Holy crap," says Jezz at last.

Patrick sounds dazed. "Yeah."

"Yeah," I agree.

Jezz laughs. Jezz's laugh is this high, crazy cackle that always makes other people start laughing with him. "I wonder how insane the crowds will get after this."

"Yeah. He really liked us," says Patrick. "Well, he really liked . . ." He jerks his buzz cut in my direction.

Here we go. Good thing I hadn't let myself smile.

"It wasn't just about me," I say quickly. I swivel the chair sidewise so I can see Jezz and Patrick without facing them head-on. "It was about *us*. And I barely talked to him."

"Which adds to the mystique." Patrick puts on a

reverent voice. "You're in *another sphere*."

"Dude." Jezz punts him lightly in the shin.

"Whatever," I say to a heap of shirts and socks on the end of Jezz's desk. "I hate it when they call me 'the front man.'"

"Well, you *are*," says Patrick simply. "You play lead. You sing. You write everything now. You stand in front."

*You write everything now.* The words hit like a dart.

Patrick and I used to write together, way back when we were coming up with our first original, totally crappy songs. Over time, as better songs started coming to me, with the lyrics finished and all the parts already complete, I switched to writing on my own. It was faster that way. And the way the songs came, overwhelming me, filling up my head, I couldn't move or think or do anything else until I'd let them out on paper. It wasn't my choice.

But Patrick doesn't get that.

"You want to write some songs?" I spin around to face him. "Seriously. You want to write something? Go for it. Go ahead."

That's not all I want to say. I want to ask if he'd like to be the one awake at three a.m., unable to stop until he gets the songs out. If he wants his brain to be like a radio where someone else keeps switching the stations.

If he practices until his whole body hurts, and if that just makes him love it more. But I don't. Because that would get too close to something dangerous.

Patrick hesitates for a sixteenth beat. "No," he says. He looks straight back at me. His voice has gone back to being as steady and cool as usual. "I don't do that. That's yours."

I take a breath.

Patrick is not the kind of guy you'd normally find on a stage. He's the kind of guy you'd find in the back of a garage, modifying an antique car or fixing a short in an electrical circuit. He's in on this because he likes the music. He likes the drums, because they're the perfect mix of physical strength and technical precision. He likes Jezz. And he likes me, most of the time. When I'm not being a jerk.

Patrick and I stare at each other for a second. His expression doesn't soften—nothing about Patrick is ever really soft—but eventually I see it shift, and then there's nothing bitter in it anymore. It's just my best friend, looking back at me.

"And *I'm* sure as hell not going to write anything," Jezz cuts in. "Unless I can just set some Dr. Seuss words to a Rage Against the Machine bass line. So it's a good thing we've got Mister Other Sphere writing for us."

"Yeah," says Patrick. "Right."

"I know I'm right." Jezz's tone brightens. "Hey. What do you call a drummer who just broke up with his girlfriend?"

Patrick blinks. "I don't know."

"Homeless."

Patrick gives a one-syllable chuckle. "Good one. So, a drummer walks into a bar . . . Ba-DUM-chick."

Jezz laughs his crazy laugh. I want to laugh, too, but I don't think the sound actually comes out of my mouth. I'm still feeling something—something heavy and dark, down in the pit of my stomach. Like the sign of something bad about to start.

Jezz slides sideways off the couch, hopping to his feet at the last second. "You guys want a can of pop? There's more Mountain Dew in the fridge."

"Throwback or regular?" says Patrick in the way someone else would say, "Cabernet or Zinfandel?"

"Both, I think." Jezz turns to me, eyebrows up. "Anders?"

It's too warm down here. My skin itches, like the words of the article are still crawling all over me. I lurch to my feet. "Actually, I've got to go. I need to get to the studio a little early today." A lie. What I really need is to be outside, alone, away from that article, away from the reminder that somebody is always watching, listening, waiting. "See you guys on Monday."

"Okay," says Jezz. "See you Monday."

"You don't need a ride home?" asks Patrick.

"Nah." I can't quite look at him now. "I can walk. Or call home. But thanks."

I charge up the basement stairs. Yvonne's case swings heavily in my hand.

It's bright outside, everything tinted yellow by pollen and clear sky and late April sun. My first impulse is to hit something. A cinder block. A cement wall. Something hard enough that what gets hurt is me.

You can't be the lead in something without it putting other people in the background.

And you can't just keep taking what you didn't earn. You need to pay for it somehow.

But you can't just stand outside punching a wall, either. Not in the middle of a small town, where everybody knows your name and your parents' names and your grandparents' names, on a sunny Saturday morning.

I stand at the end of Jezz's driveway for a minute,

taking deep breaths. Then, when I feel a little less freaked out, I turn and head down Franconia Street.

I walk downtown—or what passes for downtown in Greenwood. Six blocks of cafés, junk stores, dentists' offices. You could sleepwalk from one end to the other in three minutes. I keep my steps slow. I've got hours to waste, and nowhere to go, and a guitar in my hand, and $3.75 in my pocket.

At Sixth Street I turn right, away from Main, toward the park. You don't look like you're loitering if you do it in a park. I shuffle past the rows of old brick and clapboard houses, under trees flaming with fresh gold leaves, past alleys and yards and streets all still half asleep and Saturday-morning quiet.

I'm in the middle of a block when it attacks me. The line. Rhythm. Lyrics. Melody tangled into the words.

Damn it.

I shove my hand into the pockets of my jeans. No pen. No paper.

Goddamn it.

I spin around on the sidewalk, searching the ground, like there might be a notebook and pencil just waiting there. More words are coming. They pile up in my skull, water behind a dam.

Hold on. I could text it to myself. Every text costs money, as Mom and Dad will be sure to remind me. But hopefully it won't take more than two to get it all down.

I set Yvonne's case on the sidewalk and pull out my phone.

*Shadow Tag*

*Turn + turn again*
*as fast as I can*
*You're still beside me*
*No matter how I run*
*you're behind me*
*holding tight to my ankles*

*And if I fall*
*if I stagger into the street*
*if I stumble*
*that's when you'll finally catch me*

The music swallows me up. I'm lost in it; I'm in love with it; it's inside of me, but it's so much bigger than I am that I can't hold on—

And then a car horn blares right beside me.

I jump. Like a moron. I barely manage not to drop the phone.

"Hey," calls a voice.

Frankie's deep blue car has pulled up beside the curb, purring softly. Frankie cranes around Sasha, who's sitting in the passenger seat, and beams out at me. "Need a ride?"

"Um—not really." My vision wavers. My brain is still scrambling after the song like a kid chasing the string of a runaway kite. "I'm just . . . walking."

"I'm dropping Sasha off. She spent the night," Frankie says.

Sasha smiles at me as though this is fascinating information.

"Oh," I say. *Great answer, moron.*

"Then I'll take you wherever you want to go," Frankie says. "Frankie's Taxi Service. Come on. Get in."

I can't think of a single excuse. Not even a stupid one. I pick up Yvonne and climb into the backseat, like a little kid sitting behind his babysitters.

"So," says Frankie over her shoulder as she pulls back into the empty street, "what were you up to this morning? Being a wandering minstrel?"

Her inky brown eyes meet mine in the rearview for a second, and I finally remember to put on the rock-star face. I raise my chin. Lower my eyelids.

It's stupid, yeah. I know *why* Frankie likes me.

But I still want her to like me.

"I was at Jezz's," I say.

"Oh, yeah," says Sasha. "That big article just came out."

My chest tightens. "How did you know?"

"Jezz just shared it. He tagged you."

The back of my neck starts to prickle. I have the stupid urge to look out the rear window, just to see if someone's staring in. This freaking town.

We pull up to Sasha's house, which looks like something you could order out of a catalog. Frankie turns into the driveway, and Sasha hops out and runs inside.

"Come up here," says Frankie, patting the passenger seat. "Unless you're actually going to pay me for the ride."

I climb out and into the front, leaving Yvonne in back, hiding my raw knuckles in my pocket. Frankie waits for a moment, her perfect face turned toward me. She's wearing this funny little smile, like she knows something I don't. Her hand rests on the gearshift. There's a beat, while she just smiles at me and I try not to smile back at her, and then Frankie puts the car in reverse. I realize only as we're bumping out of the driveway that she was waiting for me to kiss her.

God, I'm dumb.

I guess I should have known. I've kissed her before. Once.

Once, if you go by number of sessions.

If you go by number of seconds, or by number of individual lip-to-lip contacts, it's a lot more than once.

It was December, at a party at Blake Skoglund's, way out in the country. It was one of those parties that nobody was actually invited to but that everybody knew about anyway. By nine o'clock the crowd got too big to fit inside the garage and started spilling out into the sheds and the snow and the woods, getting drunk and loud and frostbitten.

I'd never spoken to Frankie Lynde before. She came to the Crow's Nest every Friday night, but so did everybody else at Greenwood High School. She was always in the middle of a whirlpool of loud, laughing friends who were way more interested in one another than the music. They probably wouldn't even have noticed if we'd launched into a medley of Disney songs.

But suddenly, there she was. By herself. Walking

across the Skoglunds' garage, straight toward me.

I was standing beside a metal tub packed with snow and cans of pop.

Frankie pointed down into the tub. Her fingernails were painted silver. "Would you hand me something?" she asked.

If I hadn't been leaning against the wall, I would probably have looked over my shoulder, just to make sure she wasn't talking to somebody else. I looked down into the tub instead. "Which one do you want?"

"I don't care. I just want something to do with my hands." She smiled at me.

Frankie Lynde smiled at me.

I felt like someone had just unzipped the front of my chest.

A rush of icy December air slid through my rib cage. My heart shivered and thumped harder. Frankie Lynde, smiling, looking straight at me with those deep brown eyes. I didn't know that actual human beings could have eyelashes so thick and dark and long.

I grabbed a can of Coke.

"Thanks." She took it. Her fingers brushed my skin.

"Whoa." I gave a little jerk backward. "Your hand is colder than the can."

She laughed. "I know. My hands are always cold." She leaned a little closer. "But that doesn't mean I'm a dead girl. I swear."

Jesus. She was quoting my song to me. The most beautiful girl I'd ever seen in real life knew the words to one of my songs.

"Oh," I said, like the giant idiot I was. And am. "That's good."

"They say, 'Cold hands, warm heart,' right? I guess the moral is: Don't trust anyone with warm hands." Before I knew what was going on, she grabbed my right hand, pressing her smaller, softer palm to mine. "Hmm. Warmish. But not coldheartedly warm." She turned my hand toward the dusty ceiling lights, staring down at my palm like she was reading the lines. "Wow. Do you have any actual skin, or are your hands just one big callus?"

"Yeah. The guitar will do that to you."

"That seems mean," she said. "That something you love would hurt you."

"I don't know. Isn't that just how it works?" The words came out before I could even think about them. They made me sound way deeper and darker than I deserved.

Frankie gave a little laugh. Music. Sound perfectly arranged in time. "Maybe. I guess." She still hadn't let go of my hand. Now she turned it over and touched her fingertips to mine. "Can you even feel anything with those?"

"Yes." There was a little rasp in my voice now. "I can feel that."

She looked up at me. Smiled again.

I don't even know how it happened, but next we were in the three-season porch at the back of Blake Skoglund's house, on a low, afghan-covered couch that smelled like bonfires, and my lips were on hers, and hers were on mine, and her cold, soft hands were sliding up under my shirt, and even in the freezing air, even with my unzipped rib cage, my skin was burning, and I couldn't feel the cold even when the shirt was on the floor, because Frankie's fingers were in my hair, and my fingers were everywhere, everywhere—

And then it was late, and cars were crunching down the gravel driveway, and Frankie was smoothing her hair, tugging her jacket back on, and giving me one last small, soft, teasing kiss. And then she slipped off into the house, and a few minutes later, I'd collected enough strength in my burning, shaking body to get up and drag myself home.

And that was that.

People knew, of course. In this town, everybody knows everything about everyone. Almost.

I guess I could have said something. I could have done what the guy is supposed to do. I could have asked her out. Asked her to be my girlfriend. Even though that would have felt like handing her a can of Coke and asking her to pretend it was champagne.

I could have. Because I got the sense afterward, from the way she looked at me, and the way she kept coming to the shows, and the way she didn't avoid me, that Frankie didn't regret it. That she might actually be interested.

But she was interested for the same reason as everyone else.

Because I'm the guy with the guitar.

I wasn't going to try to build something real on top of that.

So I've just been walking around with an unzipped chest since mid-December. I'm always kind of stunned that people can't seem to see straight inside me. That they aren't backing away, grossed-out and horrified. And I've tried to make sure that I'm never alone with Frankie, which, considering her giant circle of friends, is usually pretty easy to do.

But now, here I am. Here we are.

"Okay." Frankie shifts into drive. "Where were you headed?"

"I was just killing time before my lesson at one."

"All right." She nods. "I like killing time."

Riding with Frankie is worlds away from riding with Patrick. Her car is glossy and new and smells like cinnamon, laced with the softer scent of Frankie's shampoo. A pop station plays on the stereo. It's all too nice. I feel totally uncomfortable, like I'm sitting on someone's expensive leather furniture in a pair of soaking wet shorts.

"Want to go to Roxy's?" she asks.

Roxy's is the town diner. It's got narrow red booths, sturdy white cups and saucers, and chipped beef on toast.

"Not really," I say. And not just because there's only $3.75 in my pocket. "I don't feel like just sitting."

"We could go to the park," she suggests. "There's lots of room to not sit there."

I had been headed there, but with Frankie, it seems wrong. Too quiet. Too alone. Too much temptation to lunge across the armrest, cup her perfect face in both hands, and—

"No. Not the park."

"All right." Frankie stays cool, even though now I

sound like a brat. I don't know if this is because she *is* so cool, so comfortable just being herself, or because she's humoring me. "How about we just drive around for a while? I'll even let you pick the music." She nods at the glowing display on the dashboard, the hundreds of satellite stations to choose from.

I click the volume dial to Off.

Frankie laughs. "Nothing's good enough for the prodigy behind Last Things."

She's teasing. I know it. She both right and wrong. I'm a total snob. But sometimes everything feels too good for me.

"That article was pretty amazing," she says after a minute.

"You read it?"

"Sasha and I read it together." She throws me a coy look, one eyebrow up. "They made you sound like a mysterious musical genius."

I don't even know what to say to this. I almost say, *When actually I'm just an awkward musical dork,* but I don't want Frankie to know this. Let her think that I'm a mysterious musical genius. It's much better than the truth.

"It's funny, though," Frankie is going on, because I haven't answered. "It made me realize that I don't know anything about your songwriting. Like, at all."

I shift on the seat. "You've heard my stuff."

"No. I mean, I don't know *how* you write your songs. Where they come from. If you start with the melody, or with the words, or with the concept for the expensive music video you'll make someday, or what." She pauses again. I don't speak. "So—this sounds totally corny, but where do you get your ideas?"

We're heading past the park, along a road where the houses grow thinner and the trees grow thicker. Green walls surround us.

"I honestly don't know."

"Oh. So you *are* a mysterious musical genius."

"No. I just—I can't really explain it." And then I tell her the truth. Partly. "I'm not controlling it. It just happens."

"Hmm." Frankie lifts that eyebrow at me again. "Maybe you have a muse."

"What?"

"You know, how people used to think that art came from some goddess coming to you and inspiring you. They all had weird names, like Euterpe and Calliope...."

"Euterpe?"

"I don't know why that one hasn't caught on as a baby name." Frankie shrugs with one shoulder. "So, maybe you have a muse. Maybe some force is coming in and giving you your songs."

There's a gust of wind around my unzipped heart. I take a deep breath. *Maybe some force is coming in* . . . Yeah. She's pretty close. But it's not like some filmy Greek goddess is slipping into my head. It's more like she's breaking in with a sledgehammer. I stare down at Frankie's bare knee until I can get my thoughts in a row again. Jesus. Even Frankie's knee is perfect.

"It just makes being praised for it seem stupid," I say after a minute. "I mean, if something is just *giving* it to you, then it's not really your work at all."

"I don't know." Frankie shrugs lightly. "It's only stupid if you think muses are *real*."

We skim along the road. The pavement is so dark with shade that it looks wet. Even with the sky bright above, the woods are thick enough to rinse us in their chilly shadows.

I want to reach over and touch Frankie's hand. See if it's as cold as before. I want to run my fingertips up the underside of her light brown arm, where the skin is like silk. I want it so much I can already feel it. I clench my fist instead. I keep my fingernails long, for playing the acoustic. I clench until the fingernails dig into my palm, and I keep my face rock-star blank the whole time, keep my breath steady, even when the pain starts to spear up my arm. I clench until I feel like I've paid, at least a tiny bit, for all of this.

**Something ticks against the window screen.**

I roll over beneath the quilt and look up. The window is dusted with pale morning light. A moth dangles there. It isn't outside the screen, it's inside, caught in an old, matted wad of spiderweb, and it's thrashing as hard as it can, its wings a blur, its little brown body swinging back and forth against the screen like a tiny wrecking ball. It tires, slows, stops. It dangles there, shifted only by the wind. Then it jerks again, fighting, fighting, fighting against the trap of a predator that was probably dead a long time ago.

I wait until the moth is still again. Then I detach the web from the window frame, so the moth hangs from my fingertip instead. Its wings are like old paper. Fibrous. Velvety.

I set the moth down on the windowsill, which is full

of black bits, dead leaves, old beetle husks. I manage to peel the thread off its wings. Still, the moth just sits there. Too damaged or exhausted to move again.

I slide up the screen, just an inch. Enough so the moth can slip out and flap away if it wants to.

Then I climb out of bed.

I change into clean clothes—spare pair of jeans, long-sleeved green sweater—before stepping out the door and down the creaking stairs.

There's a tiny bit of coffee in the freezer. Enough for two cups, if they're small. And there are two nubs of bread in the plastic sack in the fridge. Stale, but good enough for toast.

I start the coffeemaker and stare out the kitchen window as the water in the machine starts to hiss. The day is golden. Dew is still thick on the ground. I can see it on the ferns, on the spiderwebs strung across the grass. People used to call those fairies' handkerchiefs. Here, under the thick branches, it will stay damp all day.

The toaster pings.

There's a jar of jam in the door of the fridge. I spread jam on both nubs of bread and set them on a plate painted with sprigs of forsythia. I take the robin's-egg-blue cup and the olive-green mug from the cupboard. There is no milk. We'll drink our coffee black. I set everything on a scarred wooden tray and carry it into the living room.

Aunt Mae is lying on the couch. She's awake, I can tell. But she doesn't open her eyes all the way until I set the tray down on the coffee table beside her.

"Sweet girl," she says. "Bless you."

I pass her a glass of water first.

She takes it. I can see her hand shake. She sips a little.

"We're out of bread and coffee," I tell her. "I'll go get some more."

Aunt Mae nods. "There's some money left in the can." She turns, sitting up slightly on the couch, bunching her cocoon of blankets. I can smell the alcohol. It breathes from her pores. Sharp as pine pitch. "Your father should be sending another check soon."

I take the glass out of her hand. "Have you heard from him lately?"

She gives a little headshake. "We will soon. We need to be patient. He's got his own demons to fight."

Aunt Mae can be patient if she wants to be. I've run low on patience, at least where my father is concerned. But there's not much difference between being patient and expecting nothing.

I give her the pretty blue cup. Aunt Mae holds it in

both palms, like she's cradling an actual robin's egg. She looks at me. Her cobwebby eyes try to focus. "Good night?"

I nod. "It was good."

"Music as good as ever?"

"Better and better."

She smiles. "And how was our boy?"

I smile back. Not answering.

"Good," says Aunt Mae. She takes a small, slow sip of the coffee, as if it's medicine.

"Would you like some toast?" I offer the plate.

"In a bit, perhaps. Thank you."

I read the tremor in Aunt Mae's hand as she sets the coffee cup aside. Not just a lack of alcohol in the blood. Something bigger.

"Were the dreams bad last night?"

Aunt Mae closes her eyes. Nods.

"Anything nearby?"

"No," she breathes. "Too far. And too vague. The worst kind."

I smooth the layers of blankets that weigh her down. "Want me to draw you a bath?"

"No. Thank you." She smiles, eyes still closed. "You go on. Get on with your day."

"I'll go to town. Get the groceries." I glance at the floor beneath the coffee table. Glass bottles are tumbled there like spent bullet shells. "Do you need another bottle?"

Aunt Mae nods. "See Martin. At the Wheelhouse."

I take my piece of toast and the green cup back to the kitchen.

There are six bills in the old tin coffee can in the upper cupboard, floating on a silt of coins. I take a twenty and a handful of change. I open the other cupboard, the one with the jars and pouches and old tea boxes, and pull out a tall glass bottle, one with a metal screw cap, that held whiskey a long time ago. I fill it with water from the tap. I put the bottle in my canvas bag. Then I swallow my toast and coffee, pour the dregs into the sink, and let the rusty tap water carry them away.

Outside, the air is on the edge of cool. The trees sift the sun so that only the finest fragments tumble through. I walk around to the back of the house, keeping inside the circle of white stones.

There, beyond the edge of the overgrown backyard, just where the trees start to thicken again, the shed stands in a cluster of young pines. It sags heavily to one side. A few more years and it might tumble straight over, like someone who's fallen asleep standing up.

I unlatch its front door.

No one comes here but me.

I haven't cleaned up inside. I haven't changed any-thing. I try not even to leave footprints. It needs to look untouched, if they come searching. When they come.

In the shed's back corner are a rusted old tub, a few sacks of long-dead seeds, a torn sandbag. I move them carefully aside.

The door is beneath them.

It's almost the size of a door inside a house, the kind of door that could open into any ordinary bedroom. But this door leads down. Into the earth.

I pry it open.

The root cellar, like the rest of the shed, had been unused for years. Decades. Now it's mine.

The steps are slats, barely broader than a ladder. They groan under me. I climb down into the little bare earth room. It smells like soil. Damp. Deep. If it weren't for the open door above me and the rickety shed streaked with dusty sunlight, it would be pitch-black. Instead, it's only gray. Splintering shelves line the walls. I take the full water bottle out of my bag and place it on the shelf, in the row of items I've been building, one at a time. Two jars of applesauce. One of peanut butter. Several other old whiskey bottles filled with water. In the corner, a pillow, a few blankets, two coils of strong rope.

I climb back up the steps. The door has three bolts on the outside. I added two of them myself. They were cheap, at the hardware store, the same kind I drilled to the frame outside my bedroom door. I don't need to lock them yet.

I move the rusty old tub and ancient sacks back into place over the cellar door. When everything looks just like it did before, I leave the shed, circle the house, and climb onto the pale blue bike.

In daylight, the road that leads me to the Thorsons' house has transformed. The woods are light stunned, lively with birds. Everything else—everything big and dark and terrible—is waiting now, hidden, half asleep. But I feel them there. Patches of prickling darkness. Their deep, thrumming breaths.

I pedal around a curve, through the ditch, onto the pine needle carpet. I climb down from the seat. The bushes swallow my bike.

I lean against the big tree and look out.

A cat pads slowly across the Thorsons' lawn, his bony shoulders working up and down beneath his dull gray fur. The white car is missing from the driveway. Anders's bedroom window is dark. This could mean many things, but I know which one it means right now. The room is empty.

Anders isn't here. I can feel it now that I'm close, as plainly as you can feel an emptiness on the other side of your own bed.

I glance around, checking the woods in every direction. Nothing but singing birds and rustling leaves and creaking limbs.

But I'll find him. I can always find him.

I pull the bike back out of the bushes and jump on, steering for town. Not by the road. Through the woods.

There's no one around. No one to see me if I move as fast as I can move.

Too fast. Impossibly fast. Like Anders's fingers on the guitar strings.

I fly through the new green leaves, weaving past twigs that lash at my eyes, ducking the branches that want to rip out my hair. My tires barely touch the ground.

I hit the pavement again at the west edge of town. I ride, slower now, along Main, past Franconia and Jackson and Pierce Streets, past offices locked up for the weekend, past the Laundromat and the library, past Oak and Pine and Maple Streets, back into narrowing streets and thickening trees. I keep my eyes sharp for him. For the white car.

Almost no one is out this early. One little girl is sitting on the uneven cement of a driveway, busy with two big lumps of chalk. My shadow glides over her as I ride past. She's drawing a bird. Its blue and pink chalk wings open wide. I would tell her that it's pretty, but she doesn't look up.

The houses begin to dwindle. Trees push up between them, forcing them even farther apart.

I ride on, past Founders Park Road.

Founders Park is huge, more than fifty acres. It slides away from the edge of town, plunges into a ravine, and trails away like a knife slash into the woods, dragging the river with it. The river gets wider and deeper in another mile, where Main Street turns back into the highway and crosses the water at Miniska Bridge.

The woods don't like the river.

The river moves and shifts and swells and shrinks. It nibbles at banks. It unravels roots. It swallows trees whole. From the side of the bridge, you can spot the trees about to fall, huge trunks leaning farther and farther over the water until they are nearly horizontal, hanging on by a single stubborn foot. Death in slow motion.

Woods hide things. They keep things forever. Rivers carry things away.

I ride along the narrow margin of the bridge, past the patches of wild raspberries and grapevine and sumac, past a slough already greening with duckweed. The Wheelhouse, a tumbledown bar and liquor store, hunches here, in a scrubby grove of box elder trees. I leave my bike behind the store, where the few passing cars won't see.

It's barely noon. No one is inside. Only Martin, who has just unlocked the doors, still holding the ring of keys in his hand. He looks up at me.

Martin's hair is like steel wool. One of his eyes droops. His smile is warm.

He doesn't say good morning. He gives the shop a quick once-over, checking the door and out the windows. Then he heads behind the counter, drops something that thuds into a narrow brown paper bag, and twists the top of the bag shut.

"How's she doing?" he asks, handing the package to me.

"Not so good," I say. "Bad nights." I put the wrapped bottle in the canvas bag. I reach into my pocket, but Martin backs away, holding up both hands.

"Next time," he says. "You two take care."

I climb back onto the bike, the canvas bag slung over

my shoulder. The whiskey thumps against my ribs.

Johnsons' Market next. On the way I'll check the music studio. The Smiths' house. The Murrays' house. In a town this size, there are only so many places to check.

I pedal through town, along the other side of Main Street. A few people are out now, heading to the diner. Running errands. Ducking into bars. I scan their faces. No one looks back at me.

And then, just as I pass the post office, I see a car slowing down on the other side of the street, across the tree-dotted meridian. Dark blue. New. Expensive.

Frankie Lynde is in the driver's seat. I can see her profile through the sunny streaks on the glass. She's laughing.

Someone climbs out of the passenger side.

It's him.

I brake, pulling the bike to a stop between two parked cars. For a blink, I see myself reflected in the rear window beside me. I'm nothing. Just round shapes. Long, curling, pale hair.

Anders pulls a guitar case out of the backseat. He leans back into the car. Says something else to Frankie. I watch his lips. He smiles at her. For her.

Something painful opens inside my chest. I slam it shut again.

Keep my eyes and my mind clear.

Anders turns around. He opens the glass door that leads down to the music studio. The panes flash with reflected sun, and he disappears into the brightness.

Frankie's car purrs away.

I focus my eyes straight ahead again.

A loaf of bread. Ground coffee. Maybe some milk. If there's a little money left over, I'll buy something else for the root cellar. Something that will keep. That can be opened by feel, in the dark.

Coffee. Bread. Milk.

I pedal on, toward the grocery store.

**Underground Music Studio is literally underground. It's in the basement of an old** three-story stone building, down with the roaring vents and knocking pipes. It shares an entrance with an insurance office and a custom alterations place called Nancy's Needles, which always makes me think of Sid Vicious and Nancy Spungen. I'm guessing the Nancy upstairs didn't have the Sex Pistols in mind.

You step off Main Street, through a stenciled glass door, into a toothpaste-green hallway. Then, if you're under thirty and you're not looking for insurance or an embroidered sweatshirt, you head toward the metal door on your right. Through that door and down a flight is a big, brick-walled room full of buy-or-rent instruments and parts: guitars, drums, keyboards, microphones, racks of replacement strings, sheet music, plastic buckets with a rainbow of little plastic picks, plus some saggy corduroy couches and chairs. I've spent so much time in this room, waiting for my lessons, that it feels like my own living room. Just with way better accessories.

Around the room are soundproofed metal doors numbered one through four. Studio number four belongs to Flynn. Inside, its red brick walls are covered with posters, mostly from Flynn's past tours playing backup guitar in once-huge rock bands. Spongy acoustic panels, like unfrosted sheet cakes, hang from the water-stained ceiling.

Now, at my lesson, Flynn and I sit facing each other on padded folding chairs. Flynn has a long, square chin and a close-lipped smile that's warm even though it doesn't reveal any teeth. He's always so clean-shaven I wonder if he can grow a beard at all. Flynn could pass for thirty, if it weren't for all the gray in his hair. That and the age of his T-shirts.

I'm holding Yvonne across my lap. My knuckles are still raw. There's no way to hide them here.

But Flynn doesn't say anything about that.

"All right," he says. "Let's hear that Dream Theater piece."

I start the intro. Arpeggiated chords in an easy-to-mess-up pattern, unexpected dissonances.

"Okay," Flynn stops me halfway through. "That's great. But I think you can speed it up even more."

"I was just worried about pushing the tempo too much."

Flynn spreads his hands, smiling at me. "The other guys aren't here. You can push it all you want."

I grin back at him. "Yeah. Okay."

I play it again. Almost twice as fast. My fingertips are a blur. Everything feels strong and clear, liquid, but controlled. The joy of it pulses through me.

This time Flynn doesn't stop me. He just sits back, listening, his eyes on my hands.

I lift my fingers and break the last note.

Flynn shakes his head. He's grinning broadly. His voice is soft. "Wow, man," he says. "Wow."

Flynn is pretty scanty with his praise. I mean, he's said nice things before, lots of times. But I don't think he's ever said "wow" quite like this. I tuck my chin to my chest and let myself smile, too, just a little.

Flynn kicks up one foot, crossing his legs. "Hey," he says. "Speaking of the band, how was the show last night?"

"All right. Good crowd. I think they were close to capacity."

Flynn nods. "You must be making Ike Lawrence a happy man."

"Yeah, he keeps threatening to pay us in actual money. Especially now that we're going to do two nights a week."

"'Threatening'?"

I look down at Yvonne's neck and pretend to adjust a peg. "Yeah. And I keep telling him no."

Flynn's eyebrows quirk. "Still? Why?"

"Because that would make it—I don't know. Something it's not."

He smiles. "Professional?"

"No, just—we all made a deal to keep things *not* professional until we graduated. Plus, it's cool that there are no expectations, you know? We can just play. We know it won't be that way once—"

"Once you're huge rock stars?" Flynn supplies, grinning wider.

"Well." I shift my shoulders. "I wasn't going to say it."

"I know. That's why *I* said it."

I feel my cheeks start to flare. Jesus. You can't be a metal singer who *blushes*. "Anyway . . ." I say, looking at the pegs again. I'm so good with these excuses now, they come out like the chorus of a song. "I don't want to make that kind of deal with the audience until we have to.

Because once there's payment, things have to change, right? Like, 'Hey, I paid you, now entertain me.' Or like, 'Here. This thing I made up just sitting around in my boxer shorts deserves your money.'"

Flynn laughs out loud. "You are the least pushy lead singer I've ever known, you know that? You're sure you're not a bassist?"

"Yeah. Jezz has that taken care of."

"You could be a two-bass band. No melodies. Just great hooks."

"I'll think about that."

"Hey—maybe Ike could pay you in trade or something," Flynn suggests. "For a guy who looks like he fronts a motorcycle gang, he's a surprisingly good baker."

"Yeah." I grin. "We could be the world's only death metal band that gets paid in cookies."

Flynn throws his head back and laughs. "That could be your first album title. *Paid in Cookies.*"

"*Appetite for Oatmeal Raisin.*"

Flynn laughs so hard he has to wipe his eyes. "Perfect. Until Guns N' Roses sues you."

The tightness that's been hanging out in my shoulders loosens a little more. Dad's sighs, and Patrick's words, and keeping up the act in front of Frankie all seem smaller and less important now. God, I'm so glad I have Flynn.

Flynn has known me since I was nine years old. Half of my life. He looks exactly the same as he did back then, lanky and tan and long-haired and ageless. Except I used to think he was really tall. Now I'm the taller one.

The first time I saw him play in concert was at a big outdoor music festival. My parents made the two-hour drive to northern Wisconsin to let me stand near the stage, not moving, just staring up at him like a human video camera. I stood at the front of that screaming crowd, watching and listening, and after two songs, I wanted to quit guitar forever. Not because I was sure I would never be able to play like Flynn, which was part of it. But because I couldn't stand to imagine myself sitting in a tiny brick room picking at some crappy folk tune while this stage-lit guitar god sat on a folding chair two feet away. I felt like a worm wriggling up to a dragon and asking how to breathe fire.

But at my next lesson, Flynn was just Flynn again, with his battered Iron Maiden T-shirt and his long, messy hair. He cracked jokes. He made me feel comfortable. He taught me the opening of a Black Sabbath song. And I didn't quit.

Eventually I stopped being intimidated. The awe

faded to something warmer and more familiar, like the feeling you have for your favorite uncle or a really cool older brother. And then, last fall, there was a moment during a lesson when I noticed a flaw in his playing for the first time. It was just a slip, a split second of less-than-perfect technique. Don't get me wrong—Flynn is still an amazing guitarist. But now I'm good enough to see the tiny imperfections. Good enough to know how to fix them. If someone threw me and Flynn into a musical battle today, note for note, phrase for phrase, I'm not sure who would win.

I don't want to know. I'm too afraid it would be me.

Flynn sags back in his chair and crosses his arms over his ancient Alice in Chains T-shirt. He scratches his upper arm. He's missing part of one finger on his right hand—his strumming hand. It ends at the middle knuckle with a healed-over stump. I've never asked him how it happened. Just like he doesn't ask me about my roughed-up knuckles or the occasional dark circles under my eyes. "You play any of your newest stuff last night?" he asks.

"Yeah. We did 'Final Round.' And 'Absentminded.' And I played 'Deep Water' on the acoustic. But that one's not that new."

"What are you working on now? Anything even newer?"

I run my hand over Yvonne's glossy side, trying to look cool. I don't have to wear the rock-star face with Flynn—he's known me way too long for that—but I don't want to seem like a psycho, either. "I wrote a few more this week."

"A few," Flynn echoes. "This week."

"Yeah."

"How many is a few?"

"Five."

"Whoa." Flynn tilts his head. Spirals of long gray hair swing sideways, falling over his shoulder. "Five. Are you getting even faster?" He looks at me wonderingly. "*Five* songs? Five finished songs?"

It's not me that's getting faster. It's something else.

At least the way I play feels like part of me. It's my own hands holding the guitar, my fingers on the strings.

But the songs—even when they take over completely, they're not really part of me at all.

"They're not all great," I say dismissively. "And some are just solo pieces."

"Anders." Flynn shakes his head. He smiles again, teasingly this time. "I've never heard you play anything of your own that I'd call 'not great.'"

Anything of my own. My stomach tightens.

Flynn must see it in my face. "You okay?" he asks.

"Yeah," I say. "Kind of."

"Because it looks like you're second-guessing yourself again." Flynn watches me for a second. "You know how rare you are, right? You know how few high school bands aren't just playing a set of crappy covers, plus two original songs that are such rip-offs of Metallica or Nirvana that they might as well be covers, too?"

"I don't know." I look at my raw knuckles. If there's anyone in the world who I don't want to disappoint, it's Flynn. But that article is still echoing in my head, along with Frankie's words about muses being real, and graduation is just a couple months away, and everything is starting to feel so huge that I need to let part of it out. Just the tiniest, most careful part. "Sometimes it feels like . . ." I start. "Like this was just *given* to me. You know?"

Flynn tilts his head. "You mean your talent?"

"Talent, yeah. If you want to call it that."

"I want to call it that." Flynn grins. "Okay. Is that a problem?"

"I don't know. Doesn't that make it, like . . . less real?"

"The way you play sounds real to me."

I meet Flynn's eyes. "Yeah, but . . ." I've opened the

door, but I'm not ready to step through it. I force one toe over the edge. "What about *earning* it? Isn't something you earn more *yours* than something that's just given to you?"

Flynn's eyes flick, sharp, to the calluses on my fingertips. "Are you trying to tell me you don't practice like a maniac?"

"No. I practice. But that's what I'd be doing anyway. It's not work. It's not pain. It's just me."

"You think you need pain?" Now his eyes move to my knuckles. "You need to be the suffering artist?"

I breathe in hard. The room smells like rust.

Maybe that's all this is. Maybe I'm only trying to hurt myself. Maybe the thing I'm so afraid of, the thing I think I have to hide, doesn't even matter. Maybe, as usual, Flynn understands even more about me than I do.

Flynn puts his elbows on his knees and leans in. "I see you, kid," he says softly. "I *see* you. Your commitment to this. Maybe it doesn't feel like a sacrifice, because you want to do it, but you're still giving it everything you have." He turns up his palms. "And even if talent *is* just something that's given to certain people and not to others, what's wrong with that? I mean . . . they call it being *gifted* for a reason."

I look down at the guitar strings. I feel myself start to smile. "You know, sometimes coming here feels like going to confession."

Flynn laughs. He makes a sloppy sign of the cross in my direction. "Bless you, my son. Now give me five Hail Marys and ten B-minor scales."

And then we go back to lesson stuff.

There's not much that I can't tell Flynn. This makes the things that I can't tell him seem worse.

I've never told him about that night in the woods beyond the Crow's Nest.

I've never told anybody. It's been long enough, almost two years, that I can tell myself different versions of the story, shifting things around until it's all totally meaningless. I mean, what actually happened? A conversation. Two people talking. That's it.

If things started to change afterward—the songs, the way my hands could move, things with girls like Frankie Lynde—it could all be a coincidence.

That's what I've told myself, over and over and over.

I wish I could believe it.

**They're going to tear the school down.**

Someday. Soon. Whenever the town finds the money to replace it.

The building is unsalvageable, all mismatched brick and leaky latticed windows and hardwood floors that groan and sag. It stands five blocks from Main Street, two blocks from the entrance to the park, not far from the leafy ravine with the old swinging bridge above the river. It's just far enough from the woods to be safe. Mostly.

At school I have three classes with Anders and one without. There aren't that many options, and there aren't that many seniors, so our having most classes together isn't strange. We don't speak to each other, of course. Most days no one speaks to me at all, so that isn't strange, either. But I know exactly where he sits. In the commons. At lunch. During every class.

I'm always on the edge. Watching.

The Anders of Greenwood High School doesn't draw attention to himself. He keeps quiet in class. Never raises his hand. Keeps his eyes on the front of the room, so it looks like he's paying attention, but I can see his fingers working beneath his desk, shaping imaginary chords, tapping rhythms on the denim drum of his knee. Sometimes he takes notes when there's nothing to take notes on, and his writing comes out in columns of tight, miniature print with spaces where each verse ends or chorus begins, and then he's not actually taking notes at all. Sometimes he falls asleep with his head propped carefully up on one arm.

The last half hour of each day, I have study hall in the library. I sit at a tiny table in the reference section, between walls of sagging bookshelves. Anders has art class just down the hall. The art room is close enough to the library that I can stand in the nook beside the chipped white drinking fountains, watching to make sure he's gone through the art room door, and still get to my seat by the time the bell rings.

I've spent the semester reading Collier's Illustrated Encyclopedia. I'm on Volume Twenty: *Renner to Sibelius*. The pages are whisper thin. They smell like bread dough and dust. But I don't always keep my mind on the pages.

Because Frankie Lynde is in the same study hall.

She and her friends sit at a table in front of me and slightly to the left. When I bend over the tiny gray print, I can catch their faces, their eyes, their moving lips.

The others are Sasha, Carson, and Will. Sasha has red-brown hair and four piercings in each ear. Everything about her is sharp: her collarbones, her light brown eyes, her voice. Carson is blond and loud and big shouldered. Will has dark hair and deadpan delivery. Both guys look like they've wandered out of a men's clothing catalog, polished and combed and perfect skinned.

But neither of them is Anders. They can't even hold a candle.

I stare at the encyclopedia and listen. Their conversations are songs with five changing chords: School. Other people. Movies. The weekend. And Last Things. Everybody talks about Last Things.

They're talking about Last Things now.

"You should tell him that," Sasha is saying as they all sit down.

"I am *not* going to tell him that," says Frankie.

"Why not? They need a gimmick. And I'm sure they'd all look great in eyeliner."

"I thought their gimmick was being younger than the songs they play," says Carson.

Frankie smacks him playfully. "They don't do covers anymore. That was just when they were starting out."

"Hey, I think they should do *more* covers. I want to hear Anders Thorson sing 'Blank Space.'"

"I want to hear him do 'Happy,'" says Will. He puts on a death metal growl. "'Because *I'M HAPPY....*'"

Sasha and Carson laugh.

The librarian shushes in their direction.

"You know they don't do covers anymore," Sasha says to Carson a second later. "Weren't you there Friday night?"

"No. I wasn't. Thanks so much for noticing."

"Where were you?" Sasha demands. "Why weren't you there?"

"Because I accidentally backed my dad's truck into the garage door."

"So the truck's in the shop?"

"No. The truck is fine. There's, like, a two-millimeter scratch on the bumper. But my dad blew a gasket."

"Why do people say that?" asks Frankie. "'Blow a gasket.' What is a gasket?"

"It's the part that regulates the truck's emotions," says Will.

Frankie laughs.

The librarian's voice slices the dusty air. "Keep it down over there, or I'll have to separate you."

"Sorry, Ms. Schmidt," says Frankie.

"Uh-oh," whispers Sasha. "Ms. Schmidt's going to blow a gasket."

"Ms. Schmidt can blow *me*," mutters Carson.

Frankie smacks him again.

I turn the page. Sacajawea in faded gray ink points the way down a craggy hillside.

"God." Sasha lets out a sigh. She flips open a textbook. "Why am I even taking physics? When am I going to use any of this?"

Will tugs the pencil out of her fingers. He opens his hand and the pencil falls to the table, rolling across the scarred wooden surface. "Look. You just used physics."

"So, you'll be at the Crow's Nest tomorrow night, right?" Frankie asks Carson. "If your dad's gasket has been repaired, I mean?"

"I don't know. Maybe."

"What else are you going to do in this town on a Friday night?" Sasha pushes. "Count how many times you can drive up and down Main Street on one tank of gas?"

"Come on," adds Frankie. "Everybody's going to be there."

Carson shrugs. He leans back in his chair, trying to look bored by everything. "I've heard all their stuff a hundred times already."

"You have not. They're writing new stuff all the time. Anders says they'll have at least two brand-new songs tomorrow."

Carson sticks his hands into the pockets of his letter jacket. "It's kind of crazy that they have time to write songs at all, with their busy devil-worshipping and animal-sacrificing schedules."

Frankie tips her head. "What are you talking about?"

"I don't know. Don't all metal bands worship the devil?"

"I don't know," Frankie says. "Don't all football players keep roofies in the pockets of their letter jackets?"

Carson pulls his hands out of his pockets.

"Speaking of new songs." Sasha shoves her textbook to the side. She taps Frankie's hand with the end of her pencil. "That soft one, that 'Deep Water' one. Is that about *you*?"

Frankie tucks her hair behind her ear. It makes a perfect, pointed curl against her jaw. She smiles. "I don't know."

"I think it's *definitely* about you. There's that line about

'Her eyes are so dark I can only see myself. . . .'"

"Narcissistic," murmurs Will.

"And 'I wonder what she's hiding, deep deep down where no one wanders.'"

"And dirty," Will adds.

Now Sasha smacks him. "It is not."

"It does kind of sound like you," says Carson. His face twists into a smile. "Does he call you and read you his latest lyrics over the phone?" He puts on a lower, raspier voice. It's supposed to sound like Anders. It doesn't. No one sounds like Anders. *"Oh, Frankie. You're so dark and mysterious and fine. You're so metal you blow my mind."*

Frankie is still smiling, but there's a little defensive hardness in her face now. A jagged rock in a meadow. Frankie wants people to think she and Anders are together. She wants it to be the truth. Her eyes steer away from Carson and trail through the library shelves, drifting toward me.

I turn back to the open encyclopedia. I need to be more careful.

"I need to finish this page," says Frankie, opening her math book. "Or, actually, Carson needs to finish it for me."

"Why do I need to finish it?"

"Because you'd rather have us drive you home than ride the bus." Frankie's smile is playful now. "Right?"

"Fine." Carson spins her book toward him. "But I warn you, I'm not a math genius."

"Good," says Frankie. "Neither am I. We don't want Ms. Grover to get suspicious."

"Freaking physics," huffs Sasha. She throws herself back in her chair. Her profile faces me. Behind her, on the other side of a half-bare bookshelf, I can see Jaden Angstrom reaching down for his book bag. Its strap is hooked around the shelf's bottom corner.

Jaden pulls. The bag resists. The rickety shelf wobbles.

I see Jaden strengthen his grip. I see him pull again. Pull harder. I see the shelf begin to tilt.

And then I feel the shelf's splintery wooden edge in my hand.

Without even thinking, I've crossed the floor. I catch the bookshelf before it can smash down on the table full of Frankie and her friends.

Will jumps out of his chair. Together we push the shelf upright. A few ancient hardcovers, jostled out of place, tumble down and whack against the gray carpet. I catch two books awkwardly in my arms.

Everyone stares. Sasha, still hunched over, protecting

her head with one arm. Carson, blank faced. Frankie.

I shove the books, sideways, any which way, back onto their shelf. I make sure my movements are slow and clumsy.

Foolish. Foolish.

"Quick thinking, Superman," says Will.

"You mean Super*girl*." Frankie's words are for Will, but she's looking straight at me. "Or Wonder Woman. That's more like it."

I start to back away. "It wasn't that heavy."

"Heavy enough to hurt somebody," Frankie says. "Sasha could have been avalanched by books."

Sasha is still just staring at me. She looks like she's flipped over a rock and is studying the things scuttling for shelter beneath it.

I take another step backward.

Carson is watching me, too. He and Will are both looking at me like they've never seen me before.

And they haven't. Not really. That's been the whole point.

I turn around now, toward my own table, ready to slip back over the edge.

"Hey, wait," calls Frankie's voice. "What's your name again?"

I pause. There's nothing dangerous in Frankie's eyes. No shadows, as dark as they are. Just depths.

"Thea," I say.

"Thanks for saving us, Thea." Frankie's smile. Pearls in a red-velvet box.

"Nice reflexes," says Carson.

"Nice flannel," says Sasha, not quite under her breath.

I touch the cuff of the old gray-and-black plaid. It's a men's shirt, secondhand and a little too large, even on me. The cuffs are so worn and frayed that they feel like silk. I smile. "Thanks."

I move back to my table. I don't rush. I am as gray and soft and indistinct as my shirt.

I love this shirt.

"You know who that is, don't you?" I can hear Sasha saying to the others, in a too-loud whisper.

"No," says Frankie.

"I've never seen her before," says Will.

"Yes, you have," Sasha hisses. "That's that psycho who lives in that shack in the woods with Mae Malcolm."

"I don't know who Mae Malcolm is, either," says Will.

"*Dude,*" says Carson, disbelieving.

"Yes, you *do,*" Sasha insists. "She's that hermit who sometimes shows up around town, drunk, telling people about some awful thing she *foresaw* or whatever."

Will's voice is even dryer than usual. "So she's a witch."

"No, she's, like, a *lunatic*." Sasha hesitates, probably taking another look at me. "I guess that girl's her niece or something. You've *seen* her, you guys. She comes to every single one of Anders's shows. She's, like, his stalker."

"We go to all his shows, too," says Frankie.

"But he actually *wants* us there." Sasha's voice gets sharper.

"He wants everybody there," says Frankie. "I think that's the point of performing. To have an audience."

Sasha says something else, something in a genuine whisper this time. Carson answers her. Soon their conversation moves on, bumping away from me back to its usual course.

I sit still, my eyes on the encyclopedia. Sacraments. Saints. Saint Petersburg.

Frankie is kind.

It's too bad, really.

Because Frankie Lynde has to go.

**"Stop. Stop. STOP."**

Patrick raises his sticks. He grabs a shivering cymbal between two fingers. Their hiss dies away in the oily air of his parents' garage. "What?"

"The beat there," I say. "It changes time signature. It's one six-eight measure and then a seven-eight one."

"And then it switches back?"

"Yes. It's one-two one-two-three one-two—"

"I know what seven-eight time is."

"Then why aren't you playing it?"

Patrick's knuckles whiten. "Dude, if I hadn't heard this song for the first time *four minutes* ago . . ."

"Whoa." Jezz speaks up. "Anders, why don't you just play it again?"

I let out a loud sigh.

"I don't need to hear it again," says Patrick before I

can even start. "I need the chance to freaking *think* for a second before I can pull a perfect drum line out of my—"

"Okay, okay," says Jezz loudly. "Someday we'll be able to read each other's minds, and then geniuses like Anders won't have to feel so tortured and misunderstood. But until then, we'll just have to deal. So let's try it again."

"All right." I pry my fingers off the neck of the guitar.

I need to get this song out. It's been pounding through my body since last night, tripping up my heartbeat with its rhythm. I need to hear it outside of my own head, ringing against the walls of Patrick's garage. I need to be part of it. I need to bring it to life.

I also need not to be an ass.

"Sorry," I mumble.

"Just play the chorus again." Jezz positions his hands on the bass.

I move through it again, more slowly, speaking the words in rhythm.

*Come out come out wherever you are*
*Come out and play*
*Crawl out crawl out whatever you are*
*You win you win*
*I give in*

Jezz finds the bass line. He thrums softly along. "It's creepy, dude."

"Of course it's creepy," says Patrick from behind the drum set. "Everything we play is creepy."

"Hey! You know what we should do?" Jezz gives a little hop, and his floppy blond hair slides down over one eye. "We should write one giant, sappy, totally cliché love ballad. Like, slow-dance-at-prom, end-of-the-movie ballad. We should wait until the crowd is going crazy, like, after 'Superhero,' and then we should just slide into this love song and watch their heads explode."

Patrick's hard face snaps apart with a grin. "No. We should write a polka. We can become the world's only polka-metal band." He starts tapping out a three-four beat on the snare. *Oom-pa-pa. Oom-pa-pa.*

"You mean the world's *first* polka-metal band." Jezz adds a bass line. "We'll start a trend."

Patrick laughs. "Dude. We'll be *huge* in Germany."

I start to smile, strumming a G chord. "Ach, Hedwig, I love ya. . . ."

Jezz hoots. "Dere's no one above ya. . . ."

"You're better than *Blutwurst und Bier*."

Patrick cracks up.

The laugh warms the air. There's more laughter

from the backyard, where Mac and Lee and Ellie are sprawled on the lawn furniture. Some other kids, people I don't even know, are lounging around on the lawn. We always leave the garage door shut during band practice, but we open the door to the Murrays' backyard, so whoever's out there can listen.

People started showing up to our practices about three years ago, when we went from mediocre to almost good. Now they come every day. At first having them there felt flattering. It made us show off, made us work a little harder. Now it also makes me tired. I have to keep on the face, keep up the act.

Someone is always watching.

And I sound paranoid.

"Perfect," says Jezz. "We've got our polka-metal prom ballad. Now we sit back and watch the money roll in."

I pull my phone out of my pocket and check the time. "We should get back on track."

"What do you want to do?" asks Patrick. He plays a quick, tapping roll on the drum's metal edge.

"We need to do 'Come Out and Play' again. I want to do it at the Crow's Nest tomorrow."

"What?" Patrick's sticks stop. "We've got three new songs already."

"Three out of fifteen isn't that many."

"We won't be ready."

"We will if we practice enough now."

"Dude." Patrick scrubs his eyes with the heels of his hands. "This is, like, sweatshop music. You keep cranking out the songs, and we keep assembling the pieces."

"I have to," I say. "Or they just pile up, and it's—" I flick at the strings with my fingernails. "Okay. Fine. Whatever. We'll just play old stuff."

"I'm not saying I want to *just* play old stuff."

Jezz flops down on an overturned crate, settling in for the long haul.

"I'd rather play stuff we've actually polished. Stuff that's decent," Patrick finishes.

"Play 'Blood Money'!" shouts Ellie's voice from the backyard.

"We haven't done that one in forever," Jezz points out.

"Do we really want to play stuff we've already done a thousand times?" I ask the guys. "That's like watching the same TV show over and over and over."

Jezz shrugs. "People do that."

"*Stoners* do that."

"Dude, stoners are people, too."

"Let's just play a decent mix of old and new stuff

then," Patrick says, twirling a stick through three fingers. "Four new songs. Max."

"Or you could do some of the new songs on your own, Anders," says Jezz. His tone is light, but I feel the air turn cold again. "Much simpler."

I look down at the greasy cement floor. Seeds from the backyard's drooping birch tree are scattered everywhere, like tiny bread crumbs. "No," I say. "One solo song is enough. More than enough."

Jezz slides off the crate. "Is the writer from the *Tribune* going to be there?"

I keep looking at the floor. There's a grease stain the shape of a huge hoofprint just to the left of my foot. "I think so."

"All the more reason for us to keep the new stuff pared down," says Jezz.

"All the more reason for Anders to do more solos," says Patrick. "That's why they're coming anyway. Right?"

"That's not why," I say. But I'm not sure he even hears me.

"Come on," Jezz tells Patrick. "Anders might be an obsessive-compulsive weirdo, but he's not an asshole."

"I didn't say he was," says Patrick. He taps both feet impatiently on the pedals. The big drum pounds like a racer's heart. "I just think he likes being in the spotlight."

Now I look straight into Patrick's eyes. "I don't care about the spotlight."

Patrick's mouth curls.

"I don't." A lie. He knows it. "I just wanted to be good at *this*." I shake the guitar on its strap. "I don't care about the rest."

"Sure," says Patrick.

"I don't." I'm lying to both of us now. Without recognition, what proof do you have that you're any good? And I need that. I need to know it. "I'm not in this for some kind of fifteen-minute, freak-show fame," I say loudly. "It's not about me. It's about *us*. It's about our music." Then, because Patrick is still glaring at me, I go on. "Look. I just got a call from S&A Management. They were practically begging me to meet with them. And I turned them down."

*Shit.*

I hadn't meant to tell them this. I'd planned to keep it secret. I hadn't meant to throw it out like this, in the middle of an argument, like gas on a bonfire. And I know, by the way both the guys are turning toward me, that I've made a huge mistake.

"What?" Jezz is saying. "S&A Artist Management? Like, that agency in the Cities? You turned them down?"

"They wanted to meet with *you*?" Patrick says softly.

"They wanted *us*." I meet Jezz's eyes. I can't even look at Patrick now. "They've heard us play. I guess they sent a scout once, and we didn't even know. They wanted to get to us before anybody else could."

"And you turned them down?" Jezz says again.

Ellie and Lee and Mac have gotten up and gathered at the open back door. Their faces peer in at us, watching. Christ. Even this has to be a performance.

"You guys." I rake my sweaty hands through my hair. "S&A is small stuff. Little, local stuff. We are going to be big. There is big stuff on its way. I promise you."

Because I am going to get everything I want. Everything. Just like someone else promised me, months and months ago, that night behind the Crow's Nest.

"You didn't even ask us," Patrick speaks up. His voice is dangerously low. "You just made the call. On your own."

"We all said we'd wait until we were done with school. Right?" I'm getting louder now. "That's what we said."

"Well . . . yeah," says Jezz. "But there's only, like, a month and a half left. And it's S&A."

"Right. It's S&A. We can do better."

"Who cares what *we* can do?" Patrick's voice cuts in.

I look back at him.

Patrick's forearms are like bridge cables. Years of high-speed metal drumming will do that to a guy. The cables twist as he turns the drumsticks slowly around in his hands. "This isn't about us. You didn't even ask us. This is all about *you*."

I can't answer. He's right. And I'm caught.

"But we're here, too," says Patrick. He's still speaking in that strange, low, calm voice I've only heard him use once or twice before—and once was right before he turned around and punched a redneck jackass named Kev Burr in the face. "We were going to do this together. Take a year. See what happens. But if you make all the calls, and you mess up, you pull us down with you."

"It's true, Anders," says Jezz. His voice is lighter than Patrick's, but there's a seriousness in it I don't even recognize. "Maybe that was our chance. We shouldn't just throw it away. I mean, this is Greenwood. You work at the plastics factory, you work for the mill, or you get the hell out." He shrugs, giving a lopsided smile. "I thought we were getting the hell out."

"We are." My hands are starting to shake. "I swear. We are."

Patrick sets his sticks on the head of a drum. They make a papery thud. "Why are we doing this, Thorson?"

he asks. "Why are we practicing every single day? Why are you staying up all night writing songs and losing your mind when we can't instantly learn them? Why are we doing two goddamn shows a week for free?" His voice is getting stronger. "Why are we even a band? If you're not all in, why don't we just shut the garage doors and play some Mastodon songs? Hell, why don't we just play some *Halo*? Why are we doing any of this?"

I stare back at Patrick. I'm breathing hard. Words boil inside me.

*If* I'm all in? He has no idea.

He has no idea how much I want this. The music. The shows. The fans. I want the people in the blur beyond the edge of the stage screaming the words along with me. I want the weight of this guitar in my hands, the strap on my shoulder, Jezz to my left, Patrick behind me, both of them building the layers of sound that I can stand on and sing. I want bigger things than S&A. Bigger things than Minnesota. I want the world to know who we are. I want to be the best. I want to *know* I'm the best. I want it so much that it scares me.

So much that it's dangerous.

"I am *all in*," I say, in a voice that barely sounds like mine. "I'm . . ."

And then, instead of even trying to finish the sentence, I'm storming out of the Murrays' garage. I'm stuffing Yvonne into the passenger seat of the battered white car. I'm gunning the motor, and I'm screaming off down the street, toward the only place I can think of to go.

### The house at 751 Franconia Street is empty.

It's beige and sealed and silent. The For Sale sign is coated with a light layer of dirt, picked up by the wind and pasted in place by months of drying rain and dew. The doors, front and back, are padlocked with clunky gray key boxes, and curtains are pulled over the empty rooms.

But the fence is easy to climb.

It's a wood-slat fence, about six feet high. It encloses the entire backyard. The gaps between its planks release shredded flashes of Patrick's backyard, next door at 749 Franconia.

Last Things is practicing.

A few kids from the high school are lounging in the yard, dangling off the lawn chairs, skateboarding slowly up and down the paved walk. Their Converse shoes smack the ground after each sloppy flip. Their voices crumble over the music that pounds out of the garage like an aluminum-sided heart.

Behind the empty house at 751, at the edge of the overgrown yard, there's a sagging wooden playhouse. Scraps of linoleum on the packed dirt floor. Water-stiffened magazine pictures taped to the walls. Horses. Roses. Wedding dresses. There's one small, paneless window at the back. Every afternoon after school I sit on an overturned bucket inside the playhouse, beside this window. I can see past the window box full of long-dead and dry geraniums to the fence, through a knothole in the boards, straight into a shady patch of the Murrays' yard, just beside the garage's open back door. No one can see me.

But I can hear everything.

They play new things, old things. "Dead Girl." "Lost and Found." They play "Frozen" for the first time in a very long time. The last time I heard it was at the Crow's Nest, back in October, a few weeks after I came here.

It was the night Janos talked with me for the first time. The first time beyond *Whole, two-percent, or skim?* and *You're welcome,* anyway. I was sitting at the back of the room, near the coffee bar, on the edge of the crowd. Janos came over when the set ended. He had pockmarked skin and a rasping accent. Slovak, I learned later.

"You come every week," he said, leaning down to wipe my table.

"I like the music."

"The music. Yeah." Janos grinned at me.

He thinks it's a crush. That's all. Something small and sweet and harmless. Something to tease a girl about.

Janos is kind.

"He's good, isn't he?" Janos nodded across the room.

The stage was empty now, the band waiting for the place to clear a bit before packing up. But who he meant was obvious.

"Yes," I said. "He's really good."

Janos nodded. "He'll be famous someday."

"You think so?"

Janos nodded again, calm, certain, like I'd just asked him if the Crow's Nest would be open tomorrow. He smiled down at me. "And we'll say we knew him before everyone else."

"How long have you known him?" I asked, taking the last cold sip of my café au lait. I'd made it last through the whole night. There's never money for a second.

"They played here the first time a couple years ago."

"Were they already really good?"

Janos looked like he was considering this. "Good. Yes. Very good for sixteen. They played mostly covers. A couple months later they played again. Now mostly new songs. His songs. More people showed up. Then they started coming back every week. Like you." He looked down at me for another moment. From a distance, I would have guessed that Janos was in his thirties. Up close, past the scarred skin, he looked younger. Maybe twenty-three, twenty-four.

"Why do you always come alone?" he asked. "Watch alone? Sit alone?"

"I'm new in town," I told him.

He tipped his head back. "I know what new in town is like. But this is a small town." He gestured around with his damp rag. "It doesn't take long for people to know you."

"Maybe." I smiled up at him. "But I don't mind sitting alone."

He picked up my empty cup. "You have family here?"

"My aunt Mae. I'm living with her for now. My father's on the road."

Janos squinted at me. "Mae Malcolm?"

"You know her?"

He shook his head. "People talk. You know. Small towns."

Something about his face, his steady eyes, made me ask the question. "What do they say?"

"You really want to hear?"

I smiled at him again. "I've probably already heard."

"They say stupid things. Superstitious." He shrugged, flicking the damp rag. "She starts fires. She does magic. She found a body in the woods, someone missing for months, because a vision led her there."

I smiled a little wider. The last part is true. But better if he thinks it's just a rumor.

Janos went on. "Does she worry when you're out late? Alone?"

"No. And I'm not scared."

He glanced toward the window. Beyond the glass the autumn sky was saturating with deep blue darkness. "Not scared of the dark, or of being by yourself?"

"Right," I said.

Janos laughed. He turned away, carrying my cup. "Café au lait?"

"I don't have—" I began, but he cut me off.

"We have to pour out the old coffee anyway. You can drink it while you wait for . . ." He nodded toward the stage again.

The band had just reappeared. Jezz and Patrick and

Anders were starting the ritual of packing up.

So I stayed at my corner table. Janos set down the steaming cup, giving me a quick wink. I sipped the hot, foamy coffee as the band laughed and talked about the set and nestled instruments into cases, and I wrote the words "Thank you" with a handful of pennies, which was all I had in my pockets, and left them on the table beside my coffee cup. When the band moved outside, I slipped after them, keeping so far back in the leafy shadows around the Crow's Nest that none of them even noticed I was there.

Now, in the abandoned playhouse, I take a breath. Scents of damp paper, wet earth, old wood. My foot has fallen asleep. The overturned bucket isn't the most comfortable seat, but I will wait here for as long as I need to. As long as it takes.

They're still working the rhythms of "Come Out and Play." The music screams loud enough that I can shift my weight on the bucket without being heard, stretch my arms over my head. I point the leg with the sleeping foot, making a little circle with my ankle. The toe of my battered sneaker scuffs the dirt. Something glitters. I bend down and brush it with my fingertips.

A little girl's necklace, its chain too small to close

around an adult's throat. Strung with pink beads and tiny gold stars. Lost, or maybe buried here, like treasure. Left behind. I rub the stars between my thumb and finger until the black dirt is gone and they can shine. Then I hang the necklace on the head of a nail that sticks out of the playhouse wall. It twinkles against a picture of a sea-sprayed white stallion.

The garage next door has gone quiet. I can hear Ellie Hammond and Lee Skiff arguing about something one of them said or didn't say, and Patrick's voice murmuring something over the muted, habitual roll of drumsticks against a rim.

Then Anders's voice. Jezz's. The voices get louder. They're talking. Arguing.

I press myself against the playhouse's clammy wooden wall. Ellie is giggling. The wheels of a skateboard clack on the cement. Jezz and Patrick are talking. I catch Anders once more.

Then shouting.

"Why are we doing this?" I hear it again. "Why . . . Why . . ." Other words lost in distance, behind the barriers of walls.

They're arguing more and more lately. I get to my feet, crouching in the playhouse. I wait until I hear the sound of an engine roaring away down the street.

I duck through the playhouse door. Thin stripes of the Murrays' backyard flicker as I dart along the fence: grass, siding, arborvitae, pavement. I jump over the fence slats into the front yard, into a patch of overgrown shrubs and sour-smelling weeds. Through their leaves, I catch the white blur of Anders's car peeling away.

At the end of the street, he turns left.

He's not heading toward home. He's heading downtown.

I grab my bike from its hiding spot behind 751's garbage cans.

By the time the white car screeches to a stop on Main Street, just across from the music studio, I'm waiting in the intersecting alley.

The world is thin here. The whole town is thin; the woods all around Greenwood are binding it together like a black wire net. And there's a spot, underground, right through the door Anders entered, where it's barely held together. Where something dark and quick could push forward and slip straight out of its world into ours.

I climb off the bike. If I stay here, in the alley beside the corroded trash bins, I'm out of sight of the street. But I can see the dark things. They're trying to hide, but I can spot them, hunched behind corners, pressed against walls. Shadows where there is no one to cast shadows. Nobody's shadow would look like that anyway.

Warped. Bony. Bent almost like branches.

They are waiting.

I can feel them.

And they can feel me pushing back.

ANDERS

I shove the stenciled glass door. *Nancy's Needles. HOMETOWN INSURANCE. Underground Music Studio.* The names flash and swing in front of me. I yank open the metal door, thunder down the steps, and charge across the central room. A kid with a stack of piano books in his lap looks up from the corduroy couch as I fly past.

I pound on Flynn's door. Loud enough that I'm sure he can hear, no matter what noise is trapped on the other side.

A second later the door opens. Flynn blinks out at me. His eyebrows rise.

"Hey, Anders," he says. "You okay?"

"Not really. Can I talk to you?"

"Sure." Flynn pauses. Over his shoulder I can see a girl about ten years old perched on the folding chair, miniature acoustic guitar across her lap. Her feet swing a few inches from the floor. "We were almost done here." Flynn turns toward the girl. "What do you think, Jamie? You want to do that *Little Mermaid* piece one more time? Anders could listen to you. Give you some feedback. He's pretty good."

Jamie glances at me. I'm clenching the door frame with one hand. One of my legs is vibrating with impatience.

Jamie shakes her head.

"Want to just be done for today?" Flynn asks.

Jamie nods.

She darts past me with her guitar, sneaking one more glance at me out of the corner of her eye.

Flynn beckons me in.

I step through the door, and he shuts it quickly behind me.

Suddenly I feel wrong, like I'm missing part of my body. I realize a second later that what I'm missing is my guitar. I'm never in this room without it. I left Yvonne outside, locked in the car. My hands feel huge and empty.

"What's up?" asks Flynn.

"The band. The other guys." I want to pace, or punch a wall, or do something to let out the energy searing through me, but this is Flynn's studio, not my own bedroom. I try to stand still. "They're pissed at me. And they should be. I did something stupid. But there was nothing else I could do."

"Okay." Flynn lowers himself onto his usual chair. He folds his ropy arms and leans back, listening. "Did you guys break up? Is the band over?"

"What? No. *No.*" Just the idea throws me. I swear, the cement floor starts to rock. "I don't think so. Jesus. I hope not."

Flynn nods. "Okay. Then you'll move on. You fight, and you move on." He gives me a dry smile. "That's what bands do. They fight. With occasional breaks to play music."

Flynn is so . . . *Flynn.* He's so mellow and cool and ready to laugh at whatever deserves it, I can feel the tension inside me lessen a little bit. But it's not quite enough.

"This was more than that." I try to string words together. "I don't know if—I don't—I don't know . . ."

"Okay," says Flynn again. "Just take a breath." He nods to the other chair, inviting me to sit. I throw myself down. Flynn uncrosses his ankles and leans forward, elbows on knees. "So, this isn't really about the other guys, right?"

I writhe in the chair. I can't seem to remember how sitting works.

"Right," I say. "It's my fault."

Flynn keeps his voice light. "What's your fault?"

The water I'm wading into is cold and deep. I take a breath, like Flynn said, and slowly let it out again. "Someone from S&A Artist Management called me a couple weeks ago."

Flynn's eyebrows twitch. Flynn stays pretty chill about almost everything, but now and then his eyebrows give him away. "S&A, huh? Decent people."

"Yeah. And I told them I wasn't interested."

"Without talking to Jezz and Patrick," Flynn supplies.

"Yes."

Flynn nods slowly. "Kind of a dick move."

"I know. I *know*. We all said we wouldn't sign any-thing until we were done with school, but I still should have told them. It was just—they were just asking *me*. Like I was in charge. Or maybe like they just wanted me. Not *us*. I don't know."

"Okay." Flynn turns his hands up in a tiny shrug. "So maybe it just wasn't the right thing."

"But that's not really it." This is colder, deeper water than we've been in before. I can't see the bottom here. "I guess . . . I'm worried about what will happen when I do say yes."

"Ah." I can hear Flynn take a deep breath of his own. "I get it."

My head snaps up. "You get it?" He does?

Flynn nods again. "Oh, yeah. It happens to almost everybody, man. You climb up the ladder, you walk down to the end of the diving board, and all of the sudden you see how high up you are, and you think maybe you don't really want to jump. I get it."

I twist in my seat. God, I wish I had my guitar. Just so I had something to clench in my hands. "No. It's . . ." I scrape my fingers through my hair. My scalp is sweaty. "I'm not, like, scared of leaving town or something. I'm not scared of taking a chance. I'm—" I have to stop and swallow. "I feel like I'm about to get everything I've always wanted. You know? *Everything.*"

"And *that* scares you." Flynn leans on his elbows. He brings his face close to mine. "We knew this was coming, right? Representation, touring, a record deal. I mean, the things you've been writing, the way you can play. People were going to notice." He cracks a smile. "I don't promise any of my students fame and fortune in the music business, but if I was going to make a bet on someone . . ." He gives my knee a quick, warm pat. "Listen. Anders. If you're thinking the life of a touring musician isn't what you want anymore, that's one thing. That's fine. That's *sane*." He grins knowingly. "But if you're just doubting *yourself,* that's another thing entirely."

I stare hard at Flynn, grabbing every word out of his mouth like it might be the thing that saves me, that makes the shitty situation with my best friends seem not so shitty after all. For a second I think about Flynn's life. Single. No family that I know of. Scattered friends. No roots but the shallow ones he's put down here. Maybe music pulls people apart as often as it brings them together. Maybe I'm headed for loss no matter what I do.

Flynn leans back, the graying coils of his hair sweeping over his shoulder. "You know, life isn't a one-way street. You can play lead guitar in a metal band for a few years, touring the world, doing crazy stuff, and then you can move to some small town where the rent is nice and cheap and teach guitar to schoolkids." He shrugs, grinning. "But Anders . . ." He pauses. His face gets serious. "You need to at least *try*. I mean it. Go down that road far enough that you can see where it leads before you turn away."

There's another moment of quiet. I can hear the hum of pipes and vents, and the muffled plinking of a piano lesson in another studio seeping in under the door.

In that quiet I want to blurt out everything. I want to tell Flynn the whole truth.

But I can't.

I can't tell him about that night in the woods. If I even try, he'll know one of two things: either I'm a fraud, a pathetic lying tool, or I am batshit insane.

"You know how we talked about talent." I measure the words. "About gifts." My heart's pounding. I'm so close to going too far. "If something's *given* to you, then somebody else had to give it, right? And if they give you more and more, won't they—probably—want something in return?"

I stare straight into Flynn's eyes. I'm begging him to understand. I'm praying for him to see through the words into what I can't say.

Flynn's eyes are greenish brown and steady.

He looks right back at me.

"Giving everything is scary," he says at last. "Giving your whole self to something—it's huge. I know. But sometimes that's what music demands." Slowly, lazily, he scratches his bicep with his missing-fingered hand. "Sometimes it demands a sacrifice."

A spear of terror juts through me.

I look away. Fast.

No, I tell myself. No way. This is *Flynn*. He didn't mean anything more by it. He couldn't know his words would stick like a knife in my unzipped chest.

We sit still for another minute, chair to chair.

I finally get my breathing under control.

"Well," I mumble at last, getting up, "I should go. I don't mean to screw up your lesson schedule."

"Don't worry about it." Flynn stands up, too. He smiles, squeezing my shoulder with one calloused hand. "Sometimes you've just got to go to confession. I get it."

He follows me toward the door.

His next student, a middle schooler with angry-looking acne blistered across his forehead, is waiting right outside, guitar case in his hands.

"Any time you need to talk, I'm here," Flynn says.

But then he ushers the kid inside and shuts the insulated metal door. And I'm alone in the empty waiting room, with that knife still sticking in my chest.

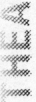

I follow the little white car away from the music studio and back to Anders's house. I'm behind the big pine before he pulls into the driveway. After watching him step safely through his front door, I steer the bike back into the trees. I keep away from the road, deep in the shade, where no one will see how fast I can ride. I don't know my own speed, but I'm faster than Anders's car. Faster than any car I've ever chased.

The air whips past me.

It's getting cold. Afternoon is turning to evening, the blue sky folding into violet. There's a trace of smoke coming somewhere not far away. Burning pine.

There's a spot where the ground folds, and a creek bed, just a muddy slash now, winds through a knot of giant oaks. I'm riding down the slope when I feel them.

They're right behind me.

I slow the bike.

A hiss in the underbrush. Crackling leaves.

I place one shoe on the ground and whip around.

Something slides behind a trunk.

Something huge and dark and hunched.

Something that's shaped almost like a human, but that gleams with thick black hair.

There's still light in the sky. So they're coming out earlier now. They're getting bold.

"I see you," I say. But I only say it inside of myself. They'll hear me anyway. *"I see you."*

The dark thing doesn't reappear.

I climb off the bicycle.

Holding the handlebars, I walk toward the tree where the thing disappeared. I leave a few feet between myself and the trunk. Sticks snap under my shoes.

The air shifts as I get closer. Warmer. Hot.

I smell the smoke.

With a last step, I slip around the tree.

Nothing.

No hunched, thick-haired, bent-legged shape.

But on the trunk are claw marks. Fresh ones.

And lying on the ground, on a bed of fallen leaves, is a gift it left for me.

It's a bird. A mourning dove. Pale gray against pale brown. Its head faces backward, its neck snapped. Its wings are spread but limp, the feathers ragged. There's blood on the leaves around it. Just a few drops. All the blood that a small bird has.

They're trying to scare me. Trying. All I feel is pity for the stupid little bird.

I am not their prey.

They can't get rid of me, and they know it. And I can't get rid of them. Not all of them. Not when they stay well hidden, slipping in and out of the gaps.

We can only touch the things that live between us. The smaller, more breakable things.

I take off the flannel I'm wearing over my black thermal shirt. Gently, with the soft fabric spread between my hands, I gather up the dead bird.

Then I climb back onto my bike.

There's an old firepit behind Aunt Mae's farmhouse that hasn't been used in years. I rip up handfuls of grass, toss out clumps of moss. When the dirt is bare, I collect sticks and pinecones, old newspapers from the rain-bleached pile on the front porch. I get the big box of matches from the kitchen, the ones we use to light Aunt Mae's ancient stove.

I place the bird on top of the heap of kindling in the center of the firepit.

The paper lights fast. The flames are so high and bright I don't have to see the mourning dove dissolving inside. Only searing gold.

When everything is burned away, I head indoors.

"I'm going to do a load of laundry," I tell Aunt Mae. She's sitting upright on the couch, her hands shuffling a deck of cards. Half a game of solitaire is spread on the coffee table in front of her. "Would you like me to wash your blankets?"

"Well, that would be lovely. Thank you." Aunt Mae rocks to her feet. She helps me wad up the crocheted blanket and the old yellow quilt. "While you do that, I'll start on dinner."

"I can make dinner, Aunt Mae."

She waves me off with one hand. "I got a special treat at the grocery store."

Aunt Mae hasn't left the house in nearly two weeks. Too many long nights, too many bad dreams. Too many stares when she does go out.

But there are good days, too. Once in a while.

"You went shopping?" I ask her.

"Yes, I did." Aunt Mae smiles at me. "I got us a frozen

potpie. And some nice apples and French bread. *And* a red velvet cake. Just for us."

So many things at once—so many treats—means money. My father must have finally come through. "You got a letter?"

Aunt Mae smiles wider. "It came this morning."

She passes a slit envelope to me.

Dad is in Missouri now, I see by the postmark. Hannibal. Making his way down the river.

My father repairs boats. Unusual boats. Old boats. Wooden boats. Paddle wheelers and replica pirate ships. Between jobs he drinks too much bourbon and stands in the water, preaching and shouting about damnation and offering to baptize passersby. Once in a blue moon, someone takes him up on it.

In the letter, one ragged-edged sheet of notebook paper, he describes his latest job, working on a Mark Twain-themed tour boat. He writes about his truck, his trailer full of tools and parts, says he's getting decent gas mileage but might need new tires soon. He talks about the water and the weather. He mentions the hundred dollars he's sending inside.

Then there's part of the letter that's just for me.

*Thea, I hope you're doing good at school. Remember who's watching out for you even when I'm not. Though you*

*walk through the valley of the shadow, you will fear no evil,*
*and surely goodness and mercy will follow you all the days*
*of your life.*


My father has no idea.

He may be Aunt Mae's brother. But he's not like us.

I slide the paper back into its envelope.

"Sounds like Josiah is doing well." Aunt Mae watches my face. "He's been working steadily for weeks this time."

"Hmm," is all I say.

"Be patient with him." Aunt Mae puts one soft hand on top of mine. "Those who don't have the gifts think that they want them. They don't know the weight."

I set the letter down.

I've been told all of this before. The lore of our family. The ways we aren't just chosen, but made.

I don't need to be told. I've always known what I am. Maybe that's another part of the plan.

"Your father never had your strength," Aunt Mae goes on. "*I've* never had your strength. I don't know of any-one, not for generations, who was made quite like you." She steps closer to me and takes both my hands. Her foot bumps the week's empty whiskey bottles, setting off a tinkly music. She squeezes my hands once, tight, before letting go.

"'Thanks be unto God for his unspeakable gifts.'"

I take Aunt Mae's blankets and my flannel shirt and my second pair of jeans down to the clunky old washing machine at the bottom of the basement steps. We don't have a dryer. Even if I hang everything up tonight, it won't be dry by morning.

But we'll make do.

When I climb back up the stairs, Aunt Mae is in the kitchen. The potpie is already baking in the oven. I can see the cake in its little plastic dome on the counter. As Aunt Mae brushes past me, getting plates, I smell nothing but talcum powder and shampoo.

By morning the sweet smells will probably be burned away in whiskey and sweat.

Aunt Mae knows the weight.

I help set out the dishes and fill empty jam jars with cool water. Aunt Mae hums something I don't recognize. I'm not even sure it's a song.

The egg timer by the stove has just pinged when there's a tap at the front door. It's so timid and small that I wonder if we were supposed to hear it. Aunt Mae is busy digging pot holders out of a drawer. I duck away.

By the time I swing the front door open, the man is halfway down the walk to his car.

He hears the hinges creak. Pauses to glance back.

It's Martin from the Wheelhouse.

"Just hadn't seen you in a few days." He sounds almost sheepish. "Thought she might need that." He points at the floor of the porch, near my feet. A brown paper parcel, the bag twisted tight around the glass neck of a whiskey bottle.

I pick it up. "Thank you."

He nods. Glances past me at the pale blue house. Golden lights stream from the kitchen windows, reaching out into the twilight. "How's she doing?"

"Really good," I say. "It was a good day."

"Good." He's still waiting. His hands are in his pockets. "That's good."

I take a step toward him, off the porch. "Do you want to come in? Have some dinner with us?" I gesture with the bottle. "Or just a drink?"

"Nah." He shakes his head. "I don't touch that stuff anymore. Not since Mae saved me."

He says it matter-of-factly. Like it's something I already know. But then he notices the blank look on my face.

"She didn't tell you about that?"

"No," I say.

He nods, looking just past me. "Almost two years ago now. Late at night, roads still icy. I'd just gotten off a long shift at the 'House, and I'd had too much to drink. Along County N my car skidded off into the woods. Made it almost a hundred feet, I guess. Down a slope. Out of sight of the road. Hit a tree. Smashed me almost through the windshield." He taps the side of his face, where the eye drags downward. "Cut my head. My neck. I probably would have bled out right there. But your aunt came along just in time."

I smile at him. "She's good at that."

"So." Martin halts again, looking beyond me, into the woods. The last tints of sunset have dwindled away. Fireflies are circling the edges of our yard. Little green-gold sparks flash against the darkness.

"Can we pay you for it?" I ask, lifting the bottle again.

Martin grins. He waves a hand. "Nah. Next time."

I watch as he climbs into his car and drives carefully away.

I bring the whiskey inside.

Aunt Mae smiles when I tell her about Martin. She sets the bottle on the coffee table. In case she needs it later.

Just in case.

Then we sit down to our hot chicken potpie, with red velvet cake for dessert.

# ANDERS

**Thursday night, after the blowup with Jezz and Patrick, and after crashing** Flynn's lesson at the studio, I drive around town for a while. I keep trying to think straight, but I just keep reliving the fight instead, like an ugly track played on a loop. I'm finally heading for home when the song attacks.

I have to pull over to the side of the road. The lyrics and melody, the bass line and thumping drums fill my head. By the time I get the car into park, I can barely see.

I have a pen, but no paper. So I write the whole thing on my arm.

*Hear the whispers*
*turning into roars*
*Volume rising*
*beating down the doors*

*Each note a scream*
*The drone is deafening*
*Beat beat beat*
*until the truth is beaten*

*Amplify*
*the things we hide*
*Tear it down*
*and turn up the silence*

It goes on and on, three more verses, another chorus, all complete.

I have to just sit there for a while afterward. My mouth is sour, and my insides are spinning. I'm afraid some cop is going to pull up beside me and decide I must be drunk. But the road behind me stays empty.

I read the words on my arm. Even though it's my handwriting, I feel like I'm seeing them for the first time. *This isn't right,* says something in the back of my head. *This isn't right.* But I've got the song.

Finally, when my hands stop shaking, I put the car back in gear and drive home.

Dad's fixing something in the garage. He gives me a nod as I walk past. Mom flutters around me while I get some leftovers from the fridge. I manage to push the food into my mouth. Then I head down the hallway, shut myself in my room, and start the usual nighttime drill.

Scratch Goblin for a while. Let him out when he starts *mrrk*-ing at the door. Fifty push-ups. Thirty crunches. Jump rope until some of the energy boiling inside seeps out. Then I sit down on the floor at the end of the bed, take Yvonne out of her case, and start playing the chords that go with the new lyrics. I play them again and again and again, until they're enameled in my brain along with the words, and my fingers are starting to cramp. Then I stop, even though I can hardly stand to. Stretch. More push-ups. My back aches. My eyes burn. I'm on fire, and it feels glorious. The song is awesome. The crowd at the Crow's Nest will love it. And it's mine, as far as anyone else needs to know.

I'm still nowhere near being able to sleep. I pull Yvonne back into my lap. Scales now. Then fingerwork, my hands flashing in the moonlight. Precise. Perfect. Then the song again, polishing the intro, and then—

Then someone knocks. But not at the door. At the window.

Yvonne jerks in my hands, the melody breaking off.

I look up.

Frankie's face smiles through the glass at me.

It's dark outside. Getting colder. When I open the window, the gust of air chills my sweaty shirt. Maybe sweaty and gross is better than damp and shirtless, like last time Frankie showed up. Either way, I feel exposed, unarmored, without a guitar between us.

"Hey," she says.

"Hey. What are you doing here?" This comes out even more unwelcoming than I mean it.

"Visiting you," says Frankie. Like I don't already know this.

I glance past her, into the woods. "Who else is out there?"

"With me?" Frankie shrugs. "Nobody."

"Nobody?" Frankie Lynde, alone. The words don't even sound right together. "Are you sure?" I ask, even though this is a really stupid thing to say.

"I'm sure." She leans her arms on the windowsill. She's wearing a soft, wide-necked sweater. Her fingernails are painted dark purple, or at least they look that way in the moonlight. "So. How's it going?"

"Not great." I rub the side of my head. "There was a stupid fight with Jezz and Patrick today."

Frankie nods. "I heard."

Of course she heard. This freaking town.

Frankie tips her head to the side. Her eyes are black ink, sharp and soft at the same time. "Do you think it will blow over?"

"I don't know. We'll see."

Frankie's eyes move over me, outlining my face, traveling down. "What's that?" she asks.

"What? Oh." She's pointing at my forearm. "Song lyrics."

Frankie reaches through the open window and grasps my arm. Her touch makes my whole body ignite.

"'Amplify . . . the hugs we hair?'"

"'The things we hide,'" I say. She still hasn't let go of my arm.

Frankie laughs. It makes the air sing. "Your handwriting is *terrible*."

"In my defense, you *are* reading it upside down."

"Maybe I should come in and read it the right way around."

"Um . . ." Something starts to fizz in the pit of my stomach. Alone. With Frankie Lynde. In my bedroom. I turn an ear toward the door. The occasional distant laugh track from the TV seeps through the wood. "I guess you could."

Frankie slides through my window, head first. She reaches out so I can grab her before she hits the floor. "Thanks." She clings to my hands, laughing at herself. "Please don't remember how gracefully I did that."

She's wearing tight pants and high-heeled boots. Her hair is glossy. I can smell it—her—even a few feet away. I take a step backward. Our hands unclasp.

Frankie takes a long, slow look around my room. "Wow," she says. "It's a metal museum."

She trails along one wall, checking out the posters, the stickers, the torn-out articles. I follow her with my eyes. She leans into the mirror, studying the ticket stubs wedged around the frame. "You've seen a lot of great bands. And a lot of bad movies."

My heart is pounding. It doesn't feel safe having Frankie in my room. It's too much like having her in my head.

"So, why are you really here?" I say. Way too bluntly.

Frankie straightens and turns to look at me. "To see you."

She moves toward me. I back up.

Frankie stops between my bed and the row of guitars. Yvonne is still on the carpet, where I left her. She glints like an oil slick. Frankie reaches out and gently touches the neck of the acoustic, propped on its stand. "It seems like there's always someone else around, you know? Like somebody's always watching. Like we're never really *alone*."

My heart pounds harder. Jesus. Is she actually reading my mind? "Yeah," I say.

Frankie faces me. She steps closer. I try to step backward again and bump straight into the closed closet door.

Frankie's a lot shorter than I am. We've stood face-to-face so seldom—because I've avoided it, in part—that I'm surprised by it all over again. But when she looks up at me, with those dark eyes, I know that I'm the smaller one.

"What are you afraid of?" she says.

There are so many answers that they crash into one another. My head's full of rubble.

Frankie is something else I haven't earned. She's something else that could disappear in a second, and it will only hurt if I try to hold on.

"I'm not afraid," I say. "I just— We're about to graduate. Leave. I don't think I can, like, promise anything."

Frankie looks like she might laugh. "Have I asked you to *promise* anything? Because I don't remember doing that."

"Okay. No. You haven't."

"So, how about instead of guessing what I want, you just let me tell you?"

My skin is electric. If my heart pounds any harder, she'll be able to hear it. Christ, my deaf cat who's hiding somewhere in another part of the house will be able to hear it. "All right," I say.

But Frankie doesn't tell me anything. She stands on her toes, and she places both hands on me, one on my neck, one on my chest, so I'm sure she can feel my pulse, and then she presses her lips against mine.

And I'm lost.

In an eighth beat, my arms are around her. One wraps behind her back, all the way around her body, crushing her against me. The other hand slides up through her sleek black hair.

She moves her palm against my jaw, tilting my face downward, so she can kiss me more deeply.

My breath is on fire.

She pulls me backward. We stumble together toward the bed. My foot bumps Yvonne, still lying on the floor. I don't even glance down.

We hit the saggy little bed with a creak.

Frankie Lynde. In my bed. Beneath me. Her body, the

shape of her, the hollows and curves, pinned under me, my weight crushing the space between us until there isn't any space left.

All my worries suddenly seem so distant and small that when I look back I can't even recognize them. Who cares? Who cares about anything but this?

Frankie moves against me, spaces notching against curves. She's breathing harder, too. She runs a hand up beneath my shirt, over my back. Each fingertip leaves a track of fire. Or ice. I can't even tell.

And then, slowly, she pulls away. She puts a finger against my lips and smiles up at me.

"Anders Thorson," she murmurs. "You really like to keep a girl waiting."

I smile back. We both start to laugh.

"Since *December*," she says. "I've been waiting since *December* to do this again." Frankie laughs some more, eyebrows pulling together. "Why were we waiting?"

"I don't know," I say, because I don't. I don't know anything.

Frankie pushes lightly at my chest. I lean back, and she gets up, smoothing her hair and tugging her sweater back into place.

"I'd better go," she says, sidling toward the window.

"But I want to see you again. *Alone* again. Not in front of a crowd. And not four months from now."

"Good." I'm still trying to get my breath under control. "Me, too."

"How about tomorrow? After the show?"

"Sure. Perfect."

"Good." Frankie's lips curve upward. I want to touch them so much, it makes me dizzy. "Then I'll see you at the Crow's Nest."

I offer her my knee, and Frankie uses it as a step to climb up and through the window.

I look past her into the blue-black woods. "Hey. How did you get here?"

"My car." Frankie nods into the distance. "I parked way back on the road, so nobody here would hear me come or go."

I grin. "You planned all of this."

Frankie grins back.

Then she hops down from the stump and flies off into the trees. I watch her go. I'm just turning away from the window when I catch sight of something else.

A pale flash behind a big pine. A shape that looks like a face. Glittering eyes.

I freeze.

I stare at that spot for more than a minute, but whatever I saw doesn't reappear. Maybe it wasn't there in the first place.

I shut and lock the window.

Then I flop back onto the bed that still smells, really faintly, of Frankie Lynde.

I take a deep breath.

What am I fighting against?

If life's trying to give me what I want, why don't I just freaking *take* it?

I roll over on the bed and grab Yvonne from her spot on the floor. I lay her across my chest. The sleek surface of her body begins to warm. I can feel my heartbeat reverberating inside of her.

There was a guitar that used to hang on the wall at the Underground Music Studio. A Fender Stratocaster. Arctic White. The tag dangling from its neck said it was six hundred dollars, but it might as well have said six million. The Fender was there when I started lessons with Flynn nine years ago. Back then the only guitar I owned was an acoustic we'd gotten for free from one of Mom's coworkers who didn't play anymore. It came with a cardboard case and a pack of spare strings and a book called *You Can Play Folk Guitar!* I'd sit on the lumpy navy couch in the middle of the studios, waiting for my lesson with my own crappy guitar beside me, and I'd stare up at the Fender's pearly curves and glossy finish. It looked like it had been made of magical snow.

For my thirteenth birthday Mom and Dad got me a secondhand electric, an Epiphone Les Paul Special. That same year Flynn helped me find a great deal on a decent Yamaha acoustic, something I could afford with two summers' worth of lawn-mowing money. Later I found out the deal was so great because Flynn had paid for half of it himself. And the whole time that snow-white Fender hung there, above the lumpy couches, just out of my reach.

I'd gaze up at that guitar week after week. I'd picture it in my hands. In my bedroom. I could see our future together stretching out in front of me, all the glory, all the music.

You can want something so much that it feels like it's already yours.

I thought I'd never want anything as much as I wanted that Fender.

But that was before Frankie Lynde.

And it was before Yvonne.

I remember how it felt the very first time I played

her. The skin of my forearm on her curve. My hand wrapped around her neck. The way her name just came to me, *Yvonne,* like someone had whispered it in my ear, like it already belonged to her, just the way she already belonged to me. It seemed impossible that something so exciting could feel so familiar. I guess that's how you know it's right. I guess that's why you should just take it, without dissecting it into pieces. Even if you know you don't deserve it.

**Before the Crow's Nest opens, the woods are louder.**

It's early in the afternoon. The coffeehouse doors
are locked, the parking lot empty. There's no one here
but me to hear the trees roar.

I sit on the back stoop. Behind me two broad steps lead
up to the Crow's Nest's kitchen door, set back in a frame
of scarred gray wood. Moss and mushrooms and tiny
white flowers sprout from the earth on either side. My
bike leans against the wall nearby. It's shady here. It
smells like coffee and pine.

The wind pulls my hair. The trees shake. They would
like to lash out and brush me away.

I should be at school right now. History class. Second
to last row, right-hand side. Mrs. Wilder probably won't
even notice that I'm gone.

The thought of Anders being there alone makes my

156

chest tighten for a moment. But being here mattered more.

This morning when I went into the living room with the coffee tray, I found Aunt Mae half unwrapped from the wadded blankets. She was shaky and dew-drenched with sweat, whispering, "No. Not too late. No." The TV babbled in the background.

I sat down on the edge of the couch. There was some whiskey left in the bottle. I poured a slug straight into her coffee. Then I helped her sit up and curl her fingers around the cup. The oily surface trembled.

"So hot," she muttered, her eyes still shut. I was ready to take the coffee back, to pull away the loose cocoon of blankets. Then Aunt Mae went on. "It melts the glass."

She didn't mean the coffee. I watched her face. "The glass where?"

"A kitchen. A little room." She shivered. "At the back of a bigger place."

I found her bony leg beneath the blankets. Rubbed the spot below her knee. "What else?"

"Too late for him. Standing right there at the stove. He's one of the good ones. And they know it." Aunt Mae's eyelids twitched. "Skin gone. Shirt charred to his body."

There was a little trail of drool leaking down Aunt Mae's chin. I patted it away with my sleeve. "What else?"

"Spreading. Out into the big room. Bottles bursting. Bags of coffee beans. *Pop pop pop.*"

I felt it. The hot breath on the back of my neck.

They're getting closer. They're nibbling away at the edges. They want to leave me nowhere to hide.

"The Crow's Nest?" I asked, although the answer already sat heavy inside me.

Aunt Mae's eyelids flickered upward. She looked out at me. Watery eyes, blue on red. "Yes," she breathed. "That's it. Yes."

"Do you know when?"

"Soon." Aunt Mae squinted. "Afternoon. The sky outside the windows is light."

I squeezed her leg again. "I'll take care of it."

Aunt Mae gave me a grateful look. Another long sigh. Then she blinked down at her coffee, seeing it for the first time.

I watched her take a careful sip. "Do you think it's an accident?"

Aunt Mae just looked at me. More sharply now.

"I'll be there before they open," I told her.

And I am.

The Crow's Nest opens at three on weekdays. Most of its customers are at school or work or asleep until then. I've been waiting since one. Sometime around two o'clock Ike Lawrence's big gray truck rumbles up the road that's slashed through the oaks and pines like a paved wound. He veers across the empty parking lot, stopping at the far end.

He climbs out of the cab. The trees hush.

He saunters toward me, face unchanging, one hand swinging his ring of keys.

Ike is well over six feet. His face is like carved oak. His black T-shirt strains around his torso. The Crow's Nest doesn't need bouncers.

But Aunt Mae is right. He's one of the good ones. You can see it, deep down, under the black T-shirt. The light.

He stops, standing above my spot on the stoop. He looks down. I look up.

"There's something wrong with your stove," I tell him.

His face doesn't change. "Well," he says. "Let's see about that."

He unlocks the back door.

I follow him up into the kitchen——a small room at the back, lined with wire shelves of paper goods, seasonings, bulk food bins. The smell of gas is faint. Easily hidden behind the rich hum of coffee, the lingering harmonies of chocolate, muffins, toasted bread.

Ike throws me a look.

He grasps the sides of the big gas stove and yanks it out, one corner at a time, onto the scarred black-and-white checked linoleum. He cranes around it.

"Huh," he says.

Then he turns to the nearest window and opens the pane wide. Forest air blasts in. I hear the woods roar. Ike opens another window. I step in to help. As I pass the stove, I can see it, too: a crook in the blue hose winding out of its back, the crack like a wrinkle in thick skin, letting out the explosive gas.

Ike heads to the basement to shut off the gas main. When he comes back, shoving through the swinging door into the main room, I follow. He leaves the lights out, striding through between the empty tables and upturned chairs to the patio entrance. Throws the doors wide.

Leaf-tinted light. More cool, piney air.

Ike walks slowly back to me. "Guess we won't be serving hot food tonight."

I nod.

He tips his head to one side. It's only a few degrees, but for someone as stony as Ike Lawrence, it's a tip. "How?" he says.

"My aunt Mae. Mae Malcolm. She—"

"Yeah," he cuts me off. "I know Mae."

There's weight to the words. He knows. Lots of people in this town guess or whisper or imagine, but there are also a few who know.

Ike looks at me for several seconds.

I almost never look at myself. I try to imagine what he sees. Scuffed sneakers. Jeans with holes in each knee. Black thermal shirt, men's, secondhand. My favorite old flannel, also made for a man, hanging loose and soft around me. The hair. White blond, flyaway, with wide curls. Unfashionably long.

"You know how to grind coffee?" he asks.

Not what I expected. I nod again.

"I've got an old hand crank around here somewhere. We'll wait until the place airs out before we start any electrics."

Ike turns, his broad back disappearing into the storeroom beside the kitchen.

He sets me up behind the coffee counter with a stool and a hand crank and a sack of roasted beans and a metal container to dump the little grinder drawer into each time I fill it.

I'm still there, turning the crank, when Janos crosses the room.

He stops. Does a dramatic double take.

"It's like seeing a statue climb off of its pedestal," he says, starting to smile. He pats the stool at the very end of the counter. "Aren't you supposed to be sitting here?"

I smile back. "Not all the time."

"Gas leak," says Ike to Janos, coming out of the kitchen. "Repair guys are coming. We'll just have drinks and baked goods for tonight."

"Sounds good to me," says Janos. He grins at me again. "Grilled cheese and I could use an evening apart."

Ike goes back to the kitchen. Janos steps behind me, checking the cooler's milk supply, sliding empty trays out of the bakery case.

"How was school this afternoon?" he asks.

"It was good," I answer. "I'm guessing."

Janos smiles wider. He begins arranging a row of biscotti on a sheet of waxed paper. I knock another heap of grounds out of the drawer.

"Think we're in for a storm tonight," says Janos in a moment, in a way that doesn't tell me whether it's a statement or a question.

I stop and try to feel the air. Here, inside the long, scarred-walled room, it's cool and shifting. Changing. Changeable. A faint sourness of gas still hangs beneath the scent of fresh ground coffee. The open windows are gray. The sky beyond them, behind the trees, is too dark for midafternoon.

"Maybe," I say.

"Oops," says Janos, with a stagy twist of one hand. "This one is broken. We'll have to eat it."

He holds out half of a snapped biscotti. I take it. Give him another smile.

For the next hour Ike leaves every window and door open. The woods breathe into the Crow's Nest, touching everything greedily but unable to carry any of it away. A work crew thumps into the kitchen. Heavy footsteps, the rasp of appliances pushed across the floor. Janos lets me help him take down the chairs from the table-tops, refill sugar canisters and stir-stick cups. It's Friday. Which means Last Things. Which means the place will be packed, and soon.

People start showing up right at opening time. Janos plugs the steamer into its socket. He switches on the coffee machines. Dark streams pour into their carafes.

Ike strides back with a handwritten sign to tape to the register: Kitchen Closed Tonight. Then he steps over to the corner where I'm wiping the backs of the old wooden chairs.

"Here," he says in his gruff voice. He holds out a folded twenty between his first and second fingers.

I don't touch it. "You don't have to pay me."

"Come on," he says. "I owe you for the help. And I don't like being in debt."

I still don't touch the money. "Anybody would have told you about the leak," I say. "If they knew."

Ike narrows his eyes just a little. "I'm not paying you for that. I can't, and I know it. I'm paying you for the prep work and cleaning you've done. Now, are you going to take this or am I going to have to mail it to your aunt?"

He sets the money on the table in front of me. Twenty dollars. I don't know when I've had twenty dollars of my own to spend.

"One other thing," says Ike, already stepping away. "That money is no good here." He gives me the tiniest one-cornered smile. "Anybody who literally saves my ass gets their coffee for free."

I pick up the money. There's a second twenty folded inside the first.

I slide the bills into my pocket and smile at Ike's disappearing back.

Janos has finished making flavored mochas for three freshmen girls when I walk up to the counter. He raises an eyebrow at me. He overhead everything.

"So," he says, "what can I get for you, miss?"

"A cappuccino. Please."

Janos gives a little bow. He turns to the steamer, packing espresso into the little basket, picking up the metal milk pitcher. When he's not looking, I slip one of the twenties into the tip can.

I take my cappuccino out to the edge of the patio. Three other outdoor tables are already taken by people with dark clothes and bright tattoos. I don't recognize any of them. The wind through the trees is blowing harder. Spatters of loose leaves click across the pavement.

Janos has made a leaf in the foam on top of the cappuccino. It's pretty. Brown-veined and delicate. I whirl it into a smudge with my fingertip.

Far off to the north, there's a rumble of thunder.

The crowd grows fast. People from school, people from town, people I've never seen. They lounge at the edges of the parking lot, smoking. They crowd around the coffee counter. They stake out spots near the edge of the stage.

Around five-thirty Jezz and Patrick pull up. I can see them park from my spot at the patio's edge. They climb out of the rusty pickup and begin to unload. Patrick's face is hard. Harder than usual. Even Jezz, who's always joking about something, looks like someone who's just witnessed a car crash.

A few minutes later Anders pulls in next to them.

He steps out of the little white car. He's wearing faded black jeans. A gray T-shirt that fits tight around the tops of his arms.

"Hey," says Jezz.

"Hey," I see Anders answer.

Patrick doesn't say anything.

The people around me have taken notice. The regulars, the kids from school, the newcomers who recognize Last Things from pictures they've seen online. They're all watching the band, trying to pretend they're not watching. They're noticing the heaps of cables, the hard black cases, the way the band swings into this wordless routine. They probably don't notice the tension strung between them, invisible and strong as spiders' thread.

But I see it. The woods see it, too. They'll use it if they can.

The guys carry their equipment to the far door. Jezz and Patrick and Ike begin the drill they perform every weekend. Placing stands. Checking wires. Anders carries loads back and forth from the parking lot, keeping his head down. He avoids the stage like it's something hot.

More car doors slam.

More and more.

I slip inside, through the patio doors, into the very back of the room.

The band gathers for a quick sound check. Anders keeps his back to the room, his head down. He tests a mic, a handful of chords, then disappears through the backstage door. A few minutes and a few notes later, Jezz and Patrick follow.

Soon the Crow's Nest is fuller than I've ever seen it. Bodies and voices ricochet from the walls. I see most of the senior class. Frankie's friends, in a tightly orbiting cluster. Frankie herself, wearing a halter-neck dress that makes one guy walk straight into a table and spill his coffee. I spot Flynn, Anders's guitar teacher, halfway up the room's right side. He doesn't usually come to the shows. I try to look closer, but he's already lost in the crowd. More schoolkids. More people in expensive boots who've driven up from the Cities. More and more and more.

When Last Things finally takes the stage, the screaming is so loud that it shuts out the thunder. The guys position themselves. They're stretched wires. Flying sparks. They look ready to explode.

Anders gives a nod so small only the band and I can see it.

They launch into "Blood Money." Then "Frozen." "Come Out and Play." "Dead Girl." There's barely a breath between songs. The music feels as tight and hard as ever, but there's a new texture to it, something that cuts deep. Anders's hands move so fast they aren't hands at all. They're just a pale blur of sound streaming out of that black guitar.

They play "Hitting Sleep." Everyone in the room seems to know this one. I scan the crowd. People are jumping in time, combat boots and Converse low tops pounding on the scarred hardwood floors. The Crow's Nest is one huge, pulsing heart.

*Knock knock knock*
*until you wake me*
*Pound pound pound*
*until you break me*

There's another smash of thunder. Closer this time. Even it seems to rumble to Patrick's rhythm.

And that's when I see her.

She's perched on a high stool at the very edge of the

opposite side of the room. Tight black pants. Tight black jacket. Sleek, short hair.

She's older than high school, older than college, but far from old. She's watching the stage with an expression I recognize. Like Anders is the only real thing in the room.

I let my eyes focus, the way I usually only do when I'm alone in the woods and no one else will see. Because I know what my face looks like when I do this. I know what happens to my eyes.

The room goes gray. There are flashes of light around me, bright beacons burning here and there. But I'm not looking for those.

I stare at the woman.

She ripples with blackness.

It seeps out of her in pools and tendrils. Too much to be held inside. It climbs up the wall. It drips from her feet, pools on the floor. It slithers in and out as she breathes.

She's one of them.

She's here to take him away.

Blood surges into my chest.

I keep still. Wait. Wait.

Watch the stage.

Watch her.

Watch him.

Last Things tears through "Bleeding Out" and "Minotaur," and, finally "Superhero."

By the time it ends, there's something in the room with all of us. Something that makes the air as combustible as a gas leak. Something that pulls the crowd's pulses into its dance.

The woman is sitting perfectly still at her little table. But the music affects her, too. I can see it. The darkness seeping through her is wilder, thicker. It climbs above her, stretching up the walls, reaching toward the stage like vines or veins.

But I can't move. Not yet.

The sky outside the windows is pure black.

The final chord dies. The crowd screams.

Last Things leaves the stage.

They don't usually play encores. Everyone knows "Superhero" is the end. But tonight no one leaves. No one turns around to pick up their bag or weaves out between other people's sweaty bodies. The screaming goes on and on and on. Everyone is on their feet. I can't see through the crowd anymore. There's only a wall of bodies between me and the stage.

Finally, amazingly, the band steps back out.

Jezz and Patrick wave. Jezz grins; he does a little hop, clicking his heels together in midair. Patrick smiles. They know how incredible tonight was. They feel the thing in the air. The strange, flammable, crackling thing.

Anders crosses slowly in front of them.

His back is straight. The guitar hangs loosely from his shoulder. Emotions glance off his face, trying to break through the smoothness. He leans toward the microphone. Smiles with one corner of his mouth.

The light in him is dim. It's almost gone.

"I guess you guys want some more," he says in that deep voice.

The screams explode.

Anders leans toward Jezz and Patrick. They whisper. Nod.

They turn around. Assume positions. Then they whip into a cover of Prince's "I Would Die 4 U" so hard and hammering that the tables beside me vibrate.

There's more screaming when they're done, but this time the band doesn't reappear. The crowd is delirious. Shouting. Laughing. Shoving.

I crane through the bodies toward the woman. Toward the spot where the woman was. Because she's gone.

I climb onto a stool. Scan the crowd. There's nothing. No sign.

No.

No. No.

How could I have lost her? How could I have let myself lose her?

Blood thunders through me. My head starts to roar. I keep my eyes clear.

When the crowd dissolves at last, rivulets of people dribbling out the doors, I look at the stage. Jezz and Patrick are there, chatting with a few fans who've clustered at the edge.

Only Jezz and Patrick.

No Anders.

I scan the room again. He's not here.

No. No. No. I rush out to the parking lot. I have to fight myself to keep my steps unobtrusively slow.

Anders's small white car is just bumping out of the gravel onto the road.

I can't lose him now.

I grab the blue bike. Throw my leg over. I rush forward, into the woods.

The first raindrops start to spatter as I plunge into the trees. I'm moving so fast that they turn into streaks as soon as they hit my skin. My hair whips behind me. The trees are just flashes.

Thunder shakes the sky. Black sky, black trees, shades of black on black.

The bike's tires leave the ground. I fly.

The wind is strong. Leaves tear from twigs. Branches strain like bones about to snap. But the woods are laughing. I can hear them laughing.

I keep within the trees, following the curve of the road as it heads toward town. In the distance, to my right, I can see the taillights of the white car, leaving their red smears on the road. Rain fogs my eyes. Branches groan. A bolt of lightning shocks the woods, bleaching everything. I blink fast, but my vision is dulled, my focus lost. Darkness plunges in, thicker than before. I hit a root and nearly fall.

But I won't let them take him.

Thunder. Another flash. A roar.

Something huge and black and monstrously heavy lunges in front of me.

I wrench the handlebars to the side.

The smoking tree trunk crashes down inches from my bike. Falling branches swipe my face. Needles lash my arms.

The bike tilts. I catch myself on my left foot, just managing to stay upright.

Another few inches and the bike might have been crushed.

I wipe the rain from my eyes.

And that's when I see it. Just for a fraction of a second.

It's crouched on top of the fallen trunk. Limbs long and dark furred and strong. Face like an elk's skull, but with a carnivore's jagged teeth. Crown of black antlers. Long fingers. Claws.

Its eyes are like hailstones. Empty. Dead white. They stare down at me.

I don't move.

I stare back.

But the spattering rain finally makes me blink.

And it's gone.

I scan the woods. No sign of it now. Of anything. The road is only a vague blur in the distance. The beacon of Anders's taillights has disappeared.

I breathe deep.

They've made their move.

I'll have to make a move of my own.

# ANDERS

I skid around a wide bend of the highway. The rain's hard enough to make the roads slick, and the Nissan's wipers barely keep up. I don't touch the brakes. I roar toward town, sometimes feeling like something is chasing after me, sometimes feeling I'm chasing something else. Either way, I can't slow down.

I'm headed toward the studio.

Flynn was waiting backstage in the tiny greenroom when we finished our set tonight. He's played the Crow's Nest himself, so he knows the way in. He was beaming so hard that I could see all of his teeth.

"That was amazing, man!" He grabbed my arm and pounded me on the back, speaking over the noise of the crowd that was still screaming beyond the door. "Amazing!"

I could feel my arm vibrating in his grip. The

adrenaline of the show was still surging through me. I could have flown through walls.

"That new one? 'Minotaur'? *Awesome*," Flynn went on over the noise. "One of the best solos I've ever heard you do."

"Thanks." I bent down to put Yvonne in her case, which let me hide my face for a second. I was grinning like an idiot. It *was* one of the best solos I'd ever done. Clean and strong and lightning fast. I could feel it. "I didn't know you were going to be here tonight."

"Yeah. I thought I'd surprise you." Flynn leaned closer so that Jezz and Patrick and Ellie and Lee, who'd snuck into the back room, too, couldn't overhear. "There's somebody you need to talk to tonight."

I blinked at him. "What?"

"She was here. She heard the whole show. Now she's waiting for you at the studio." Flynn grinned. "I set it up. Hope you don't mind. We thought it would be easier to talk somewhere quieter."

Flynn's words could barely reach me through the noise and the buzz. "She?"

"Yep. She came all the way up here to hear you guys."

"From Minneapolis?"

"Chicago." Flynn grinned even wider. "She's with one of the big ones."

I glanced at the guys. They were goofing around with Ellie and Lee, not paying any attention. "A record company, or—"

"Artist management. She knows her stuff. She knows *exactly* what to do for you." Flynn's eyes hooked into mine. "Listen. I know it's still a couple of weeks until graduation . . . but I'm telling you, this is the deal you've been waiting for."

I was already so laced with energy, my heart couldn't pound any harder. But I heard my voice catch. "Seriously?"

"Seriously." Flynn's smile looked ready to burst like a firework. "These guys work with *huge* names. Huge. This is it, Anders. This is the door."

Ellie laughed at something Jezz said. I looked up at him, his sweaty blond hair sticking out of his head in a million directions, like he's just gotten out of the shower and toweled himself halfway dry. Patrick was smiling at them both, stretching his arms behind his back, one at a time.

"All right," I said. "I'll get the guys."

Flynn's hand caught my arm. "Anders. She just wants to talk to *you*."

"Wait." I blinked at him. "What?"

"She asked for a meeting with *you,*" Flynn said. "Just you. At least at this first meeting. Even I'm not tagging along. You can handle this on your own."

"I can't do that," I told him, my voice low. "You *know* I can't."

"I know you *should*." Flynn's gaze was steady. "If you want to talk about the band, fine. Discuss that with her. But at least meet with her. Learn what she's offering." He still hadn't let go of my arm. "You owe this to yourself, man," he added. "You owe it to what you can do."

Maybe it was because this was Flynn, who knows me better than almost anyone. Maybe it was because, deep down, this was exactly what I already wanted. Maybe it was just to stop the twisting feeling in my stomach. Whatever the reason, I heard myself saying, "Okay. Fine. I'll go."

I made some kind of excuse to the guys, something about the car, Dad needing me home early. Jezz and Patrick were still high on the energy of our set. The night had been good enough to wipe out their anger about the last time I went behind their backs. They both gave me quick, sweaty hugs. We pounded one another on the shoulders.

And then I ducked out the back door.

Now I'm skidding around another bend, veering closer to the streetlights of downtown.

I park in front of the studio, behind a glossy black Audi with Illinois plates, and jump out into the rain. Most of Main Street is asleep at this hour, even on a Friday night. The signs of a few bars glow through the wetness. I duck my head and run for the door.

I've never been in the studio late at night. It feels strange, pushing open the stenciled glass, stepping out of the pouring rain into a hall that's only lit by safety lights.

I open the metal basement door.

There's usually noise. Guitars and drums and key-boards leaking out of the lesson rooms, making a messy soup in the air. But now, except for the hiss of the rain, it's silent. A few of the lights in the central room are glowing.

I step off the staircase and into the waiting room.

A woman is sitting on one of the couches.

She's wearing tight black pants and a low-cut leather top. She's got black hair that swings at an angle across her forehead and fancy high-heeled boots, and eyeliner that flicks up into little points at the ends.

And I am young and shabby and totally stupid. There's a hole in the left cuff of my jeans. My hair is flat-tened with rain. My T-shirt is stuck to my back. I can feel the sweat that's pooled in the band of my boxer shorts starting to chafe my skin.

For the first time all of this feels real.

She's here. I'm here. My real life is about to begin.

"Um . . . hi," I hear myself say. I sound like a little kid who's meeting Santa Claus at the mall. If Santa Claus was hot.

The woman stands up. She'd be tall even without her high-heeled boots. Which make her really, really tall.

"Anders Thorson." She smiles. "I'm thrilled to meet you."

"Nice to meet you."

She reaches out to shake my hand. Hers is a little chilly, but firm. Mine is wet.

The woman sits back down. She gestures casually to the chair across from her. I've always wondered how you get to be one of those people who makes everything around you seem like it belongs to you.

"I'm a huge fan," she says as I sit down. "We all are. Everyone I work with. Seeing you play tonight just confirmed everything we've thought about you."

"Oh. Thanks." Why am I suddenly so nervous? I don't know where to look. There's something about the sharpness of the woman's eyes that makes me not want to look straight into them. But I really don't want to stare down the deep *V* of her top, either. I aim for somewhere around her shoulder.

"Did Flynn explain why I'm here?" she asks.

"Kind of. Yeah." My heart hammers a quick double beat. *Don't look down her shirt.*

"So. To put it in really basic terms"—she crosses her legs—"we help musicians achieve everything that they can achieve. And we'd love to do that for you."

Anything I could say—*Really? Me?*—sounds idiotic. So I nod and keep my mouth shut.

"I hope you recognize your own potential," she goes on. "We certainly do. We've heard your material. We've been keeping an eye on you. For *years,* as a matter of fact. You're something special. With our help, you could go far."

I dig my nails into the meat of my palm. Here it is. "How far?"

The woman smiles, this curling, catlike smile, like we already share a secret. "For you, Anders, there may be no limit."

My heart is beating so hard, I feel its pulses in the tips of my fingers. *This is it. This is it. This is it.*

The woman spreads her hands. "We would love to

work with you. I'm telling you that straight out. I would like to sign you here and now. So." She pauses to smile at me again. "What do you think?"

This is where I should jump.

But instead, I feel my knees lock. Maybe Flynn was right. Maybe I'm looking down from the end of the diving board, letting fear stop me. Maybe I just need to know what I'm jumping into first.

"I think I need . . ." My voice sticks. I clear my throat. "I need a little time to think. Do some research. Talk to some people."

"Of course." The woman's tone is perfectly polite, but her face looks the tiniest bit amused. "Do what you need to do. But if you'll let me make our case . . ." She leans on the arm of the couch, angling closer to me. "You've got the magic combination *right now*. Youth. Energy. Incredible talent. Good looks."

My cheeks are heating up. Goddamn it.

"You've got a growing following," she goes on. "You've got building online interest. You've got everything. But we know how quickly these things can change."

I clear my throat again. "Last Things is just getting started."

"You're adults," she says. There's a special little tang

in the way she says the word. *Adults.* "You're just a few weeks from graduating. And then what? Do you plan to stay here?"

*Here* describes everything at once. The shabby underground studio. This dying little town.

"No," I blurt, a little louder than I'd meant to.

"I didn't think so." She gives a little laugh. I can hear the mockery in it, subtle, but there. "So the choice isn't *what.* It's *when.* It's now, or it's later. Which may be too late." She sees me hesitate and leans even closer.

"Anders. You're *meant* for this." She slows her words so that each one has time to land. "Why would you deny yourself everything you've always wanted?"

My throat clamps.

*Everything you've always wanted.*

That was exactly what the guy in the woods had said. *You're going to get everything you want. Everything. It's going to be something to see.*

I fight to keep my hands from shaking. The woods. That night in the woods. I want to turn around and fly out of here. But something keeps me stuck to my seat.

The woman is still smiling at me. She reaches toward a black leather briefcase that's tucked beside her on the couch. She pulls out a paper and a silver pen.

It might as well be a scalpel.

Fresh sweat breaks out on the back of my neck.

"I at least need to talk to the guys," I manage.

"Your band?" She taps the pen lazily against her other hand. "I'll be honest, Anders. They're good for small-town, teenage musicians. But we all know what *you're* becoming."

Rain spits against the tiny basement window. I hear a sound like wind through tall trees.

"The skill. The speed. The songs," she says. "They're just pouring out of you, aren't they? You couldn't stop them if you tried." She unfolds and recrosses her long legs.

The bottoms of her heels are coated with mud. Mud and pine needles.

The sweat on my back turns to frost.

"Everyone in this town knows your name," she goes on. "You're a god to your classmates. The most beautiful girl at your school is practically throwing herself at you."

My heart pounds at the top of my chest. It's going to seal off my breath.

She leans even closer. "And this is just the *intro,* Anders. The song hasn't even started yet."

I smell pine pitch. Wet earth. The woods.

I look her up and down. The briefcase. The clothes. It all felt so real.

But she never even handed me a business card.

"Who are you?" My voice comes out in a whisper.

The woman looks like she might laugh. "You want my name?" I can't tell if the question was stupid, or too personal, or too unimportant. She shakes her head, smiling. "You know who I'm with." She holds out the paper and pen. "Everything you've always wanted. That's what we can give you." She stares into my eyes. I finally make myself stare back. Hers are black, iris to pupil. Like slate.

I've never seen eyes that color. I don't think people have eyes that color.

She doesn't blink. "All you need to do is sign. Give us your word. Let us know we can call you one of ours."

I lurch to my feet. The second I do I can't remember what was keeping me in that chair.

"No," I say. My voice breaks as the word comes out, just a little too loud for this quiet underground room. I sound, literally, like a jackass. But I say it again. "No."

I take a backward step.

The woman looks surprised, like the rain has suddenly started falling indoors. "You're going to risk losing everything?" she asks. She tilts her head. "Because that's what you stand to lose, Anders. All the things you love. One by one."

"No," I say again. Even though I guess the answer to her question is *yes*.

The woman leans back. Her muddy shoes click against the floor. "Oh, Anders," she says, and now she sounds almost sad. "You are going to be so, so sorry."

Jesus. Her eyes.

I'm half expecting to look down and see a blade sticking out of my side or to hear the beep of a detonator just as the room explodes in fire.

Before she can move or speak again, I run.

I turn around and bolt through the doorway, up the stairs, through the toothpaste-green hall out into the night.

I grind the key into the Nissan's ignition. The engine roars. I peel away from the curb, into the deserted Main Street. Rain bashes against the windshield. Wind shoves the car sideways. The trees around me thrash. I clutch the wheel, roaring out of town, driving as fast as I can without skidding off the wet road, until I'm bumping up my own driveway.

It's only when I'm in my room, with the door and window locked, sitting on the bed with both feet pulled up so nothing in the darkness underneath can grab me, that I finally slow down long enough to think.

And what I think is that I'm acting like a total psycho.

Did I actually just run away from a professional meeting set up by my guitar teacher—a meeting with a gorgeous woman who offered me a music contract—to hide in my bedroom?

Yes.

Yes I did.

I go back and sort through the things she actually said. *You know who I'm with. You're meant for this.* Okay, a little weird and intense, but she was both trying to flatter me and to push me into signing something by making me afraid I'd lose my chance. That's what dealmakers do, right? There's nothing in her words that should make any sane "adult" run away in terror. But I let some stupid phrase like *You are going to be so, so sorry* and the color of her eyes scare the shit out of me.

Plus, Flynn set up the whole thing. Flynn vouched for her. Flynn, who's right up there with Goblin in the circles of people I trust.

Goblin. I lean down and look under the bed. There are no yellow eyes glimmering back at me, no stinky cat breath wafting out. It figures that just when I need some comfort, my cat decides to spend his night somewhere else.

Jesus. I press my forehead into my hands.

So she had mud on her shoes. So what? That doesn't mean anything. It doesn't mean that there's something out there in the woods, watching me, creeping closer and closer.

What the hell is wrong with me? Why do I take every good thing—a record deal, representation, a free guitar, Frankie—and turn it all into some kind of threat?

I'm paranoid. I'm mentally ill. I'm messed up.

Because when I focus on the things I actually *know,* instead of things I *imagine,* I've got next to nothing.

And that's what I'm still telling myself when something pounds at my bedroom window.

I've been standing behind my usual tree, in the leaf-filtered rain, waiting for the light. My clothes are soaked through. My hair twists into damp ropes against my back. I could walk right into the river and not be any wetter than I am right now. But the rain doesn't matter. I barely feel it.

At last his bedroom light flicks on. A golden patch in the blue-black dimness. It's so dark out here. Dark enough that he doesn't see me creeping closer on the other side of that illuminated glass.

I stride across the grass, my feet sinking into the soggy ground.

There is no music.

Not his stereo. Not his fingers on the guitar strings. Nothing that I can hear over the whisper of the rain in the trees.

Slowly, so there won't be even a flicker of shadow on

the pane, I glide closer until I am looking straight inside.

Anders sits on the bed. His head is down. His fists are clenched against his forehead. His hair is wet, clinging messily to his neck, his cheekbones. His shirt is soaked. Almost as soaked as mine.

I hesitate.

This is dangerous. It's been safer, simpler, to watch and work from the edges. But I'm running out of time.

I lift my hand and knock at the pane.

Anders's head jerks up.

The look in his face is pure terror.

Then, confusion, as his eyes narrow, realizing I am not who he guessed I might be.

Then, an instant later, anger.

There's annoyance in it. Embarrassment that I've caught him like this, scared and vulnerable. Exhaustion. Self-protectiveness. I understand it all.

I know him so well.

He jumps off the bed and stalks across the carpet. Turns the lock. Shoves up the window. A series of cold droplets spatters the sill.

"What the *hell*?" he asks.

He's never spoken to me before.

His tone is anything but warm, and still I feel the words

light up something inside me, matches touching wicks.

He's speaking to me. No one else. Me.

His eyes search my face, checking my hands, the empty night around me. Looking for an explanation. I'm sure I look odd: my hair so drenched it's changed color, water dripping off the end of my chin. But he's looking straight at me. He sees me. He frowns harder.

"What are you doing creeping around my house in the middle of the night?" he asks.

He's not happy. But I have to fight not to smile. Anders is speaking to me. I am going to speak to him.

I weigh my words. I plan each one. I keep my voice low enough that he has to lean closer to hear. "I came to warn you. I know what's happening to you."

"What?" He stares at me like he's trying to translate the words into another language. "You know what's *happening* to me? What's that supposed to mean? I don't even know who you *are*."

He's not supposed to. Still, the words sting.

"I mean—I've seen you," he amends, and I wonder if I let the sting show. If he's being kind. "At the Crow's Nest. You're what's-her-name's niece. Mae Malcolm. That old lady who lives in the woods."

Now he is piecing things together. Rumors about

Aunt Mae . . . her visions, her one-hundred-proof breath. Glimpses he's caught of me here and there, everywhere he goes. His face hardens again. "Okay," he says. "What do you need to warn me about?"

I feel strangely rattled. I've never been stuck like this. I've watched him from a distance for months, memorized every motion, learned every secret. Now I'm close enough to smell him. His skin. Salt and soap and rain. And he doesn't even know my name.

I can still see the anger in his face.

Anger because he's afraid. I am making him afraid.

Fine. Let him be angry. Let him feel something, anything, for me.

"There's a darkness at work here," I tell him. "It's been getting stronger. Now it's ready to act."

"Here," he says tersely. "In my house."

"In this town. In the woods."

There's a flicker in his eyes. The woods. He wonders what I know, but he can't ask. He can't admit that this is something we share.

I watch the flicker turn from fear to doubt and then into disbelief. He flattens his feelings into sarcasm. A smile that's almost a smirk.

"A darkness," he says. "Okay. Next are you going to

tell me that metal is the music of Satan and invite me to come get born again at your church?"

"No," I say. "It has nothing to do with metal."

I've gone about this all wrong. He's not going to listen; he's not going to admit that he believes me, not even to himself. I should have known better. But I wanted this. I wanted him to open his window.

Anders looks at me now like he can hardly believe he's still listening, standing here, letting cold rain splash through his window.

"All right," he says at last. "Well. If you've ever got something else really important to tell me, maybe you could do it in daylight, at the Crow's Nest or somewhere, instead of sneaking across our lawn and staring into my bedroom window."

The words shove me backward for an instant.

For that instant I'm only what he sees. The crazy niece of the crazy local drunk. The obsessed, rain-drenched fan peeping into his bedroom in the middle of the night.

He reaches up to close the window.

"Did you give her anything?" I ask.

He freezes. His hands are still on the window. "What?"

"That woman," I say, slow and clear. "Did you give her anything? Even your word?"

There's a long, silent moment. Wet wind gusts between us. He drops one arm, keeping the other on the window frame.

"No," he says at last.

"Good." I step closer again, putting my fingers back on the windowsill. Closer to him. "But they won't give up. They'll keep trying until they claim you."

*Or destroy you.* But I don't tell him that. It's kinder, I think. Besides, his face is hardening into skepticism again.

"So, the music business people are the darkness you were talking about." He smiles. It doesn't get anywhere near his eyes. "Okay. I've never heard it put that way before, but I bet some bands would agree." His arm tenses, and he starts to pull the window down. "Thanks for the warning."

"Be careful," I say. And then Aunt Mae's words, my father's words, the Bible words, fly out of my mouth and into the rainy darkness. "'You know not the day nor the hour.'"

Anders doesn't reply to this. I'm not even sure he heard it. He shuts the window. The lock clicks. He pulls the curtain between us.

I stand there for a minute.

It's still raining. I feel heavy, and for the first time, I feel cold.

I spoke to him. He spoke to me. He knows who I am now. The thought that he recognized me brightens the little fires again.

But he's not *meant* to know me. I've gotten greedy. I've let things that will never happen, *can* never happen, get in my way.

And he didn't believe me. Of course he didn't. Just like every other time, every other place. I should have known better. I *do* know better. But I let myself think, just for tonight, that there was some sort of connection between us. That he might see me for what I really am.

Now I'll have to make another move.

I sort through the pieces. *Click click click.*

I have to get to the other side of town. Fast. I have to reach the bridge before she does. I have to be waiting.

Then I'll bike home, passing Anders's house one more time, just to check. I'll bring another load down to the root cellar. Buckets and blankets and tarps, some nylon cord fine enough for binding wrists. And then I'll tiptoe inside, down the hall, and curl up in the living room armchair before Aunt Mae wakes up.

You know not the day nor the hour.

# ANDERS

**I pull into the parking lot of the Crow's Nest around six-thirty the next evening.** The sun is low in the sky, streaking everything red. There's still more than an hour until we play, but the lot is already packed, and I can hear the noise coming from inside. I park the Nissan in the grass at the far end, near the backstage door.

Jezz and Patrick are standing near the doorway. They're alone. No Ellie or Mac or Lee or other hangers-on. They're dressed for the show—jeans, favorite T-shirts, Jezz's collection of leather and silver bracelets. Patrick holds his sticks in one fist. Their eyes follow my car. They're talking to each other, but when I open the door and climb out, they stop.

I move slowly around to the trunk and lift out Yvonne and my amp. Even with the preshow energy pulsing through me, the equipment feels heavier than usual.

Everything that happened last night—the show, the artists' rep woman with the mud on her heels, my running away, the insane conversation with the soaking wet stalker girl at my bedroom window—has started to seem like a strange and stupid dream. It's just like that night in the woods almost two years ago. Now that I'm half a day away from it, I can't remember what seemed like such a big deal. I can't remember why I freaked out. I can't remember much of anything except the woman's eyes, and the fact that Goblin wasn't waiting for me under my bed as usual, and that pale, wet girl telling me that something "dark" was coming for me, and then lying on my bed with Yvonne's calming weight across my chest, practicing exercises until it was almost dawn.

If the way that girl showed up, staring in my bedroom window in the middle of the night, wasn't so messed up, I'd almost feel sorry for her. I mean, yeah, Frankie has showed up at night at my window, too. But there's a huge difference between Frankie Lynde and this girl. There's a difference between someone you *hope* looks your way even once in a while and someone you don't know who watches you without you realizing it. What that girl told me just made it worse. She's obviously under some kind of delusion, talking about dark forces, telling me to be careful, thinking she's the one who can save me.

What does it say about me that I was almost ready to believe her?

I trudge across the lot toward Patrick and Jezz.

"Hey guys," I begin. Trying to sound normal. "What's up?"

Patrick folds his meaty arms. "You tell us."

"What?"

Jezz glances between me and Patrick. "Rumor is another talent scout was here last night," he says. "And that you went and met with her alone."

Goddamn it. This is the last thing I need.

I guess I could pretend not to know what they're talking about. But that would make me even more of a jerk than I already am. Besides, these two know me way too well.

I set the end of Yvonne's case on the ground. "I . . . Jesus." I press one thumb against my temple. "I didn't even know about it until after the show. Flynn set it up. He totally sprung it on me."

"But you went."

"Yeah. I went to find out what they were offering and to tell her that I definitely wasn't going to sign anything without my band."

"Were they even interested in the band?" Patrick asks. "Or were they just interested in you?"

I look at Patrick's scarred fists. "We didn't really talk about that."

"I bet you didn't," says Jezz.

His words sting more than anybody else's would. First, because this is Jezz, who usually makes the best out of any crappy thing. Second, because it's so unfair. I *did* bring up the band. And I don't want to hurt them. That's why I can't tell them the truth.

They wouldn't understand. They *don't* understand.

The guys are quiet. Patrick cracks his knuckles. Jezz combs one hand through his hair and looks away.

At the same time, the crowd inside the Crow's Nest is getting louder. I can hear the mass of voices pressing against the walls. The place must be packed.

My chest starts to tighten.

Patrick mutters something under his breath, something I can't catch.

Jezz nudges Patrick's arm. His tone softens. "Dude."

"What?" Patrick turns to face him. "I'm serious. I don't want to do this anymore."

Panic hits the adrenaline in my bloodstream.

"What?" I force the words out. "You're not going to do the show?"

Patrick finally turns his eyes on me. They're so hard, I feel like I've been punched. "Why don't you do it solo?" he says. "That's how you do everything else."

There's no way I'm doing the show alone. The songs need a band. That crowd, roiling and yelling and waiting—if we don't get up there and play, play *together,* they'll tear this place apart.

Maybe I should apologize to the guys. Maybe I should beg. Tell them how much I need them, how the songs would be incomplete and lifeless without them. But suddenly I'm so angry at Patrick for even threatening to back out on Last Things that all I can imagine is punching him in the face. I might try it, if I didn't know he could rip me apart with one hand.

Jezz faces him. "I get it, dude," he says placatingly. "I do. But everybody's already here. They're waiting for us."

Patrick stares back at him. His jaw flexes.

"Come on," Jezz says softly. "Maybe Last Things has run its course. But let's at least do one last totally amazing show first."

Patrick's eyes slash to me again.

I glare back at him. Patrick, the pulse of this band,

can't just *quit*. I can barely fit my brain around the idea, it's so impossible and selfish and ridiculous. It would be like your heart deciding it was sick of all this beating BS and climbing out of your chest and stomping away.

*You can't do this,* I think, staring into his eyes. *You can't do this to me.*

He's probably thinking the exact same thing.

There's a burst of noise from inside. The crowd is yelling for us. Another jolt of adrenaline hits me. My hands twitch, hungry to hold the guitar, to feel Yvonne's sleek neck slide through my palm, to feel the stage rumble under my boots with Patrick and Jezz's rhythm. Maybe for the last time.

Damn it. This could really be the last time. I want to grab it with both arms and dig my fingernails into it and hang on to it forever. I need this. I need my band. And I hate them both for how much I need them.

"Fine," says Patrick at last.

He turns and walks away. Jezz follows him. They're heading toward the back door, and I'm staggering a few steps behind, when I feel a soft touch on my arm.

I whip around.

Frankie.

She's wearing a dark top that curves down her chest,

showing a slash of soft golden-brown skin. She looks amazing. And kind of unhappy. But I'm too full of rage and loss and hunger for this to really sink in.

"Hey," she says.

"What?" It comes out harsh. Too loud.

Frankie gives a tiny flinch. "So. I was just wondering," she says. She smiles a little and touches her hair in a way that would normally make my skin get hot. "What happened to you last night?"

The rage flares. She knows about the stupid meeting, too? Jesus. Is there anyone in this town who *doesn't* think they know everything about my life?

And then I remember. I was supposed to meet up with Frankie after the show last night.

Oh, goddamn it.

"I can't—" I glance back. Jezz and Patrick are disappearing through the door. "I have to get set up. We'll talk later."

Frankie's voice stops me again. "Are we *actually* going to talk later this time? Or are you just going to mysteriously vanish again?"

My fingers clench. I can feel the energy of the crowd blasting out from inside. "I said *later*."

"Okay," says Frankie. Her smile is gone now. "Later.

And if you ever want to speak to me again, maybe you'll actually show up."

I don't answer.

I just slam through the back door, Yvonne's case in my fist, the noise of the crowd stretching out to engulf me in its roar.

**Friday night the Crow's Nest was packed. Saturday night is explosive.**

Ike has brought in extra help for the kitchen, but even with two cooks and both Ike and Janos at the coffee counter, the lines are long and tangled, and the atmosphere is impatient. Charged. The darkness that entered yesterday is still here, and it's hardened now, like something burned down to cinders.

I thread my way around the edges of the room. No one glances at me. Janos and Ike are buried in backed-up orders for lattes, mochas, espresso shots. I check the space, body by body. The woman is not here. No one like her is here. Just the too-large, too-loud crowd of metalheads in battered denim and tour T-shirts, locals and outsiders.

Frankie is here, of course. She's with her entire court tonight, Sasha and Carson and Will and Mason and Gwynn. Mason and Gwynn are taking pictures of themselves and each other. Carson's mustard-yellow letter jacket looks out of place. He stays between Frankie and Sasha, whispering in both of their ears. Sasha laughs dramatically every time he does, flipping her hair back over her shoulder, her mouth open wide. Frankie doesn't seem to be listening. She's as pretty as ever—delicate features, shiny dark hair. But she looks different tonight. It's because she isn't smiling.

She and her friends encircle a table. Frankie's back is toward the stage. When Last Things appears and everyone else in the room bursts into screams, Frankie doesn't even turn around.

I heard them talking from my spot on the patio, Anders arguing with the band, Anders confronted by Frankie. The anger against him is building up, his friends turning away. He's more and more alone. Just how the dark things want it.

Patrick takes his seat behind the drum set. Jezz clutches the bass. Anders strides up to the microphone, moving so fast that it looks like he's going to attack it. Without a word to one another or the crowd, they launch into the first song.

It's "Dead Girl." The screams get even louder.

I take another look at Frankie. She turns a wooden

stir stick in the foam on top of her drink. Her spine is stiff. Her eyes stay down.

I glance from her to Anders. He's got the same choppy brown hair, one of a dozen well-worn T-shirts, the usual thick-soled boots. But there's a change in his face tonight, too. It's hollower. Harder. The rock star might not be a mask anymore.

*Don't say good night*
*she says, she says*
*Why don't you come inside*
*she says, she says*
*I can change your mind*
*or time can change your mind for you*

Anders flies into the guitar solo. His fingers tear at the strings. Fast. It's always fast. But tonight the tempo feels a little higher, the motions more elaborate, the beat a little harder. It's on the very edge of impossible.

Patrick, behind the drums, already glitters with sweat.

*Just walk me home*
*Just walk me home and I'll be warm*
*Just walk me home and I'll be warm*

They move straight from "Dead Girl" to "Deep Water," then to "Cutting Edge." "Shadow Tag." "Minotaur." The songs fly like bullets aimed at something we can't see. Jezz and Patrick look focused, taut, buried in the music. Anders looks like a burning fuse.

The last strains of "Minotaur" rip through the room.

The audience roars.

Anders halts, swaying back and forth, both hands clenching the guitar. Patrick and Jezz watch him. They're waiting for the signal, the title of the next song.

But Anders doesn't speak to them.

He speaks into the microphone instead.

"Hey," he says, deep and quiet.

The crowd screams back.

They never do this. He never does this.

He goes on, over screams that don't stop.

"I'm going to try something," Anders says, in that same slow, deep voice. "Something we haven't done before. This is called 'Devil's Due.'"

I see surprise flicker on Patrick's face. He and Jezz trade a look. Then, like everyone else, they stare at Anders again.

Anders positions his fingers on the guitar's neck. He says something over his shoulder to Patrick. Patrick gives a nod. He starts a plain, rapid beat. Jezz backs up, taking his bass to the dark at the edge of the stage.

Anders begins to play.

I haven't heard this intro before. It's winding and quick, with a jagged, forward force, almost like staggering foot-steps. I haven't heard it during band practice or when Anders plays in his room late at night. In an instant I know why.

Because it didn't exist before.

Anders has never played it, never even imagined it, until this moment. It's coming out of him. Coming through him. Coming straight at us.

*Holding on*
*Holding on to the only sound*
*the sound of your heartbeat*
*Breathing in*
*Breathing in before everything*
*everything crashes down*

*And you are not*
*You are not who I'm waiting for*
*I can't lie to you anymore*
*Should have gotten to me before*
*before it was too late for*

*Afterthoughts*
*That's all I've got*
*A fistful of regret*
*But regret is not a reckoning*
*Don't forgive me*
*Don't forget*

*Falling in*
*Falling into the dark again*
*again I am lost and*
*Getting close*
*Getting close to the end of it*
*the end of it all*

*And this is not*
*This is not what I meant to say*
*but who's listening anyway*
*Who's hearing the songs you play*
*beneath all the noise and*

*Apologies*
*don't mean a thing*
*when the injuries don't end*
*Weigh my heart, tear it apart*

*Don't forgive me*
*Don't forget*

There's another guitar solo, this one so piercing and fast that the crowd's thrashing can't keep up with it. I see Jezz staring from the corner, his bass dangling on its strap. I see something like panic on Patrick's face. I see Frankie turn to watch the stage over her shoulder. And I see Anders's hands become a blur. They move so fast, so viciously, they look more like claws.

As he plays, something presses in against the walls of the Crow's Nest. It's huge and dark and hungry. It could crush us all.

The woods have moved in.

The chorus lashes back, Anders screaming the last words into the microphone.

*Weigh my heart, tear it apart*
*Don't forgive me*
*Don't forget*

It ends.

Anders lets go of the guitar. It swings against him on his strap. He's breathing hard. His arms are slack.

There are blue hollows under his eyes.

I watch him. I breathe with him. I stand still, my back pressed to the trembling wall.

For a few seconds Anders simply wavers there. If it weren't for the look on his face, he could be basking in the applause, which is long and loud and frenzied. But he looks sick. He looks stunned, like he's just woken up and he can't remember where he's supposed to be.

Jezz strides across the stage. He nudges Anders's arm. Anders seems to jerk awake.

"'Frozen'?" Jezz's lips murmur.

Anders nods.

Another few heartbeats and they are back on, back into their usual polished rhythm.

But Anders is shaken. I can see it. And the woods press in.

They finish with "Superhero." By the end of the song, the energy is raging so hard that the air could ignite. The last notes scream through the room.

"We have been Last Things," says Anders, into the microphone. "Thank you. Good night."

The band exits through the stage door. Even though the screaming goes on and on, as on every night but the last one, there is no encore.

The crowd is slow to leave. There's an edge in the air, something rough and fierce. Ike scans the room, his eyes sharp, his big arms folded, ready. A fight breaks out somewhere near the doors, and Ike moves so fast I lose sight of him for a second. Then there he is, side by side with Janos, hauling three stubbly-headed guys out the door by the backs of their T-shirts.

Frankie's circle is still at their table, talking, sharing something on their phones. Frankie keeps quiet. Finally, when half the room has emptied, I see her whisper something to Sasha. Then she turns and heads outside.

I follow.

The band is in the parking lot. Patrick, Jezz, and Anders have been cornered by a bunch of people I don't recognize, fans who might have driven hours to get here. The woods have crept in so far that the air is black. Even the moon looks like it has been rubbed with a lead pencil.

I watch Frankie approach the crowd.

Anders spots her. Something freezes on his face. I see him glance at the others, then move away from the group, following Frankie into the thicker darkness at the edge of the parking lot.

Nobody looks my way as I drift across the patio, between the rusty sculptures and the bathtub full of weeds.

At first I'm too far off to hear their voices. I see Frankie gesturing, the smooth skin of her bare arms catching what little light there is. I can see the *V* of Anders's back, the broad line of his shoulders. The way he hangs his head.

Frankie steps closer to him. She throws her hands out.

The trees rasp and groan.

Then Anders speaks.

I see Frankie lean back. She sways a little. As if the words physically hit her.

A needle of excitement hits my lungs. But I can't let it distract me.

I creep closer, divided from them by one parked car.

"I'm not pushing," I hear Frankie say. "I'm just asking you a question."

"And I don't have to answer it." Anders's voice is rough. "Maybe you're so used to getting everything you want that you haven't even noticed this. But *I don't belong to you.*"

Another needle. If he's not hers, he's a tiny bit more mine. Even if he doesn't realize it.

Frankie's eyes widen. "What is *wrong* with you? Two

nights ago you were a totally different person."

"This is me," says Anders. "This has always been me."

Frankie shakes her head. "No, it hasn't."

Anders lets out a little laugh. "And this is proof."

"Proof of what?"

"How little you know me. You *think* you know me," Anders goes on before she can speak. "Because you watch me play. You watch me perform. That's it. You've never known anything else."

"That's because you push people away!" Frankie lashes back. Her hands fly out again. "You won't talk to me. You won't come out with me and my friends. You won't even answer me when I ask one stupid little question about where you went last night."

"Yeah," Anders answers. "I'm sorry. I'm sorry that I don't want to spend my time with your shallow poser friends."

"Right. Because you'd rather sit by yourself in your mildewy little bedroom, pretending to be some tortured rock star—"

"Oh, fuck off, Frankie."

Frankie sucks in a breath.

Across the parking lot, Jezz and Patrick and the clustered fans have gone quiet. Everyone is watching.

The back of my neck prickles.

He's losing everything. He's doing it to himself.

"You wanted the rock star," Anders goes on. "Just like everybody else. You don't know me. You just imagine that you do. And then you're mad when what you imagine doesn't match the truth."

Frankie's eyes are huge and flashing. "I didn't want *the rock star*," she says, loudly and clearly. "I actually thought that I wanted *you*." She leans back. Her shoulders straighten. "But you're right, Anders. I didn't know the real you. Because the real you is a piece of shit."

Then Frankie turns and strides away, toward the spot where her friends are waiting.

Anders stares after her for a beat. He laughs, a short, ragged sound. "You have no idea."

Frankie doesn't look back. I see her say something to her friends. Sasha looks worried. She reaches out with a skinny hand and touches Frankie's arm. Frankie murmurs something back. Then she climbs, alone, into her car.

Frankie Lynde, alone.

Driving off into the woods.

Alone.

Anders is already striding back toward the Crow's Nest. His face is a streak of moonlight on shadow. He slams through the door, toward all the loading and packing that's left to do.

And I'm already on my bike.

# ANDERS

**For the second night in a row, I barely sleep.**

I'm electric and furious and totally alone. My head is hot. My wrinkled old bedspread might as well be made of fiberglass. I thrash against it. My guts are a knot.

The way that song came out of me—"Devil's Due"— it felt like something had made an incision in my body and started removing parts of me, right up there on stage, in front of everyone. And all I could do was stand there and let it happen. I had to *help* it happen. I've never had a song come like that, in front of a live audience. I'm usually sick and dizzy after the songs come, but this— this was a thousand times worse.

What the hell is wrong with me? What else can I screw up?

I've lost my band. I've lost my sort-of girlfriend. Even my cat has abandoned me.

And I deserve to lose them all.

Everything I did. The way I talked. The way I acted. It's like someone I don't even recognize. Someone I've never even pretended to be.

I pull Yvonne onto my chest. I don't play. Just having her weight on me, the texture of her strings under my fingers, makes me the tiniest bit less alone. Sometime between three a.m. and dawn, I guess I finally pass out.

And I wake up starving.

In the kitchen I thump through the cupboards, pulling out the coffee filters and the big tub of Folgers, setting out mugs for Mom and Dad.

I find a skillet. There's a half stick of butter in the fridge, and most of a carton of eggs, and a loaf of white bread. It's been a couple of years since I made French toast, but I think I still remember how.

I'm halfway through the first pan when Mom drifts into the kitchen in her worn blue bathrobe.

"You started coffee? And French toast?" She leans over the stovetop, beaming. She rubs my back between my shoulder blades. "What's the occasion?"

I shrug. "I was hungry. And I wanted to do something for you two."

Mom's smile quivers. She actually looks teary. Guilt

spears me, that such a stupid thing means this much to her. I turn my eyes back to the next slice of bread.

"You were out late last night," says Mom, patting her eyes on her cuff and pouring coffee into her mug.

"Yeah. You didn't wait up for me, did you?"

"Oh, I went to bed around midnight. I just noticed that you weren't home yet. I assumed you'd stayed late at the Crow's Nest."

I *had* stayed late at the Crow's Nest. And then I'd spent another hour or two driving around town, long after all the businesses were locked and the houses had switched out their lights.

"Yeah," I say.

"How did it go last night?"

"Fine."

Fine. Except that my band—my best friends, the guys I've spent every day with for the past four years, musicians who can back me even when I'm playing some song I've never played before—is blown to shrapnel.

But I'm not going to think about that.

I can't. I can't even think.

"Whoa-ho," says Dad, shuffling into the kitchen. He's already dressed in his jeans and button-up plaid shirt. I don't think I've seen him wearing anything else in years, not early in the morning, not late at night, not even on the days when he's got no work to get dressed for. He probably showers in jeans and a button-up plaid shirt. "What's going on out here? Did we hire a chef?"

Mom pours Dad a cup of coffee. "Come and sit." She pats his usual spot at the table. "We'll all eat the very same thing at the very same time!"

Mom sets out the fake maple syrup and the fake orange juice, and I put down the plate of French toast.

We all dig in.

"Not bad," says Dad, nodding at me over a forkful. "I think you've got a backup career here, if the guitar thing doesn't work out."

This isn't really a compliment. And I know Dad doesn't really mean it as one.

Mom makes a little tutting sound. "So, Anders," she says brightly. "We need to talk about your graduation party."

I swallow a mouthful. "We do?"

"Yes, we do. We need to talk about when you want to have it, and what you'd like to do, and how many people you want to invite, and if you want Last Things to play. . . ."

My chest gets tighter with each word. "I don't know."

"We could set things up in the garage for the band. Couldn't we, Brian?"

Dad nods slowly. I can tell that he's mentally moving his truck and parking it somewhere else, putting his power tools in the basement, shunting the long-dead boat motor out of sight. "Sure," he says.

"I think that would be perfect. There are relatives who haven't heard you play in ages. I'm sure they'd love to hear how far you've come. They'll be blown away."

I shrug with one shoulder. I'm still starving, but the French toast feels like a gooey lump in my mouth.

"We could grill out," Mom goes on. "Brats. Burgers." Her face is still smiling, but now there's a little question in her eyes. A little worry. "We could swing that. Right?" She sends a silent message to my dad.

I shake my head. They don't need to spend a bunch of money on something that doesn't deserve celebrating anyway. I've got no plans left. No future that I can even really picture. "Everybody grills out. Let's just have cake."

"Well," says Mom, "that just leaves the big question then." She pauses dramatically. "What *kind* of cake?"

The kitchen phone rings before I can answer.

Mom pops up. "I'll grab it."

Her voice comes back to us from around the corner.

"Hello? Yes? Oh, good *morn*ing! How are *you*?"

Dad points at me with a loaded fork. "I mean it," he says. "This is good."

I give him a half smile. "Good."

"You know, you could get a restaurant job this summer. Maybe at Roxy's. Maybe at the golf course. Pay would be decent."

I slosh some orange juice into my glass. "Restaurants always want you to work weekends."

"Hmm." Dad pauses. "And you're still planning to play those two shows a week. For free."

The realization hits me. I won't be playing those two shows a week. I won't be playing any shows at all. The future is as empty and flat as a sheet of paper.

I nod anyway.

"So," says Dad. "Did you talk to Ike Lawrence about him covering your expenses?"

The tightness in my chest pulls again. "No."

"Are you going to get on top of that?"

Mom reappears around the corner. The receiver is pressed against her chest. "Anders," she says, in a hushed voice. "Did you see Frankie Lynde after the show last night?"

I set down my fork. What townie gossip is calling

my house to ask my mother about our stupid fight?

"Yeah," I say warily.

"About what time did you see her last?"

Something in me stiffens. "I don't know. After we played. Probably around ten."

"And then she left?"

"Yeah. I think so. Yeah." I stare at Mom. "Why? Who's on the phone?"

"It's Mrs. Lynde." Mom blinks back at me. "Apparently Frankie didn't come home last night."

The room goes gray.

"What?" I say.

Mom just goes on looking at me. Dad sets down his fork, too.

"Maybe she just—" Maybe *what*? I can see Frankie's face—her perfect, furious face—turning away from me under the dim lights of the parking lot. And then what? Then I was alone with the anger and the sickness burning me up from inside. But what about Frankie? Frankie is never alone. My voice sounds brittle. "She probably spent the night at a friend's or something."

Mom nods. "That's what her parents are thinking, too. That's why they're calling everyone she knows."

"She's not at Sasha Nelson's? Are they sure?"

"I don't know. But you saw her leave at ten? Was she by herself?"

The parking lot. The rage thumping through me. I try to remember.

"I think so," I say. "Yeah. I think so."

I hear Mom repeating my words into the phone.

Dad sips his coffee. I look at my plate.

The fight. The stupid freaking fight. The smell of French toast suddenly makes my mouth fill with bile.

After another minute Mom comes back to the table.

"Well, they're worried," she says. "Of course. But they're still thinking that maybe she went to a friend's who they haven't thought of yet, and that she just fell asleep or forgot to call." Mom leans over and puts her hand on top of mine. Which is so much more than I deserve, it almost makes me scream. "I'm sure that's all it is, Anders."

None of us eat any more.

After another minute I get up and clear my plate.

Back in my room I sit down on the end of the bed. Still no Goblin creeping out from underneath. Maybe he's avoiding me, too.

Or maybe something's wrong.

I think back. I last saw him on Thursday night—the

night Frankie climbed through my bedroom window. So, all day Friday, and all day Saturday, while I've been obsessing over that stupid meeting and the blowup with my band and whatever's going on with Frankie, my bony old cat has been missing.

. . . *That's what you stand to lose, Anders. All the things you love. One by one,* says the music executive, her dark eyes on me. *Oh, Anders. You are going to be so, so sorry. . . .*

Last Things. Goblin. Frankie.

For a second I can barely breathe.

I jerk to my feet.

I could search the house and the yard, even though I already have the sick, certain feeling that I won't find anything. Then I could head out there, into the woods. I could search for Goblin. I could go farther, all the way back to the Crow's Nest, and look for any sign of Frankie. I could look and look and never find anything. Or I could find something that I don't want to find.

I glance out the window, into the darkness of the trees. And then I see it.

It's drawn on the glass.

It's just faint enough that I might have missed it if I hadn't looked at it head-on.

An *X*. It crosses my window from edge to edge. It's

drawn in something red brown and flaking. Something that looks a lot like blood.

My heart pounds harder. My head starts to swim.

*Oh, Anders. You are going to be so, so sorry.*

**I move through the trees.**

Pine needles and dead leaves whirl under my feet.

There is nothing here that can scare me.

Delay me. Yes. But only if I fall behind.

And I'm fast.

I'm faster.

I'm lighter.

I barely touch the ground.

I skim through the shadows. It's not morning yet, but the darkness in the sky is starting to weaken, rinsed at the edges like a stain in cold water.

Light will come. Inevitably.

But now they're here. They're everywhere. Seeping out of the roots, hiding in nooks and hollows. Teeth and claws and too-long arms. Silent, black-furred feet. They'd like to snap my neck. They'd like to tear me into pieces.

But they can't. Not them. I know them. I know everything I need to know.

It's been a long night. My arms ache. My hands are
sore. But the scratches and scrapes, the one bad slash
under my eye, have already healed. It's the delicate little
ones like Frankie who sometimes put up the toughest
fight.

I circle the sagging shed, again and again, dead leaves
flying, scattering drops of river water from one of Aunt
Mae's empty bottles. The ring of stones gleams.

Very faintly, through the layers of walls and soil, I
can still hear her screaming. But she's getting tired. She's
hoarse. She'll stop soon.

And no one else will hear even this wisp of sound.

No one can get close.

No one will find her.

**Big things start small. That's how they get in.**

You make one little choice. You choose to take guitar lessons. You choose not to quit the lessons, even though you suck so bad that at first you'll only practice shut inside your bedroom closet, where no one else can hear. Every day you make the choice to practice instead of going off with your crappy bike or your skateboard or your computer games like the other kids. You choose to put on that same metal album eight hundred times. You choose to learn every solo. You start hanging out with other guys who like the same kind of music you do, other guys with instruments that they actually practice, too, and then one day you choose a name for your band.

After a couple of years, you choose to play in public for the first time. You do it again. And again. You choose working and pushing and failing and writing and playing again until you're actually *good* and you'd do anything, anything, to be even better. And then you start to get famous, and everybody around you knows who you are, and then one night you do something idiotic in front of a giant crowd of people who all know your name, and just like that, all at once, your whole life starts to disappear.

Your whole life.

All those tiny, stupid choices turn into one huge, god-forsaken mess, and when you look back at it, you can't even see where things started to go wrong. But you know it was your fault. Because you did it. All those little, gigantic things. Every single step of the way.

That's how it started at the Crow's Nest: Small. Embarrassingly, pathetically small. We played a local talent night. I think there were five people in the audience, not counting the other musicians who'd come to play. And there we were, me and Jezz and Patrick, scrawny sixteen-year-olds with crappy amateur instruments and a name—Last Things—that we'd finally decided on after fighting over it for weeks. We played an Opeth cover, pretty badly, and one song that Patrick and I had cowritten that was called "Apocalypse," which truly sucked, and some decent Deftones. We were just decent enough that Ike Lawrence asked us to play again for the next local talent night.

We practiced like crazy in between. I convinced the guys to start meeting three times a week, and Patrick talked his parents into letting us take over half their garage.

And I practiced. I'd been working an hour or two each day. Now it was three. Sometimes more. I'd wake up in the middle of the night with cramps in my hands and realize that I'd been playing imaginary chords in my sleep. Music followed me everywhere. I could literally feel it thumping in my bloodstream. And that was all I wanted: to be part of it. To be a conduit for it. To be one tiny piece in whatever it was that made it real.

We played our three songs at the Crow's Nest. We got the longest, loudest applause of the night. It was incredible.

Ike offered us a night of our own.

It was a Tuesday, when the Crow's Nest would be half empty, almost dead by eight. But we took it. We felt like gods.

I went straight home from that local talent night and wrote three songs, all of them crap. Then I wrote one that was a little less bad. Then I wrote one called "Blood Money." I could tell it was all right, because I went around humming it to myself for days, its rhythm stuck like a burr in my head. Patrick added some great lines.

We played it on Tuesday night.

People went nuts.

We did tighter and tighter covers. Patrick and I wrote more songs, sitting up late in his bedroom or mine, surrounded by empty Mountain Dew cans, scribbling and testing and trying again.

Ike gave us a Thursday night.

Somebody came from the local newspaper. They wrote about us: "Young Locals Take Aim at Heavy Metal Fame." They wrote that Jezz's name was Jess, and that Patrick had said he was inspired by Slipknot, when Patrick actually hates Slipknot and had just said that the drummer Joey Jordison was awesome. Jezz laughed about it. Patrick was pissed.

Then someone came from the Bemidji newspaper, which has about eight times the circulation of the *Greenwood Gazette*.

And then someone posted a clip of us playing on YouTube, and things started to spiral.

By the end of summer, a couple of metal bloggers had made the drive just to see us. Another came in early September. He wrote for an actual online magazine, one we'd even heard of. He looked only a little bit older than we were, with stringy dark brown hair and a round face and thick-framed glasses, and he had an ancient black leather jacket that he said had once belonged to Dimebag Darrell.

After our set he hung out, chatting, helping us move the drums, wind the cords. He was too excited about metal to even bother pretending to be cool, which made me like him a million times more.

When we had everything packed up in our cars, he still made no move to leave. Now he was talking about metal movies, documentaries, the best tour DVDs. Patrick finally had to leave, taking Jezz with him. The writer shook their hands. Then he pulled them both into big, back-pounding hugs.

"This was awesome, you guys," he said. "Awesome. Really. Can't wait to hear what you do next. Awesome."

And then it was just the two of us, standing in the parking lot.

"Would you mind talking a little longer?" he asked me. "It would be awesome to hear more about your song-writing. We barely covered that."

"Sure," I said. This guy was so baby faced and metal nerdy, I didn't feel uncomfortable, even when I was talking about myself.

"One thing—I hope you won't care, but I've been jonesing for three hours now." He pulled a pack of cigarettes out of his pocket and gestured to the edge of the woods, away from the No Smoking signs that Ike put up around the patio and that everybody else ignores. "You mind?"

"No," I said. "Go ahead."

We shuffled into the trees.

It was the very beginning of fall. A few sugar maples were starting to change color, but most of the woods was still thick and green. It smelled like fall, though: that sharper, smokier smell on top of summer's rotting sweetness. The trees rustled around us as we walked away from the Crow's Nest. There was a half-moon. The writer guy flicked his lighter, and for a second I could see his round, orange-tinted face beside me, and then his cigarette flared and the light went out.

"So," he said. "Anders Thorson. That's even an awesome metal name. *Anders Thorson.* It makes you sound like one of those Norwegian black-metal dudes who burned churches."

I laughed. "Yeah. I don't think that was my mom's goal when she picked it."

He laughed, too. "How did you feel about tonight?"

"You mean about our set?"

"Yeah." He nodded eagerly. "Were you satisfied?"

"I'm never satisfied."

"Ah." He smiled and blew out a puff of white smoke, which disappeared up into the dimness. "So you're a perfectionist."

"I don't know. Maybe." The term *perfectionist* has always seemed dumb to me. Like wanting things to be perfect is so weird that it needs its own special term. I kicked a clump of ferns. "But I know what *good enough* is. And I know when we're not there."

The guy's eyebrows went up. "You're really close."

"Well, thanks. Another five or ten years of insane practice, and then . . . maybe."

"Oh, I don't think it will take that long." The journalist took another drag. "What's your main passion: playing, singing, or songwriting?"

I scratched a hand through my hair. "I don't know," I said again. "I don't think I'm a great vocalist or anything, so—"

*"Dude,"* he cut me off. "You reminded me of Trent Reznor tonight. Especially Nine Inch Nails' late-nineties stuff. Like, *The Fragile*-era Reznor."

"No way." I was glad it was dark so he couldn't see my idiotic smile.

"Seriously. When you're straight-up singing, you sound like him. Well—not quite as low."

"And not quite as good." We both laughed. "Thanks. But I'm a mediocre singer. And an okay guitarist."

"And a really bad judge of yourself." I could see the guy's teeth as he grinned. "But that's okay. I like that. We *need* that. People who don't already think they're too good to get any better." He let out another puff of smoke. "So. Where do you see yourself in two more years?"

I'd been feeling so happy. So *almost* content. Now anxiety covered me like a swarm of mosquitoes.

Two years from now. Done with high school. Starting out on my adult life.

I couldn't tell the truth. It was too raw and pathetic and predictable. I couldn't say it out loud, not even to this guy.

*I want to be a rock star. I want to be the best who's ever been.*

Nope. No way.

"I don't know," I said slowly. God, how many times had I said *I don't know*? I don't know. I don't know anything. "I'd really—I want to keep going with this. See if it could be something real."

He nodded. "I think, for you, it definitely could be."

I started to say something dismissive, but he went on.

"You're the type, you know?" he said, stepping a little closer. "You really want this. You give everything you've got to this. You'd give anything *for* this. Right?"

I smiled. "You sound like my guitar teacher."

"I'm sure," he said earnestly. "I'm sure he sees it, too. You're primed for this. You're *meant* for this."

He dropped his cigarette. I watched the glowing orange butt hit the ground, touching the carpet of pine needles, before he crushed it with his boot.

"I mean, if this all went exactly the way you wanted it to"—the guy waved his hands, taking in the night, the Crow's Nest, me. "If you could have everything you've been dreaming and daydreaming about, what would that be like?"

I laughed, rubbing my hair with one hand. "You want to hear my when-I-grow-up fantasies?"

"I'm serious," he said. "What do you want? What do you *really, really* want? What would you give at least one kidney and one lung for?"

"A lung? I don't know. I'd kind of like to keep both of them." I looked around at the thick black trees. There was no one to hear. The words were building up inside of me, and as soon as I opened my mouth again, I heard them escape into the chilly air. "I guess . . . I want to be good at this. Really good. Not just decent for sixteen years old. Not good enough for the small-town metal scene. I want to be top tier. World-class."

The journalist nodded, listening. This time he didn't jump in. So I went on.

"I'd like to be faster, I guess. Better technique. I'd like to be a better songwriter, too. A better singer. All of that. I want it all."

I laughed again. He didn't.

"The stuff that comes with all of that would be nice, too," I went on when he just stood there, listening. "I mean, the money. And the fame. And the travel, and the girls and whatever. But, really, it's the music that I want the most. I want to be good. And I want to *know* that I'm good." I took a breath. "That, and a decent guitar."

Now the journalist grinned. Moonlight flickered on his glasses. "Know what?" he said. "I think that's all going to happen for you."

I gave that kind of snort people give when they're trying not to sound too dickish.

"I'm serious," he said. "You're going to get everything you want. Everything. It's going to be something to see." He flicked his lighter, sparking another cigarette. He took a drag, nodding at me the whole time. "I'm telling you, dude. You're going to do it. You're going to fly out of this place like a bullet. Like a bomb going off. You're going to be something."

There was a crackling in the pit of my stomach where I could feel his words hitting my ambition like a match on kindling. All of a sudden I *believed* him. I actually, totally believed him. I was going to be something. For a second all the old rock-star fantasies came flaring up. Giant, screaming crowds, me looming onstage in the spotlights and smoke. A gorgeous guitar in my hands.

Then, somewhere in the woods, there was a snap. I gave a little jerk. At first I thought the journalist must have stepped on a twig, but he was moving past me now, back toward the Crow's Nest, and the sound had come from somewhere deeper in the trees. I held still for a second. Listening. Watching. But I couldn't see anything in the darkness except the swaying branches, and the journalist was calling to me over his shoulder.

"Hey," he said, speaking loudly enough that his voice covered any other sounds from nearby. "I've got something for you. Come on."

I hurried after him.

The parking lot was empty except for the dingy white

Nissan and one beat-up gray sedan, its back coated with music bumper stickers. Even Ike and Janos were gone.

The journalist popped the sedan's trunk. Inside, lying on a pile of dirty laundry and a bunch of battered CDs, was a silver hard case.

The journalist picked it up. I could tell from the way he lifted it that it was heavy. Solid. Valuable.

He slammed the trunk and set the hard case on the closed lid.

"Open it," he told me.

I unlatched the case.

Inside, cushioned on a red-velvet lining, was the most beautiful guitar I'd ever seen.

An Ibanez JEM. Glossy black. Its solid silver pickguard inlaid with twisting vines and flowers.

I'd seen guitars like this—God, I'd *studied* guitars like this—on blogs and online shops and band sites. I didn't know exactly what it was worth, but every glinting, gorgeous detail whispered *money. Lots and lots of money.* Maybe thousands. More than I'd ever had, and maybe would ever have, to spare.

"Nice," I heard myself breathe.

"Yeah," agreed the journalist. "Take it."

The words didn't even sound like words in my head.

It was like at a birthday party, when your friends and family jump out and scream "Surprise!" and for a second you're so startled and confused that you actually feel *angry* instead of happy, because being ambushed by something good doesn't make any sense.

*"What?"* I said.

"Take it." He shrugged, smiling. "It's yours."

"Dude. I can't *take* it. This thing is worth—"

He was already shaking his head. "Who cares? I got it in trade from a rich-kid friend of my roommate who wanted my old XBox collection. *Seriously.* Plus, he sucks at guitar. Not that I should talk. I don't even play." He laughed. "See? This thing *deserves* to be played. By *you.*"

I stared down at the guitar.

I wanted it.

I wanted *her.*

More than I'd ever wanted any single object in the world.

In my head I skimmed through everything I owned. I had fourteen dollars in my wallet, all that was left from two recent lawn-mowing jobs. There was a little change in the Nissan's armrest, probably another two bucks or so, although that wasn't technically *mine.* I had nothing at home. My garage-sale speakers, maybe. The account number for a "college fund" that wouldn't cover a single credit, if I ever ended up going. Mom and Dad sometimes kept a little cash at the back of the junk drawer for emergencies, but I knew I couldn't take that, either. They'd been cutting corners everywhere. Cancelling subscriptions. Keeping the thermostat at eighty-two degrees all summer to save on air-conditioning. There was no help there.

It hit me like an actual, physical pain: I could not have this thing. Even now, when it was right in front of me.

"I can't just take it," I got the words out. "I have to pay you something for it."

"Dude." The journalist spread his hands. "You becoming a world-famous guitarist with this thing will pay me for it. You can thank me in your liner notes someday." He snapped the case shut. I instantly wanted to shove it open again. To see her again. But then he turned and held the case out to me. "Here," he said. "It's yours."

The silver box was just inches away. I knew I couldn't take it. I couldn't. But without even really trying, my hands opened and turned over, and I reached out and grasped the guitar case.

"Seriously . . ." I started, but I had no idea how to finish the sentence.

"Seriously." He smiled at me, his round, babyish face catching the moonlight. "It's meant for you." He jingled the car keys in his hand. "I've got to hit the road. But we'll be watching for you. In a couple years we'll check in again. See how far you've come."

I was still standing with my feet glued in place, like if I moved all this might collapse around me. "Maybe by then I can pay you back for this."

The journalist opened the driver's side door. "Don't worry about it," he called back to me. "I'm just glad it will have a good home." He climbed into the car. "It's been awesome, man. *Awesome*."

When the car's taillights came on, I finally jerked myself out of place. I stumbled out of the way as the journalist backed up, giving me one last big smile and wave from his window, then watched him peel out of the parking lot.

And I went home with the guitar.

Dad was still up. He used to go to bed early. Ten at the latest. Even earlier if he had a job to get to in the morning. But lately he'd been staying up past midnight. Sometimes I'd still hear the sound of the living room TV when I climbed into bed.

He glanced up from the saggy armchair when I walked in. Some late-night movie glowed on the TV screen. I was carrying my amp and two guitar cases, the Les Paul's battered black one and the shiny silver. Flashes from the screen glinted on its edge.

"What's that?" Dad said.

It figured that he would notice. Even the Ibanez's case was too nice for me. It stuck out in our house like a giant jewel.

"A guitar," I said back.

"I see that. Whose is it?"

"Mine."

"How did you afford another guitar?"

"Somebody gave it to me."

Dad's eyelids tightened. "Who? That Jezz?"

Jezz's family has money. Greenwood money, anyway. They have a bigger house. They take vacations by airplane instead of by minivan. Jezz has given me other stuff over the years. His clunky old laptop. Nikes that didn't fit him quite right.

Dad has never liked those shoes.

"A journalist," I said.

"Some journalist gave you a guitar."

"He didn't need it. He just ended up with it." I held the handle of the silver case tighter. "He wanted somebody who actually plays to have it."

Dad stared at the gleaming case for a second. Then he turned back to the TV screen. "I think you better find out if anyone has reported that guitar stolen," he said slowly. "Seems like someone was trying to get rid of it."

I grasped the handle so tight it hurt. I already couldn't imagine losing that guitar. No way.

"That's not it," I told him.

Dad's eyebrows rose and fell, like the tiniest shrug. He didn't look at me. "Just sounds too good to be true."

In that second what I really wanted to say was, *What do you care? It doesn't cost you anything either way.* But I didn't want to deal with the fallout. I just wanted to get down the hall to my room, shut the door, and play the new guitar.

So that's what I did. I didn't say anything else to Dad. I walked quietly away, holding the guitar tight.

Inside my own room, I sat down on the carpet beyond the end of my bed and unlatched the case. I'd almost expected it to disappear, like some magical dream, but the gorgeous Ibanez was still there. I lifted her into my lap.

The weight of her. The texture, the smell—it practically made me dizzy. I plugged into the amp, keeping the volume low as it could go, and played a couple of lines from an old Metallica song.

Each note sounded the way I'd only imagined notes sounding. The way they sounded when I heard them in my head. I played and played, until my fingertips burned and my eyes were starting to fog over, and I wanted never to stop.

And then the song came.

"Carrion." It showed up in one piece. Melody, lyrics, drum line, all at once. It made my head ache, like my skull was too full, like the liquid around my brain was boiling. I scribbled the words and chords in an open notebook.

Then I picked up the guitar again. I played the song to myself.

My fingers felt faster than they had before. Stronger. More precise.

And that felt good. Really freaking good. It balanced out the boiling, out-of-control feeling in my head.

*Okay,* I thought. *Okay.*

Just to check, I picked up the acoustic guitar resting on its stand and played the new song again. The feeling didn't change. It wasn't just because of the Ibanez. I was playing more consciously, more perfectly, than I'd ever played.

*Okay,* I thought again.

So maybe this was normal.

Maybe this was how it worked for everybody. Maybe you practice and wish for something for years, and then, suddenly, all at once, it happens. Maybe it wasn't as strange or huge or too good to be true as it felt.

That's what I kept trying to tell myself.

That's what I repeated when, in the days after that, the songs kept searing into my head and my fingers worked like perfect machines. It's what I told myself a few weeks later, when I realized I could play faster than Flynn. It's what I told myself when I jolted up at 2:00 a.m. to write three complete songs in a row.

I told myself that maybe, if I paid for these gifts by practicing like crazy, staying up half the night, working until my fingertips cracked, then it would all make sense. They wouldn't really be gifts if I had earned them. They would be under my control. And I wouldn't accept anything else until I felt like I had earned it, too. I wouldn't take money from Ike Lawrence. I wouldn't take too much praise for the songs. I wouldn't notice the girls. Not really.

Not even Frankie Lynde.

I'd take it slow. I'd keep everything under control.

But I was just lying to myself.

I was given these things. The guitar. The skills. The songs. And everything that the music has brought me.

They were given to me.

So they can all be taken away.

## On Monday they organize search parties.

Everyone from Greenwood High School signs up to help. Everyone but Anders.

No one expects him to join in. He's been shut in his house for two days, not even coming to school.

This has let the gossip spread more quickly. The stories about Last Things breaking up are only drowned out by the stories about Frankie. At first the stories traveled in whispers, soft and sympathetic. *Poor Anders. He must be brokenhearted, losing everything at once like that. He must feel so guilty, having that big fight with Frankie in front of everyone. Maybe she ran away to punish him. Maybe she hurt herself. By accident or not.* But by the end of the school day, the whispers shifted. They grew louder. Larger. *Maybe he knows something. Something no one else knows. Maybe he did something himself.*

In the early evening on Monday, everyone collects at the Crow's Nest. The parking lot is full—as full as it would be for a Last Things show, even though the coffee-house is closed for the search, its doors shut and locked. Everyone is forming pairs or groups, getting ready to walk into the woods, holding hands, turning on their phones for extra light. Jezz and Patrick are there, along with Ellie and Lee and Mac. I see Ike, with a black flashlight the size of a baseball bat, and Janos, with a camping lantern. He nods at me.

I don't have a phone. I don't have a flashlight. I don't have anything that would give the woods something to push against. They'll already be watching me.

There are police in the parking lot, two men in uniform, standing next to their squad cars. They didn't organize this. The official theory is still that Frankie ran away. She's an adult, technically. She has money. Her own car. But they're here anyway. In case.

Everyone lines up around the lot, along the edges of the road. This is the last place Frankie was seen. The last place they could trace her phone.

At someone's signal, everyone walks into the woods. More than two hundred people. They make a wavy ribbon, all colors and textures, before they weave into the trees, moving deeper and deeper, until at last the woods swallow them up.

I wait until everyone else is gone and the police have turned away to watch the searchers disappear. Then I walk in the direction no one else is walking. Away from town. Away from the direction Frankie turned her car. I walk north.

Pines. Layers of them. Sunset is still an hour or more away, but the sky is already tinged rose orange. The light catches in the pines. They shake and flicker. It's like walking through a forest of burning candles. The farther I go, the hotter they burn.

I climb over a creek bed narrower than a sidewalk. The underbrush is thick. Poison sumac, poison oak. I hold the cuffs of my sleeves tight. The woods will stop you any way they can.

Ahead of me is the fallen trunk of an oak tree. I remember it from Saturday night—its texture, its scent. It's covered in moss and seashells of fungus, its surface spongy and wet. It crumbles where my heels sink in.

Just past the fallen tree, in the distance, is a little clearer spot in the trees. And in the clear spot, I see it. A shriveled apple tree.

"Apples," Aunt Mae had muttered, still deep asleep,

when I brought her coffee to the living room that morning. "And he's so hungry . . ."

I didn't wake her. But I went back to the kitchen and took one of the pink-gold apples from the crisper drawer, still left from the sack she'd bought last week. I washed it and left it beside her coffee cup.

Now I know this wasn't what she meant.

I didn't notice the apple tree the other night. It was dark. Very late. I only noticed the clearing. The rusty remains of an old threshing machine, like the dried carcass of a grasshopper. The convenient stones left from a house or barn that must have tumbled down in this spot long ago. But Aunt Mae must have seen the withered apple tree. She must have known. She's helping to guide me back.

On the ground, several yards from the apple tree's bent trunk, I find the pile of stones I left behind. I brush aside the disguise of leaves and needles and twigs. The cell phone, dead faced and shiny as a mirror, lies beneath. I pick it up and slide it into my jeans pocket.

I straighten and take another look at the apple tree.

It's clearly ancient. It's warped and gray and nearly dead, cut off from sunlight by the canopy that's grown above. Its arms twist sideways, reaching for something, never quite catching it. A few tiny, worm-blackened apples dangle from its twigs.

I'm still looking at it when I hear the sound. A small sound. A shift in the leaves.

I skirt the apple tree. Ahead of me is a crumbled stone wall. Past the wall, in a deep hole that used to be a cellar, coated with mud and moss and decaying leaves and other long-dead things, is a creature.

It's small and furred. It's the color of wet dust.

At first I'm not even sure if it's alive. But then it moves. Two reflective gold eyes stare up at me.

*Mrrk?* it breathes.

It's a cat.

It's *his* cat.

I've seen it stalking around Anders's yard, bony shoulders working, long tail flicking. But even without those memories, I'd know this cat. His touch is all over it. I swear, I can even smell him.

This is what Aunt Mae saw. This is where she was guiding me.

"Hello," I whisper. I crouch on the edge of the hole. It's deep, rotting, slick sided. With a wrong move, I might be stuck down there, too. And wouldn't the woods love that.

I glance all around. Nothing nearby. No one to see.

I stride back to the hulk of the ancient combine.

It's heavy. Its bottom edges are buried in years of damp earth. It takes me more than one try to lift it out of the ground and then to drag it to the edge of the crumbling cellar. I tip it in.

It creaks as it hits the mud below, but the old machinery stays intact.

I climb down its side into the cellar. Rotting leaves sink under my shoes. Mud and standing water suck at my feet as I step, slowly, closer to the cat.

I remember its name. I've heard him use it. I've seen him, through his window, stroking this same gray fur.

"Hi, Goblin," I whisper.

The cat is a long way from home. It didn't come here on its own, of course. They caught it. They brought it here. The woods would have swallowed it up for good.

But they've lost this one.

The cat inches toward me. It's wet, cold, hungry. It lets me gather its body into my arms. I wrap the sides of my flannel shirt around it, keeping it warm and close, and it begins to purr.

With Goblin in one arm, I climb back up the combine.

We walk back through the woods to the Crow's Nest.

A few searchers have already given up and come back to

the parking lot. They stand around their cars, talking, checking phones, kicking bits of gravel. I can hear others shouting and crunching in the trees. Most of them haven't gone far. No one glances at me. It's twilight now, dark enough that the air is thick and smoke colored. Lights flicker through the woods, here and there, brighter and larger than fireflies.

With my fingers kept inside my cuff, I pull the phone out of my pocket. I leave it just beyond the edge of the parking lot, near a jumble of lilacs that will bloom like wild in another month. Someone will spot it soon. They'll hand it over to the police. The police will comb the area, search the ground, the lot, the grass. They won't find anything else.

I climb onto my bike, Goblin still hunched against my rib cage.

I could take him to Anders now. I could leave him on the stoop, or even knock on the window. But I don't want to let go just yet. I want to bring the cat home, feed it, dry it, comb the bits of broken leaves out of its fur. I want to feel it sleeping on my bed, curled up near my side, just like it does with Anders. I want to sense his touch when I run my fingers over the cat's smoky fur, just for a few more hours.

This is where I fail, even when I win.

I'm not good at letting go.

**I'm not sure how I get to school on Tuesday. I don't know how I get to my** first class. All morning it's like someone with an invisible remote control is pushing a Pause button on my brain. Flash: Pulling a clean T-shirt out of my dresser. Flash: Sophomores chugging energy drinks in the commons, whispering *Last Things . . . breakup . . . Frankie Lynde.* Flash: I'm in the science room for physics class, in my usual desk. Everyone is pretending not to be staring at me.

Everyone except Sasha.

She sits two desks to my right. Her eyes are like razors.

I slide lower in my seat.

Now the invisible remote control hits Rewind. I'm passing Frankie in the high school hall, and she turns to give me a smile so long and bright anybody around us could see it, and I'm sure most of them do. I'm with her in my bedroom, late on Friday night. I'm above her on that smoky-smelling couch on Blake Skoglund's porch, her body under me, pressed against me, even though it feels like I'm the one being completely enveloped by her. I'm telling her to fuck off in the dark Crow's Nest parking lot.

And everyone is watching.

My head pounds like the beater against Patrick's bass drum.

*All the things you love. One by one,* says the music executive with the slate gray eyes. *Oh, Anders. . . . You are going to be so, so sorry.*

I heard someone found Frankie's cell phone last night, near the Crow's Nest. Near the spot where everyone saw us fight. Still no sign of her car, though. No sign of Frankie herself. It doesn't seem possible that Frankie Lynde could go from the center of everything to someplace where no one can find her at all.

Mr. Norales is at the board, talking about mass units and velocity units, and I can't follow anything. I stare down at my open notebook.

I haven't written a song in days. Not unless you count that song I played to the live audience on Saturday, the last time I played with Jezz and Patrick. Maybe the last time we'll ever play.

Now I can barely remember the words to that song. Only the chorus sticks around. *Don't forgive me, don't forget.*

Freaking perfect.

When the bell rings, I stumble into the hall. In the last couple of hours, somebody has posted flyers everywhere. There's Frankie's name in big print above her family's phone number and the police tip line, a picture of her gleaming blue car, and three photos of her smiling into the camera, like anyone who goes to this school doesn't already know her on sight. Somehow I make it up the stairs, to the right classroom, to the right desk. I sit through American Literature. Then I find my locker. It takes me three tries to get the combination right.

Lunchtime. I almost don't go to the cafeteria. I could find some corner or classroom to hide in, but before I can settle on one, autopilot steers me through the swinging cafeteria doors.

Across the huge room, I see Jezz and Patrick and Lee and Ellie and Mac already clustered around our usual table. There's a huge bag of tortilla chips open in the center of the table and a metallic rainbow of cans from the vending machines.

From a distance, Patrick glances up at me. He doesn't

even frown. His face stays blank, like he's looking at a total stranger, someone he's never spoken to and probably never will. He glances away again. The rest of them don't even look up.

"What did you do with her, Thorson?"

The voice comes from behind me.

I turn around.

"What did you do? Did you eat her?"

The voice is nasty and loud enough to cut through the cafeteria buzz. It's coming from a table of guys in camo and hunting gear. Chase Pokolski, Kev Burr, Dustin Barrino. And Austen Marks. It was his voice. His wide, pasty face is grinning at me.

He's talking about Frankie. At first I think he means something dirty. I learned half of the rude terms I know from being stuck on the same school bus route as Austen and Chase. But he keeps on grinning at me, with that mean, eager face, and then I realize he means something else.

"You did, didn't you?" he goes on. "I bet you chopped her up, put the nicest pieces on your Satan altar, and ate the rest. I bet she was tasty. Wasn't she."

They're all grinning at me. All those bared teeth.

I keep my face blank. I raise my middle finger slowly,

steadily in their direction, almost like I'm giving them a salute. Then I turn and walk away.

I'm not sure if my friends—or the people who used to be my friends—overheard. But everyone at the closer tables did. Their faces are a quiet blur as I stride by.

I head through the doors, back down the hallway, moving against the stream of people still heading into the cafeteria. More blurred faces. One flash of long, pale blond hair. More whispers. More stares.

I've just made it around the corner when someone says, "Hey. Anders."

It's a different voice. Another guy's. It's familiar, but I can't place it yet.

Then I'm flying forward so fast that it's like the floor has folded in half. My forehead slams something hard and sharp. It rattles. I reel back. There's a flare of pain above my eyebrow, where my head just hit the corner of an open locker door. The freshman getting his books out of the locker stares up at me, his eyes wide.

I cup one hand over my forehead. Wet and warm. I turn around.

Will and Sasha and Carson stand in front of me. Sasha's mouth is pinched tight. Will looks blank and observant, as always. Carson is closest. His face has a look of surprise on it, like maybe he meant to shove me, but not into an open metal door. His eyes flick to my forehead. I can feel the blood trickling down now, sliding over the edge of my cheekbone. I don't wipe it off. Behind me, the freshman slams his locker shut and scurries away.

"What do you know, Anders?" says Carson. He's trying to sound hard. But I can see that he's shaken.

"You're going to have to be more specific," I say, dry and calm as I can make it.

Sasha jumps in. "About *Frankie.*" She's speaking so forcefully, her entire body is quivering. "Everybody saw it. You know that, right? First you sing this song about how nobody should forgive you for what you've done. Then you have this huge fight with Frankie, in public." Her voice is getting higher and tighter. "And then she disappears, and you go into hiding, and—what? We're supposed to think it's some kind of *coincidence?*"

"I'm not telling you what to think."

Something in Sasha's twitchy face seems to snap. She lunges forward, grabbing a fistful of my shirt. Maybe she's the one who shoved me. "Where is she?" she hisses up into my face.

"Look—" I'm trying not to let them rattle me, but I

can hear it in my own voice now. "If I knew where she was, I'd be there, too." I get the words out. Even though I'm not sure they're true.

Sasha doesn't let go of my shirt. "Everybody knows about you," she says. "Everybody knows. We all know how you've been toying with Frankie for months. Staring at her, writing songs about her, hooking up with her and then ditching her, never making anything official, never treating her like an actual *person,* because you think you're some superspecial *rock star,* right?"

A crowd is starting to gather. I feel like I'm onstage, but without the armor of my guitar. Totally bare.

"I don't know anything about where Frankie is," I say. Blood is trickling over my eyebrow into my eye. "You can believe me or not. I can't tell you anything else."

Sasha's eyes are slits. "Everybody knows there's something wrong with you." Her voice is as fast and hard as a drumroll. "I used to think you were just some pretentious loner. But that's not it. You're messed up. You're not normal. Look at you. You're not even a *person.*" She finally lets go, pushing me backward at the same time. Hard enough that I hit the row of closed locker doors. "What is *wrong* with you?" she screams. "Do you even *care?* Do you have any feelings at all?"

Will grabs her, his encircling arm pinning hers down. "Hey," he says softly, "it's all right."

I take my chance. I turn left, striding off into the hall.

"Yeah, run away!" Sasha shouts after me. "Run away. You coward!"

I don't run. But I keep walking.

I walk until I'm slamming through the doors, out of the school, into the cool April air.

I drive home.

Mom's at work. Dad's gone, too. He must actually have a job today. Thank god.

I head down the hallway to my room.

The guitars on their stands look like a bunch of hunting trophies, like dead things propped up in a row. I don't even want to touch them.

And Goblin's still not there.

I crouch down and look under the bed. Not there, either.

I go to the window. A faint trace of that rusty *X* still crosses the pane. There's no sign of Goblin through the glass.

I check the kitchen, the garage, the basement, just in case. Then I head outside.

I know there's no point calling his name. He's too deaf

to hear, and he never comes when he's called anyway. But I need to do something.

"Goblin?" I shout. "Goblin!"

The woods around the yard creak and sway.

I run into the trees. Immediately daytime feels like evening. A few blades of sun try to get through, but the shadows are so thick, they dull everything. It's chillier here. A few birds scream.

The shadows and creaks and my own panic trigger my imagination, filling it with the stupid stories Greenwood kids tell each other about all the secrets lurking in these woods: animals, monsters, serial killers. It's too easy to picture bad things happening here. In my head Goblin and Frankie start to overlap, mixing with those old stories. I can see them both running through the underbrush. Trying to hide. Falling into the leaves. Teeth—or knives—flashing closer.

My heart thunders. I look around, the adrenaline burning through me, but there's nothing to fight. No one to save.

*Oh, Anders. . . . You are going to be so, so sorry.*

I can't save my band. I can't save Frankie. I can't even save my fucking cat.

"Goblin!" I shout again.

The sound of my voice disappears into the wind. But there's something else out here, I can feel it. Something wrong. Something nearby.

I hear a snap.

My heart almost shoots out of my chest.

I spin around but there's no one there. The trees just whisper, shifting in place like an audience that hears your music but doesn't care. My brain is playing tricks. I'm an idiot. I'm pathetic. Paranoid.

And then—

"I have your cat."

The voice comes from right beside me.

I think I jump straight into the air.

I don't know how she got there without my hearing or seeing her, but there she is.

Stalker girl.

She's wearing her usual baggy, dark clothes. She's dry this time, so her long, white-blond hair floats around her in frizzy ringlets. It looks like curled fiberglass.

It's so weird, so much like I summoned her with my thoughts, that I almost blurt out a laugh. Why is she here? Why isn't she at school? How does she know exactly where to find me?

I'm flipping through one question after another. And

then I notice that she's holding a big gray cat in her arms.

Goblin.

He's alive.

I make some other noise, something that's not any kind of laugh at all, and throw out my arms.

The girl passes him to me.

Goblin grabs hold of my shirt. He puts one paw on either side of my neck and sniffs at my mouth, like he's checking me for ID.

"Goblin," I whisper. I'm fighting not to cry. "Hey. It's you."

*Mrrrk?* says Goblin.

He feels bonier than usual, but he's whole. Not mauled by wild dogs. Not bleeding from an open gash. I'm so stupidly, overwhelmingly grateful that I'm on the edge of sobbing, right here, in front of this delusional girl in her giant flannel shirt.

"Where was he?" I ask, still checking Goblin over, using the excuse to keep my face down.

"He was stuck in an old caved-in basement in the woods," says the girl. "He must have fallen in during that storm."

Her voice is soft and polite. It has a faint accent. Then I realize that she's just speaking so precisely that it sounds like she has an accent. She sounded the same the other night, I guess, but I was too startled and angry at the time to really notice. And it was too dark to get a good look at her. She looks a little foreign, too, or a little old-fashioned, with that long pale hair and soft face and no makeup.

Maybe I should be angry that she's here, in my yard, almost scaring me out of my mind again. But she's the opposite of threatening.

Plus, she just handed me my bony old cat.

"How did you find him?" I ask.

The girl pauses for a beat. "I heard him."

I glance around. My house is in view, through the trees. A prickle of distrust comes back. "So . . . you were just wandering around out here behind my house, and you heard him?"

"No. My aunt heard him," the girl says. "Or saw him." Oh, yeah. Mae Malcolm, who's supposed to be crazy, or a witch or something. I don't know what to believe about that. I don't know what to believe about anything. I try to put on a skeptical look, but I feel it crumbling off my face as soon as Goblin takes another sniff at my chin.

"She gave me the clue," the girl says, softly and steadily. "And he wasn't here. Behind your house."

I rub Goblin's head. "Then where was he?"

"Miles away."

Miles away? I want to ask Goblin what the hell he was thinking. The cat sags against me. He's purring so hard that I can feel the resonance in my rib cage.

I look straight at the girl instead.

Her cheeks are pink. Tendrils of hair blow across her face.

"Is that how you knew about the other night, when you showed up at my window?" I say, before I know that I'm going to say it. "About the music executive, and the contract. Because your aunt *saw* something?"

The girl pauses again. She doesn't look surprised, or like she's trying to come up with a cagey answer. She just looks straight into my eyes. "Some of it," she says at last. "Some of it I saw and heard myself."

"So you have, like, psychic powers? Like your aunt's supposed to have?" I hit the words *supposed to* extra hard, to show that I'm not quite buying all of this. I'm not sure if I'm showing her or myself.

The girl just smiles. "No," she says. "I'm not like her that way."

"Oh. Then . . ." I start, trying to look like I don't put any stock in her answer either way, "you don't know anything about Frankie Lynde, do you? Like—where she might be? Or what happened to her?"

The girl gives me another long look. The edges of her smile have softened away. "No," she says. "I'm sorry."

"Okay." I feel myself deflate, but I try to hide it. "I just thought . . . no stone unturned. Or whatever."

I start to turn away.

"I do know one thing." Her voice stops me. "I know that you had nothing to do with it."

For half a second the words are comforting. Then they turn creepy, because how the hell could she know that? And who would believe some obsessive stalker, anyway? I wonder if a stalker can give you an alibi.

"Okay," I say again. "Well . . . thanks for saving my cat. Really. It's been the only decent thing in this whole messed-up week."

For a second the girl looks weirdly surprised. Her pale eyebrows go up. She smiles. Her face gets even softer. She looks like I've just given her some grand personal compliment, not a simple thank-you.

"You're welcome," she says.

I start to walk away again, but this time I stop myself. "Hey." I turn to face her again. "What's your name, anyway?"

I can see her suck in a breath. "It's Thea," she says.

"Thea," I repeat. "I'm Anders."

Now her smile shows her teeth. She looks like she might laugh. "I know."

"Okay. Well." I jut my chin at Goblin, who's bumping his head against my chest. "I'd better go feed this guy."

I head toward the house. Dead leaves shuffle under my feet. I hold Goblin tight against my body with one hand, rubbing his ears with the other. I don't see or hear the girl leave. But when I get to the front door and glance back at the woods, she's gone.

Goblin laps up an entire dish of fresh water while I find a can of special wet cat food at the back of a high cabinet. He devours it and then eats a whole serving of his usual crunchy cat food, and then he finally passes out next to me on the living room couch.

I keep one hand on his side.

We're both still sitting there, me staring at a movie on the TV screen, Goblin snoring, when I hear the garage door open.

My heart jolts upward. I check the TV clock. 3:18. I might have gotten home from school by now if I'd left just a little bit early.

Dad walks heavily—but fast—across the kitchen and into the living room. He halts when he sees me. He's still got his Day-Glo work vest on. His phone and keys are in his hand. His face is tight. I can't quite read it.

"Found Goblin," I tell him before he can do the math in his head and ask me anything about why I'm home so soon. "Somebody from school found him in the woods. He was stuck in an old basement, I guess."

Dad nods. I don't think he even heard me. He looks like he's making a decision about something else. I see his jawline flex. He's not looking at me. He clears his throat.

"Looks like they found that Lynde girl, too," he says. "The cranes are in the river."

**The day they pull her out of the river is sunny and clear. Police boats have been** searching since last night, looking for the dark blue car in the dark blue water, and they've finally found something. Something hidden down there in the currents and the long-sunk trees and the shadows cast by the big blue bridge.

It's nearly three o'clock when they drive the crane over the bank. The dive teams are working. White boats bob nearby. Traffic on the bridge slows.

Everyone watches. Everyone stares down into that deep, quick water.

Word spreads. Cars gather on the shoulders. Once school lets out, there are more. Clusters of people hurry out on foot, with cameras, with phones. News crews screech up in their painted vans.

Sun sparkles on the water.

I'm watching from the bank on the far side of the bridge. It took me just a few minutes to get from Anders's place to the river, riding straight through the woods. It's grassy here on the bank, and shaded, with clusters of birch and box elder and oak. Lots of people have collected here. Kids from school. TV reporters. We have a clear view.

Uniformed people on the boats point and gesture. Divers go under. The hook on the crane goes down. Down. Down.

Of course they'd find the car eventually. It was only a matter of time.

Rivers keep moving. Things lost in them move, too.

The divers surface. A huge motor revs.

The car rises slowly, like a sliver pulled out of thick skin. Waves boil around it. It's upside down, so the tires come first, then the black undercarriage, and then, slowly, its body, dark and dripping.

The car isn't deep blue. It's black.

I can hear the gasps around me.

They know it isn't Frankie's car. That's not Frankie inside of it.

It takes ages for the river water to drain away. The black Audi with the Illinois plates dangles there, swaying very slightly on the crane's thick cable.

**LAST THINGS**

The windows slosh. They're tinted anyway. Nothing to see inside. Not yet.

The headlights are dead now.

They were burning on Friday night. Just the low beams, not the brights. The rain was too thick. On the bridge, where mist gathers over the water, the air was like gray gauze.

She'd taken her time leaving the Underground Music Studios. Maybe she'd stopped to reapply her red lipstick or to comb her sleek dark hair. And I'm fast. Faster than any car. I had plenty of time, even after the talk at Anders's window, to make it to the bridge. To be standing there. Ready.

She didn't see me until it was too late.

The roads were slick. The pavement on the road that leads out of town is old, worn into soft divots that trap the rain. Her tires were already skidding.

As the Audi streaked closer, she met my eyes through the windshield. She saw me standing there. At the entry to the bridge. Waiting for her.

I could see her face. I could see her eyes. I could see the instant when she recognized me.

Then she hit the accelerator.

I watched her through the wet glass—sleek hair,

spread red mouth, glittering teeth. Then I took a step forward, as fast as I can move.

Fast.

My hands hit the black hood so hard they left twin dents. I shoved the car to the side. It skidded off the road, away from the bridge, down a slope of scrub grass and gravel. I watched it veer straight over the bank and into the river.

There was barely a splash. Just a rushing sound, lost in the roar of the rain. The gold puddle of the headlights fading to black.

The car disappeared fast.

I waited for a while, past the foot of the bridge. Making sure nothing came back up.

Now it has.

But it's been long enough. My heart is calm.

Everyone else is pushing closer to the water. Craning. Lifting up their phones. They want a glimpse of what's stuck inside those draining windows.

I don't need to know.

All I wonder is whether she stayed belted to her seat. If she was knocked out on impact. If she tried, too late, to shove the door open against the steel-hard pressure of the water.

I hope the end was quick.

I walk away.

It will be all over the news in less than an hour. The police need help identifying a woman: late twenties or early thirties, dark hair, alone in an expensive black car.

I know who she was. I know *what* she was. But no one else needs to know.

I get my bike from the bridge railing, climb on, and pedal slowly toward home. Toward the shed. Toward the root cellar.

But no one needs to know that, either.

**Wednesday is another sunny day. It feels like an insult.**

I didn't set my alarm last night, and nobody wakes me up. By the time I shove the covers off my head, Goblin is *rrruckk*-ing at the closed door, begging to be let out, and flickering sun is streaming through my bedroom window.

I check the clock. It's 12:38, which means I've already missed more than half the school day. Apparently Mom and Dad have decided to let me skip again.

Last night, as soon as the pictures of that black Audi hanging over the river started to appear on the news, I think part of my brain came unplugged.

It wasn't Frankie.

That's all I could think, over and over. I couldn't even move.

Dad kept trying not to look at me, like he was too afraid he might find me crying with relief, and Mom kept putting her arm around me and squeezing me and rubbing the back of my neck, and I could barely even feel it happening.

But then, when the news cameras zoomed in on the car—a glossy black Audi with Illinois plates—I started to think something else. Something that just went *ohmygod ohmygodohmygod* over and over. And when they posted the police description of the body found inside the car—a woman, around thirty, short hair, black clothes—my brain shorted out entirely.

It was the music executive. It had to be. And now she was dead.

I didn't know what to feel, or what to do, and fear and relief and silence and guilt were all wadded together in my gut like a meal I wished I hadn't eaten. And on top of all that, Frankie was still missing.

Sometime after midnight I finally staggered into bed. I dreamed about water and about being onstage at the Crow's Nest, and I woke up so desperate to be up there that the memory of Last Things breaking up landed like a cinder block on my rib cage.

Now I open my bedroom door. Goblin darts out ahead of me, streaking toward the kitchen. I follow him.

A note in Mom's cursive is taped to the fridge.

*Hope you got some rest. We thought you needed it. I
called the school and spoke to the secretary already. We'll be
home late (Frank Rohmer's retirement party, remember?),
but your dinner is in the freezer.*

*Love, Mom*

There's an open two-liter of flat Coke in the fridge,
next to the half-empty can of cheap tuna for Goblin. I
scoop some tuna onto his dish of dry cat food. Then I
take the bottle of Coke back to my room.

I don't even want to turn on my computer. In a town
this size, everybody will be talking about the same thing:
the mysterious car in the river. Everyone's feeds will be
full of pictures of the black Audi dangling on its rope
over the water like some giant mutant fish. Everyone will
be spreading rumors, pasting made-up theories of serial
killers and underground drug rings onto the few actual
facts. Everyone will be saying that they think they recognize the woman or the car just so they can feel like
they're part of this.

If I can't turn on my computer, I can't listen to music.
But I need some other sound to erase the awful echoes in
my head.

For the first time in three days, I grab Yvonne. This

is the longest I've gone without playing ever since I first picked up a guitar. Ever since our last show—our *last* show—I haven't even been able to think about playing. It's dragged too much bad stuff along with it. The withdrawal hits me all at once. A sick emptiness runs through my whole body.

But Yvonne feels different in my hands now. Resistant. Awkward.

I strum a simple G chord. My left hand is clumsy. It's almost like the fingers are asleep, except there are no pins and needles. I shift chords. D minor. C minor. The slide of the strings under my fingers is familiar, but distant now, like a word you've used a million times but suddenly can't remember. And my right hand won't do what I want it to.

It reminds me of middle-school dances, when a slow song would come on and you'd rock stiffly back and forth with your hands on some girl's shoulders, if you were lucky enough to be dancing with a girl at all. I spent most of those nights with Jezz and Patrick hanging around near the DJ's table. We'd watch him press buttons and cue songs, begging for Metallica or Black Sabbath or at least "Free Bird." I was a skinny kid with knobby shoulders and big feet. I didn't know how to use my own body.

I don't think I figured out what my body was *for* until I learned to play guitar.

I play the melody line from "Deep Water."

The timing is off. My touch is heavy. My third and fourth fingers won't lift.

Maybe I'm just rusty, I tell myself, trying not to panic. Maybe it's the lack of sleep. Maybe I'm just preoccupied. But underneath, I know it's something else.

Because I haven't written a song in days, either. Or I should say a song hasn't come to me. This isn't normal. Three empty days is not normal.

I try to clear my mind, let a melody come to me, but all I can see is that woman in the basement studio, holding out her silver pen.

I didn't grab that pen. I didn't sign, and now I'm being punished.

*All the things you love. One by one. Oh, Anders. . . .*

I get up so fast Yvonne thumps onto the carpet.

I need to talk to someone. Someone who knows at least part of what I know.

I glance at the alarm clock. I'm still more than an hour early for my four o'clock lesson with Flynn, but I latch Yvonne into her case and rush out to the car.

I throw the Nissan into reverse. My tires squeal as I

bump out of the driveway onto the road, shifting into drive.

Flynn must have a few answers. He's the one who set up the meeting that set off this whole goddamn chain reaction, after all. My hands clench the wheel. I'm angry at Flynn, I'm *furious,* even though I know this isn't totally fair. Flynn couldn't have known exactly how things would unfold. But he must know about the woman in the black car by now. Maybe he'll know more than I know. He'll do what he always does, and stay mellow, and help me step backward until everything looks smaller, more like something I can handle.

Jesus, I hope.

I haven't even gone thirty feet from the drive when I see someone standing there, in the road.

It's stalker girl. Thea.

She's holding the handlebars of her old baby-blue bike. Snakes of white hair twist around her. The rest of her doesn't move. She just stands there, in the middle of the winding country road, watching me barrel closer.

I slam on the brakes. A car horn is wailing.

After a second I realize the car horn isn't mine. The sound is coming from behind me.

I glance in the rearview. A rusty black truck is streaking toward my bumper.

I screech to a stop.

So does the truck, just a few inches away. Through its dirty windshield, I can see two faces—Jezz and Patrick—staring down at me.

I roll down my window and crane out. "What the hell?" I shout. "You almost hit me! What are you trying to do?"

Patrick raises one hand, a little motion telling me to stay still. Then he swerves into the oncoming lane, pulling up beside me.

"Dude," says Jezz, leaning out his own open window. "You need to back up."

"What?" I shout back.

"Back up into your driveway," says Jezz, loud and clear. "Somebody sabotaged your car."

There's a sick thump in my chest. *"What?"*

*"Just do it,"* says Jezz so firmly that I stop asking questions. I just do it. As I put the car in reverse, I notice that the girl in the road has disappeared. She's not on the shoulder. She's not anywhere in sight. I blink hard. Then I focus my eyes on the rearview mirror.

I drive backward up the slope of our driveway. Patrick

and Jezz bump up after me. By the time they're climbing down from the cab, I'm out of the car, waiting, my arms crossed tight enough across my chest that they might be able to hold down my pounding heart.

"What the hell are you talking about?" I say.

Patrick doesn't answer. He just walks past me and crouches next to the driver's side wheel. He touches one of the bolts. I can see it spin in his fingers. It's loose, almost falling off.

"Better get a wrench," he says, without looking at me.

I pull a wrench down from the pegboard in the garage. I hand it to Patrick. He tightens the bolts, fast, one after the other. When he's done, he stands up and hands the wrench back to me. He still doesn't meet my eyes. His face is like cement.

I don't know what to say. *Thanks* is too small. And awful as I know this is, I'm still so furious at Patrick for destroying Last Things that I'm not sure I can say it even now, when he might have just saved my life.

Instead I say, "How did you know?"

Patrick folds his arms, too. He looks past me, toward the empty road. "Somebody left a note in my locker."

"Saying what?"

"Saying somebody was going to mess with your wheel."

"Somebody? Who?"

Patrick shrugs.

We're all quiet for a second.

"I guess it could have been Sasha or Carson," I say.

Jezz gives a little nod. "Carson is a jackass, but this has to be illegal or something."

I turn the wrench over in my hands. "They think I did something to Frankie. I get it. I'd suspect me, too. I've been expecting the angry villagers to show up with their torches and pitchforks anytime now."

Jezz lets out a breath. "Yeah, that's the other reason we're here."

I throw him a look. "Where's your pitchfork? In your pocket?"

Jezz nods, faux serious. "It's small. It's a pitchspork, actually. More versatile."

When I don't laugh, he says, "We know you, dude. We know you didn't have anything to do with Frankie disappearing. And we just wanted to tell you, maybe other people are saying bad things about you, but we're not. And we're not buying any of it. We know that if there's anybody who's upset about all this, it's you." He smacks Patrick lightly on the arm. "Right?"

"Right," says Patrick softly.

"So." Jezz shuffles his Converse shoes in the gravel. "That's why we're here. Moral support or whatever. We were talking about coming out here even before Patrick got the note, but then—yeah. Then we were sure."

I get what he's saying. Jezz was ready to forgive me. Patrick needed another nudge. But here he is.

I look back down at the wheel because I'm afraid of what my face might be doing. "Thanks, guys," I hear myself mumble. "Really. Thank you."

"And just because Last Things might be on hiatus doesn't mean we can't speak to you or anything."

"On hiatus?" I swear, my heart actually leaps.

On hiatus. Not over. Not forever.

Then I glance at their faces and see what this really means. Jezz's face says the door is still open, at least for him. Patrick's face says the door is still shut. And locked. And that maybe there is no door.

Of course, none of this even matters if I can't compose or play anymore. I force down a flare of panic.

"I mean . . ." Jezz looks at Patrick, too. "Never say never. But we can talk about that later. When everything makes sense again."

It's a small step. A better-than-nothing. "Okay," I say. "Good."

We're all quiet for a minute.

I frown down at our shoes, my ancient knockoff Dr. Martens, Jezz's red Converse, Patrick's scuffed work boots, all of us shuffling in the gravel. And suddenly the craving to jump back into our usual routines is so powerful that it almost knocks me down. I want to talk about music with them. Listen to a new track with them. I'd give pretty much anything I own just to get out our instruments and play.

But they aren't my band anymore.

I still can't wrap my head around this. It's like learning that your mom isn't actually your mom, and that she'll never be hugging you or helping you with anything again, and she'd really like it if you moved out of her house ASAP.

"So," I ask when I can finally talk again, "who do you think left the note?"

Jezz looks at Patrick. Patrick doesn't speak. "I don't know," Jezz says. "Maybe it was another one of Frankie's friends or something. Like Will. He's not a total psycho. Maybe he knew about their plan and wanted to stop it. In a kind of chickenshit way."

I nod. "Maybe."

Patrick makes a little grunting sound. Jezz and I

know exactly what this means. It's the sound that means Patrick disagrees, but he's not going to say anything unless we ask him to.

"What?" I say.

He lifts one shoulder. "It didn't look like a guy's writing."

We all think for a second.

"Anyway." Jezz rocks on his feet. "Crazy, about some *other* car being in the river."

My heart sinks. "Yeah."

"I mean, I don't think you had anything to do with Frankie *or* with that, but maybe there's some kind of connection. I mean, things like this just don't happen all the time. Not in this little town. Right?"

I'm starting to feel sick again. "I don't know."

"You know what I think?" Jezz hurries on. "I think there's something weird happening around here. Around this whole town. I mean, like, bad spirits or something crazy like that. I think it's affecting all of us." He nods at my wheel. "I mean, even an ass like Carson Bergdahl wouldn't normally do something that could *kill* somebody. And—I'm just saying—you *do* seem different, dude." He raises his hands, quickly, placatingly. "Not, like, *dangerous* different, but like . . .

Dude, what was with that song on Saturday night? 'Devil's Due'?"

I focus my eyes on the hood of the Nissan, just to have somewhere else to put them. "I don't know," I say. "I didn't plan that. I had no idea it was coming. It was like I wasn't in control of it at all."

"Maybe you're epileptic," says Patrick, out of nowhere.

Jezz blinks at him. "What?"

"Like that guy from Joy Division. He'd have seizures onstage and stuff. Curtis Ian."

"Ian Curtis," corrects Jezz. "You think Anders has seizures?"

"Maybe." Patrick raises his shoulders. "Just saying."

"Yeah," I say softly. "I don't think that's it. But maybe."

"I think it's something else." Jezz looks weirdly thoughtful. "Okay. Maybe it's nothing supernatural or whatever. Maybe it's just some crazy local weirdo."

"Like that stalker who was just hanging out in the middle of your road," says Patrick softly.

The skin on the backs of my arms goes cold.

He saw her, too. So she was really there. That's something, I guess. Something strange.

I shake my head a little harder than I need to. "She's weird, but she's harmless. She actually saved Goblin. He was stuck in some old basement in the woods all weekend. She brought him back."

The guys are mute for a second. Then Patrick says, "Or maybe she kidnapped him."

I turn toward him. "What?"

"So she could return him." Patrick's voice is measured. "Maybe she loosened the bolts on your wheel and then left me the note. So she could save you herself."

The fragments of these ideas whirl around in my brain, slashing through everything else. Nothing holds together anymore. Nothing makes sense. "Jesus," I breathe. "That's . . . messed up."

"Yeah. Exactly." Patrick stares straight into my eyes. "Like her aunt. Like her."

*"Dude,"* Jezz jumps in. "You know what I heard?" He leans closer, like there's anyone nearby to overhear. "There was this series of fires around town back in the eighties, barns and sheds and other places, mostly out in the woods, and everybody knew Mae Malcolm did it. But there, like, wasn't enough evidence to convict her."

I frown. "Then how does everybody know she did it?"

"I don't know." Jezz raises his hands again. "I'm just saying. Everybody knew."

We go quiet, staring at the woods all around us.

I step back into the garage to hang the wrench in its spot. I try to walk smoothly and slowly, but my heart is hammering in my ribs.

I can't avoid this anymore. There are too many pieces, too many signs.

*You're going to risk losing everything?* It was a threat. I knew it was. *Oh, Anders. You are going to be so, so sorry. . . .*

I need to talk to Flynn.

I take a stumbling step toward the Nissan. "I've got to get to the studio. But thanks again for coming here, guys. I mean it. Thanks."

They both nod. Jezz even reaches out and clasps me on the shoulder. "We've got your back," he says. "You know that."

"I'll keep you posted if anything happens." I'm trying too hard to sound normal. I just sound stupid instead. "I'd better get to my lesson."

I climb into the car and head out.

When I glance into the rearview mirror, the guys are still standing there, watching me. Then the road twists, and the dark blur of the trees comes between us, and they're gone.

## My father used to bring me stones.

Nearly every day he'd come home from repairing a boat somewhere and in his pocket there would be a stone, smooth and water polished, from whatever river or lake he'd been near.

"Baptized in the waters of the River Jordan," he'd say. Because all rivers are one river, really. Every river, every raindrop, all flowing to the sea.

It took time for me to see the power in them. In the flowing water and in the stones. But then I started to build the circles. Circles of river-washed stones, around my bed, around our house, around the scrubby edges of whatever yard was temporarily ours.

As long as the circle was whole, we were safe. The darkness couldn't reach inside.

My father didn't approve. He thought it was pagan.

Witchy. More magical than holy. But I know the truth: there's not much difference.

My father's always been this way. He argues with Aunt Mae about her cards and her whiskey and her Bible scrying, when she asks the book a question and opens it to a random passage. He argues with me. At me.

I understand. He isn't one of us.

He's always on the lookout for the things he calls *evil*. He sees them on TV. In music. In other peoples' churches. But he can't see what we see. The places where the evil slides in. The spots where the world is a little too thin and too dark and too full of hiding places.

My father and I used to move around a lot, river to lake to river. In each new spot he would find a church and then slowly begin to disagree with the pastor's way of doing things until he'd launched a whole holy war in his mind. Then he'd go off on his long nights, drinking, preaching, standing thigh deep in the river. Every now and then he'd get a warning or a fine from the police. Public intoxication. Disturbing the peace. A few times something larger happened, something that might have tied him to some old barn or building that had suddenly burned down, and we'd leave town with the smell of smoke still billowing behind us.

Sometimes I had to leave before my own work was done.

I lost some. The ones I couldn't keep inside the circles. The ones who were already half gone.

It just made me work harder.

My father had been gone on a weeklong bender/baptizing spree when I learned about Anders, up near Aunt Mae's place in Greenwood. Mae had been seeing things, hearing things. But she couldn't go out and do the work herself—a fragile old woman lurking around a high school, hanging out at a noisy coffeehouse.

She called us. Spoke to my father. Told a white lie about her health to him and the truth to me. We all decided I should move in with her. Back home. If the Malcolms can be said to have a home.

Aunt Mae and my father were born just outside Greenwood. The family has lived in the area longer than anyone can trace—in part because they had to change names and homes so many times. My ancestors had a gift for getting run out of town. When someone is present wherever and whenever bad things happen, always turning up stained with blood or ash, always arriving too promptly for coincidence, people decide one of two things. Either that someone has a gift for helping, always being in the right place at the right time. Or that someone is behind the bad things themselves.

I know what people usually choose.

Still, Aunt Mae has stayed in Greenwood, keeping to herself in that house outside of town, because she knows she's needed here. Darkness takes whatever space it's given.

Small towns. Back roads. Deep forests.

The woods outside Greenwood have given it plenty of space.

Maybe I'll try to explain this to Frankie later tonight. I've told her about the searches, all the hundreds of people lining up to comb the woods.

It's good for her to know that people are looking. To think that they're getting closer to finding her. It keeps her from getting desperate. From trying to break out on her own.

I visit the root cellar twice a day. Make sure her ropes are secure. That she has water and enough to eat. Then I sit on the steps, just for a few minutes.

She always tries to keep me talking. She wants to keep me there for as long as she possibly can. She's asked all about my family, about me and Aunt Mae and my father. I give her fragments. The whiskey that soaks through both of them. My father, fixing boats. The way he'd bring me pretty stones. She's told me about her family, too: her mother and her father and her brother, Leo, her grandparents, her adorable little cousin, Emilio, the way they all get together for Sunday dinner twice a month.

The cellar still smells like earth. But there are other smells in it now. Smells of fear and sweat and passing time. Frankie's legs are tied with rope much too thick to break or fray, no matter how she picks at it, and the rope knots around each of her ankles and weaves behind the shelves that are bolted to the wall. She can move around the cellar. Get water or food, use the lidded bucket in the corner. But she can't climb higher than the first step.

By the time I've shut the door and covered it again, I can barely hear her screaming.

I think of all this as I ride through the woods, paralleling Anders's path toward town. I'll beat him to the music studio. Hide in the shadows of the alley and wait until he steps inside.

I will watch. I will watch, because evil will use any weakness. The moment I stop, that's when they'll slip in.

**Door number four swings open before I can knock a third time.**

"Anders." Flynn looks out of the lesson room at me. He looks the same as always. Tan, T-shirted, ageless. His face is just a little more surprised than usual. "I didn't expect you today."

"It's . . ." I look at the clock hanging out in the waiting room. "It's Wednesday. Three o'clock."

"Yeah, I know it's Wednesday." Flynn gives me a tiny smile. "I just thought, with everything—you know—you might not show. Should have known better." He steps back, letting me through. "Come on in." The door clangs shut with me on the inside.

I set Yvonne's case down. But I don't sit. I can't.

I need to ask him about that woman, the one in the black Audi, but I can't get there yet. Instead, I hear myself blurt, "Last Things broke up."

Flynn looks less surprised about this than about me showing up for my lesson. "Ah," he says. "Whose idea?"

"Not mine." I pace across the room, toward a wall of concert posters. "And maybe it's just a hiatus." Panic twists in my stomach. "But that might not even matter. Not if I can't play anymore anyway."

"What do you mean, if you can't play anymore?"

"Like, my hands won't work. They won't do what I want them to." I clench and open my fists. "Everything's screwed up. *Everything*."

"Well," says Flynn, calmly, slowly, "maybe you're just a little too tense. No offense, but you seem pretty stressed out."

This is exactly what I needed to hear. A nice, normal, fixable explanation.

"Yeah. I have been. I am." The words give me my next opening. I pace back across the room. "You've heard about that girl, Frankie Lynde, right?"

"Yeah. Crazy stuff." Flynn sits in his chair and leans back, crossing his legs in their worn blue jeans. "Every kid I teach is pretty freaked out about it."

"Well, she and I were kind of—hanging out." The words clunk out of me. "Like, not *together*, really, but . . ." I trail off.

"Right," says Flynn slowly. "Yeah. You told me about that."

Of course I did. I tell Flynn almost everything. Months ago, at my lesson, when I opened Yvonne's case and a note with pink hearts on it fell out—a note from some girl I'd never even talked to—and Flynn started laughing, giving me crap about all the girls throwing themselves at me, I admitted something about Frankie. I remember blushing and smiling and trying not to look like a total dork, and feeling my heart thumping harder the whole time. Now my heart feels like a dead grenade.

"Anyway." I swallow. "On Saturday night she was at the Crow's Nest, and we ended up having this huge fight, and everybody overheard." I have to stop and swallow again. "And that's the last time anybody saw her. So, of course, people think I have something to do with—with her—disappearing."

Anybody else would probably ask me, *So, did you?* But Flynn doesn't need to ask. He knows me way too well. He just looks at me, tipping his head slightly to one side, laid-back as always.

"What did you fight about?" he asks.

"We . . . *God*." I rub my hair with one hand. "I was trying to tell her that I'm not into the whole *relationship*

thing right now. I mean, she's only interested in me because of the music thing, you know? And I don't want to have a whole relationship based on that."

"Hell, Anders." Now Flynn smiles. "If it weren't for the whole *music thing,* most guys in bands would be permanently undateable."

He looks so relaxed, sitting there in his frayed jeans and scuffed leather boots, I wonder if he's even hearing me. But of course he's hearing me. He just doesn't understand. He has no idea how much of this is my fault, how much of a dangerous moron I've been.

So I push on. "And they found that other car in the river." I drop my voice without even meaning to. "It was *her,* wasn't it? That music business woman?"

"Yeah. Sad news." Flynn nods. Now his face looks more solemn, at least. "The police called me about that. My name was in her calendar, I guess."

"You didn't—" My heart is thundering. I can barely believe I'm going to say this next thing, it's so pathetically cowardly. "Did you tell them about her meeting with me?"

Flynn pauses, scratching his upper arm before answering. "Nah. I just told them she came up to see you play. Nothing about the one-on-one. They don't need to know about that."

"Oh. *Good*." Air whooshes out of me. "Thank you. I mean—that's, like, the last thing I need. The police hearing that I was probably the last person to speak to *both* of them."

I finally sink down on the other folding chair. I brace my forehead on my fists and stare at my lap.

I shouldn't have said *good,* I realize, sitting there. I should have at least said "I'm sorry" to Flynn about losing his friend, or his business contact, or whatever she was. I should have said something about it being so terrible, the way she died. But I didn't. Panic is turning me into an even worse person. Or maybe it's just revealing how bad I actually am.

Flynn sits quietly, comfortably, next to me. His chair creaks as he crosses his legs again.

"That's where you made your big mistake, kid," he says slowly.

I drop my fists. I look up at him.

"You should have said *yes,*" Flynn says, even slower. "You should have just said *yes* to both of them. Then none of this would ever have happened."

I stare at him, trying to breathe.

Flynn stares straight back at me. "Think about it. How much have you said *no* to? Representation. Recording deals. At least two TV appearances that I know of. Even this girl, Frankie Lynde." Flynn shakes his head at me, grinning now. "What the hell are you doing, Anders?"

I blink at him. There's something wrong here. Something about the way Flynn's looking at me. I'm not sure what it is, because he's never looked at me like this before.

"That woman," I start. "The music rep . . ." Her eyes. The mud and pine needles on the soles of her boots. "It wasn't right. Something about her. It just wasn't right."

"Sure." Flynn nods. His voice is so dry, I can't tell if he's serious or sarcastic. "There's always something, right? They only like you for the music, or they don't like your music in the right way, or it feels like the music isn't really *you*. There's always something."

"But it's—" I don't know how to finish. My thoughts are just a storm of noise.

"You know what it really is, don't you?" Flynn scratches his arm again. The missing half finger twitches over his bicep. "It's *you*. You're sabotaging yourself. You're keeping yourself from being what you're meant to be. And that's your choice, dude, but I'll tell you what: I've never seen that choice end well."

I choke on the words. "What do you mean?"

"You know what other people would give up to get

what you have?" Flynn's words are sharp. Or maybe I'm so raw it just feels that way. "You think opportunities like the one you just blew are going to keep piling up around you forever? You think you just get to take and take and take?"

A cold, numb feeling is traveling down from my shoulders, through my arms, into my hands. "I didn't ask for any of this."

"Oh, come on." Flynn grins at me. His eyes are narrow. "Nine years of lessons. Practicing for hours every day. You can't say you didn't want this. Don't even *try* to tell me that, Anders Thorson. Don't even try."

My hands clench my knees. I can't look away from Flynn's eyes, even though I want to. Nine years, like he said. Nine years, and I've never seen his eyes look at me like this. So cold and flat and hard. I barely recognize them.

Abruptly, Flynn sets both boots on the floor. His palms hit his knees with a slap. "All right. That's it."

The stare is broken. I'm reeling, lost. "What?"

"We're done here." Flynn gets to his feet. "I've taught you everything I can. I've done everything I could to help you. Most kids, if they want to just play the guitar for fun, goof around, never practice, and pay me my thirty bucks a week to waste both of our time, I don't care. But you? I'm not going to give pretend lessons to you." He picks up my guitar. "You could have been the real thing. But you made your choice."

He pushes the guitar case into my hands.

I get up, robotically, like someone with a remote control is moving me toward the door.

"Wait. Flynn . . ." I hear myself say.

Flynn yanks the door open ahead of me. "It's probably too late for you anyway," he says. "You've burned your bridges. Set things in motion. Might be tough to stop them now." His hand guides me through the doorway. "So long, Anders. Good luck."

And the door slams shut.

When I tell Frankie about Carson and Sasha loosening the bolts on Anders's wheel, she starts to cry. Her face is outlined by the faint evening light that slips down through the open cellar door. One tear glitters as it falls.

"Oh my God," she says, wiping the tears onto the back of her hand. "You have to let them know I'm okay. Please. Someone will get hurt. Can't you—can't you just let them know I'm okay? They don't have to know where I am. Just—please."

I stare back at her. Frankie hasn't had a shower in four days. Her dark hair is matted, and her face is streaked with salt and dirt. She's still beautiful.

"No," I say. "No one can know."

Frankie lets out a sob. When I first brought her here, she didn't cry. But now she's getting exhausted. She still tries to hold the sob back, so the sound comes out crushed and thin. "Could you just . . . could you tell my mom . . ."

"I know you don't understand," I tell her calmly when her voice chokes off. I'm so tired of having this conversation. But I'll do it again. "I'm keeping you safe."

Frankie makes a sound that might be a snort. Derisive, or dubious. She doesn't want to anger me. She's probably tired of having this conversation, too.

She turns her face away, wiping her nose on the back of one tied hand. In a lower voice, she says, "This is all about Anders. Isn't it?"

I don't answer.

"Do you . . ." She's trying to find the right words. The words that won't make me mad. The ones that will lead to a magic way out. "Are you in love with him?"

I move the words around inside myself. They're a handful of keys that don't fit anywhere. *Are you in love with him? Are you in love with him?* Without trying, I can picture him onstage, raised above everyone else, his hair catching the light, his strong, quick hands moving over the guitar.

He's beautiful, and awful.

"I'm protecting him," I tell her.

And I am. Aunt Mae saw the white Nissan skidding out of control, Anders inside, smashed against the steering wheel. Just like she saw the fire at the Crow's Nest. Just in time.

I could have fixed the loosened wheel myself, when I went to Anders's house to find out what had been done to the car. But I put the note in Patrick's locker instead. I saw the chance to bring Last Things back together, even for a few minutes.

"You're protecting him? Like you're protecting me?" Frankie's voice is almost bitter now. "Thea. I want to believe you. But it's hard to believe that you're just trying to protect me when you kidnapped me, and tied me up, and left me alone down here in the dark for *God knows how long*."

She stops herself. She thinks she shouldn't insult me. Shouldn't call me crazy. She knows crazy people always think they're sane.

"I know you don't understand," I tell her again. "But maybe someday. Maybe soon."

I turn and start to climb the stairs.

"No," says Frankie quickly. "No. Don't leave. Thea. I'll give you anything. I'll never speak to Anders again. I'll do whatever you want. Just please. Please."

But I'm already shutting the door.

I pull the bolts. Make the cut on my palm. Draw the fresh *X* across the door's wooden surface.

I drag the boxes and bags back into place.

I shut the shed door behind me and turn its wooden latch.

It's just nearing twilight. The woods are darkening, but I can see the circle of stones, glowing and unbroken, in what's left of the powdery light.

The woods are strangely quiet. There's only stillness. No wind. No birds.

I move over the crackling ground toward the house. Then something shifts in the distance, to my left, almost out of the range of my sight.

I turn in time to see it duck into a swale in the ground. It's long limbed. Bony. It's covered in thick, pitch-black hair, although the way it moves, one bent limb at a time, is less like a mammal than a spider.

I wait, staring at the spot where it vanished.

It can't get to her. Not with both me and Aunt Mae here, not with the protections I've put in place. My heart-beat is steady. I breathe deep and slow. It won't have any of my fear to feed on.

We're safe.

When two whole minutes of stillness have passed, I move on, stepping in through the house's back door.

Aunt Mae sits at the kitchen table. Her cards are spread

out on the Formica, in a pattern that isn't solitaire. There are two empty teacups beside her. The open, battered Bible.

She's perfectly still. She gazes at me, but her eyes don't take me in.

"Aunt Mae?" I say softly.

"They're coming for him," she says, in a cloudy but steady voice. "I see them getting close. Thieves in the night. They're coming." We've known this, of course. It was only a matter of time.

"When?" I ask.

"Soon." She inhales, a shiver filling her body. "Tonight."

I touch her shoulder. Aunt Mae doesn't stir. "I'll go," I tell her. "I'll keep him safe. You keep her safe."

Aunt Mae gives a tiny twitch. She's trying to pull herself out of something heavy, something that clings and drips from her like mud.

"Aunt Mae," I say. *"Keep her safe."*

Now Aunt Mae turns and looks up at me. Her eyes clear slightly. She gives a short nod. Then she reaches up and squeezes my hand.

Before I leave, I put a folding knife in my pocket. It's no use against them, of course. But it's good to have it. Just in case.

Then I slip out the door and onto my bike.

ANDERS

## For a while I just drive.

I tear away from the studio, down Main, then left, right, left. I zig back and forth through quiet neighborhood streets like I'm in a hurry, but I'm not headed anywhere. I've got nowhere to go. Can't hang out at Jezz's; things are still too weird with us. Can't waste time at the studio. Not ever again, now that Flynn has cut me off. And I can't be at home, alone, boiling with all of this.

But I've only got a quarter tank of gas left, and no money to refill it.

Finally I pick a spot a few blocks past the high school, beyond the empty, soggy soccer field, where almost nobody comes. I park.

And then I sit.

I sit until the sky above the Nissan has soaked through

310

with indigo, and the few cars I can see in the distance are switching their headlights on.

*We're done here.*

Flynn's words might as well have been a kick in the ribs. My chest actually aches.

It's an empty, rejected, broken feeling. Like if one of your parents could dump you.

Nine years. *Nine years* of lessons, hours and hours of talking, laughing, confessing. Now it's like all of that has been erased.

And I'm totally alone.

Frankie. Last Things. The songs. The way that I could play. My teacher. I've lost them all.

*All the things you love. One by one . . .*

The memory of the black-eyed woman's words makes me sick.

I'm barely even myself anymore. What else can they take?

I slump back against the headrest. Beside me, Yvonne's case leans against the passenger seat. Its surface catches a purple gleam of sky.

At least I can give one gift back.

I start the car.

I'm not going to look at Yvonne again. I'm not going

to take her out of the case and play one last time. I'm not. I'm not even going to look down at the case, or I might back out. I veer back into the street and head north.

The sky darkens as I drive. Sunset glows through the trees. By the time I reach the Crow's Nest, it's nearly black.

The parking lot is sparse. I can see Ike Lawrence's truck parked near the kitchen door and a few other cars scattered here and there. I don't want to run into Ike. I don't know if Jezz or Patrick have told him about the breakup, or if the word has gotten out some other way, but I don't want to be the one to tell him about Last Things. He's been good to us. Really good. And now that we've become his big draw, we're ditching him without any warning.

I park way down at the opposite end of the lot. I try to find the very same spot where I parked on the night I got Yvonne. I kill the engine. Yvonne's case gleams in the thin light. I'd kind of like to give her back in the same way that I got her, but I can't just leave her here, at the edge of a parking lot. And I have no way to contact that journalist. I never even got his name. Just like the woman from the management company.

I should have known. I should have known sooner. But I didn't want to know.

I get out of the car. My boots crunch on the black pavement.

I pull Yvonne gently through the door. I scan the lot. There's no one on the patio, or smoking on the cracked pavement. For once, no one is watching me.

I head into the woods.

There's no path. I'm not sure if I'm taking exactly the course that journalist and I took all those months ago, but it feels right. It feels familiar. The trees, the thick shadows, the cold breeze all feel the same. The only thing that's different is Yvonne's deadweight in my hand. It feels like I'm carrying someone's body into the woods to bury it. The body of someone I loved.

I walk until I can't see the Crow's Nest anymore. It's dark. Roots and rocks slide under my boots, and I stagger. Damn it, I should have brought a flashlight. I pull out my cell phone. The screen gives me a little blob of gray light. Not great, but it will help. There's no signal out here, I notice. Not a huge surprise. It's patchy enough all around town.

Following the splotch of light, I head forward. The ground is soggy and soft with all the recent rain. My heels keep sinking in, like the ground is trying to hold me here. I tell myself to stay calm, stay logical, act like an adult, but half of me is ready to crumble. Every sound I catch—chirps and buzzes and creaks and snapping noises in the branches—seems to have some terrible possibility hiding in it. It takes all my energy just to keep walking, not to turn around and bolt back to the car like a kid running out of a scary movie.

I need to finish this. But I can't dump Yvonne just anywhere. I need to find a place for her that feels right. Finally I stumble into a little clearing where someone must have built a bonfire a long time ago. There's still a little divot in the ground, with a few logs pulled around it like bench seats. The surrounding trees are pines, tall and sturdy. Their needles whisper.

I stop there.

My fingers clench and unclench on the case's handle.

I've never understood the rock stars who smash their guitars at the end of a set. All those beautiful, expensive, state-of-the-art instruments, smacked into chunks of plastic. It's such a giant middle finger to every broke music nerd who can't afford a decent guitar of his own. I'd never hurt Yvonne. I can't even stand to set her on the ground out here, in the mud and the dew and the rotting leaves.

But I have to.

I have to stop thinking of her as mine. I have to stop

thinking of her as Yvonne. I have to stop thinking of her as *her*. I have to give this back before they can take any more.

God. I don't think I can do it.

I pick out a spot that seems a little drier, a patch of moss and leaves in the shelter of one huge trunk. I put the case down gently.

And then, even though I'm still telling myself not to do it, I open the clasps and lift the lid.

She's so gorgeous. Faint light from my phone glimmers over her dark finish. Her strings glint. I will never have another guitar like this. It will take me years to save up for anything close.

But it's done. We're done.

I pry my hands off the lid. My whole body is fighting me. What it really wants is to grab Yvonne, wrap her tight in my arms, and run off to some dark, safe place where we can sit and play for the next ten hours. Or ten years.

The lid thunks shut. I flick the clasps.

Okay. Okay. Damn it. There's a lump in my throat.

I creep backward far enough that even if I reached out again, I couldn't touch her.

Okay. It's done.

I'm just about to turn around when I hear the twig snap.

**I used to know what it was. To be afraid.**

I was afraid of so many things. Nightmares. The dark. The emptiness under my bed. The inside of my closet, where anything could hide. The voices that I heard whispering to me in the night, that seemed to come from outside the house or under my pillow or, sometimes, inside my own ears.

My mother always knew when the fear had grabbed me. At least, that's what I remember. I didn't have to find her, force myself out of bed over that treacherous dark gap. She would just appear there beside me, settling down on my bed, under my rumpled quilts. I remember the smell of her hair, which was long and pale, like mine, and the feeling of her hands as she'd rub my forehead, over and over, until I finally fell asleep.

I was five when she died. Cancer. Fast. And after that,

I wasn't afraid anymore. Because the worst thing had already happened. There was nothing left to fear.

Now nothing can touch me. Nothing even comes close.

It's already night as I ride to Anders's house. And they are everywhere. The dark things. All around me. Clinging to the high branches, swaying back and forth with the wind. I can see their twisted bodies and their milky white eyes. I am not afraid. I've stared back at the darkness for so long now that what I feel is barely a feeling at all. It's just recognition. Familiarity.

*I know you. I see you. You mean nothing.*

The Thorsons' house is dim. No cars in the drive. I pedal to my usual spot, leave the bike in the shrubs, and creep though the trees.

I'm less cautious than I used to be. I don't have time to be crafty. Both sides already know me anyway.

I can feel the emptiness even before I reach Anders's bedroom window. I glance through the pane, just in case. A lamp burns on the bedside table. There's Goblin, asleep in the twisted bedding. Rumpled clothes on the floor. The row of guitars. One missing. Yvonne.

My *X* on the window is faded but present, just starting to flake away. I slice my palm with my pocketknife. The cut from half an hour ago has already healed. I retrace the *X* on the glass before this cut can close, too.

Then I step back, my mind whirring. I watched Anders step through the door of the Underground Music Studio a few hours ago. He won't be there now. He won't be at Jezz's house. But he's out here somewhere, with his white car and Yvonne.

And suddenly I know exactly where he'll be.

Anders wants to believe that I don't really know him. He can believe it all he wants.

I climb onto the bike. The dark things roar as they chase after me. They can't move faster than I can. They'll have to use surprise instead. I keep my eyes sharp, looking up, down, ahead, everywhere. I ride so fast that the trees melt into a smear.

At first, when the thud comes, I think I've hit a tree. This is something that hasn't happened since I was little, first figuring out how fast I could move, unable to dependably control it. But then I realize that something has hit *me*.

It has plummeted from above, dropping on me like a panther. Its black body strikes the bicycle, its hands scrabbling at the handlebars for an instant before leaping away. The front wheel of the bike jags left. I pull it back, steadying, planting my right foot in the mud.

The thing is hunched a few paces behind me. I hone my eyes. I can see its long, long fingers. Its claws. Its eyes are chalky and wide, the shells of two rotting eggs. It makes its sound. A wet, thrumming growl.

I drop the bike and lunge after it.

The thing races away. Back up into the trees. I just have time to make out its bent, bony shape. A few rustling leaves trace its path, and then everything is still.

It wasn't up for a fight. It was only here to distract me. To slow me down.

I jump back on the bike.

I'm still not afraid.

The dark things aren't quite real, anyway. Not on this side of the cracks.

But when you're empty inside, dark things will find a place inside of you. Like water. Like air.

Dig a hole. There will always be enough darkness to fill it up.

That woman at the Crow's Nest was so filled with them, she practically breathed darkness. Usually the darkness is harder to see; it only shows in flashes, or it's gray instead of black, like an almost-dead coal.

And of course, most people can't see it at all.

That's why the dark things want Anders. Darkness loves to hide in plain sight. It loves being watched and worshipped and heard, without even being seen.

I need to find him. Fast.

I fly past the Crow's Nest, into the woods.

I can feel him close by.

I stop the bike, climb down from the pedals. Through the trees, I catch the flash of a silver guitar case, one shard of light in the enclosing dark.

They're hungry. White eyes. Dark teeth. Dark claws.

But I will catch him first.

**She's standing just a couple of steps behind me, holding her bike by the** handlebars. Just enough starlight falls through the woods that I can recognize her outline. Even in the dimness, her hair looks white.

*"Jesus,"* I gasp. "It's you. God*damn*. Maybe you could learn how to approach someone without giving them a heart attack."

She looks down at me. I'm still crouched on the ground, a couple of feet from where Yvonne's case leans against a tree. Her eyes move between us.

"This probably looks weird," I say, because I feel like I need to say something.

She shakes her head. "No. I understand."

*I* barely understand. I get to my feet. "You do?"

"You're trying to give it back to them."

Oh my God.

The things I've half imagined, half guessed, and felt like an idiot for thinking about at all become real.

She knows.

My knees buckle. I have to take a wobbly step to stay upright.

"That won't work," Thea goes on. "They won't take it back. It's not what they want."

My phone is still in my hand, but now—maybe just because I'm not alone—I feel like I don't need it anymore. I shove it into my pocket. My fingers are shaking.

"What do they want?" I ask.

Her face stays as calm and smooth as always. I realize what she reminds me of: one of those old porcelain dolls with little painted mouths and round cheeks and too-big, droopy eyes. Then she says, "They want *you*." She moves a few steps closer to me, rolling her bike. "They want you to join them, so they can act through you. That's what they do."

My head's tilting, or the ground is tilting. "Why me?"

"Because you're special." She looks into my eyes. She almost smiles. "You want big things. They can use that." The wind shifts, lifting a tendril of her hair. "They gave you gifts. You took them. You used them. Now they think you owe them in return."

"They think I owe them what?"

"I told you," she says, calm as ever. *"You."*

"Like . . ." I can't believe I'm having this conversation. I can't believe that I believe it. "Like, they want my soul?"

Her eyes run over me, quickly, from my head to my feet. "They want all of you."

I rake a hand through my hair. My fingers are freezing, but I can feel the sweat on my scalp. "If they want to *act through me,* or control me, or whatever . . . are they, like, *demons?*"

This sounds so ridiculous, I want to smack myself.

But she doesn't laugh. "They're creatures of darkness," she says. "They exist to bring evil into being. You can call them demons, if you want."

"And—you're saying these things are real. They're not just, like, *metaphorical* demons? They're not normal, human people doing bad things?"

She shakes her head. "Not *normal*. No. They're thick here, around this town. They've gotten a foothold." She casts a quick glance over my head. "They're all around us."

"Right now?" A pulse of fear rocks me. "Can you see them?"

"Yes." She points. "There's one hanging in the tree just above you."

Instinctively, I duck.

But nothing happens. I'm just waiting, with my shoulders up to my ears and Thea watching me, and the trees shushing softly.

Finally, carefully, I look up.

There's nothing. Of course there isn't. Above me a bunch of branches make their messy black lace against the sky. "I don't see anything," I tell her.

She nods. "Most people don't. Unless they see like I see."

I take another, longer look. The woods are dark, sure. But there's nothing moving in that darkness, except the branches swaying softly back and forth.

And all at once, like I've pulled off a pair of sunglasses that were distorting my vision, I can see just how absurd this is. I mean, I have to be crazy, leaving my expensive, gorgeous guitar lying in the mud behind me. And this girl, with her giant clothes and her stalking and her stories about demons, is definitely, utterly, totally insane.

"So . . . I'm just supposed to believe you?" I say. "Because you tell me you can see something that's not really there?"

Thea just gazes back at me. She keeps so still now, if it wasn't for her drifting hair, she'd look like some weird statue.

I push on. "I mean, if these invisible things are demons, then what do you think *you* are? An *angel* or something?"

She hesitates for a second. "Angels don't exist," she says.

"Right. Exactly." My words accelerate. "Demons don't exist, either. And all of this, everything that's happened, is my fault, because I've screwed up my own life without any help from Satan. And you are just some fan who's come to enough shows and listened to enough gossip and spied on me enough to weave this story. And that's it."

I stride past her, toward the Crow's Nest.

She's in front of me again so fast that it doesn't seem possible.

It *isn't* possible.

I stop, blinking. Nobody can move like that. But there she is, with that old blue bike beside her, standing right in front of me.

I stagger backward. My heel hits a root, and I fall, landing on my ass in a heap of wet leaves.

Thea looms over me.

"Listen," she says, leaning down over her handlebars so that her face is close to mine. Her voice is low and fast and hard. "You started studying the guitar with

Flynn Martin nine years ago. You practiced. You got better. When you were fourteen, you and Jezz and Patrick formed a band. You tried writing music of your own, but nothing came out the way you wanted it to. Still, you practiced, and you kept getting better, and soon you had a little following."

"Everybody who's ever read an interview knows—" I start, but she goes on as if I haven't spoken.

"Then, in the fall of your junior year, you met a journalist who walked with you here, in these woods, not far from where we're standing now."

My throat squeezes shut.

"He asked you what you wanted *more than anything*. And you told him." She pauses to let each of the words hit me. "He told you you'd get it. Everything you wanted. And then it started to happen. An expensive guitar. Inspiration for songs. People raving about you online. Pretty girls throwing themselves at you."

My whole body is ice. Nobody knows this. Not all of it.

There's no way. There's no way.

"They knew you would love it," she says. "They knew that once you had it all, you'd do almost anything to keep it. That's what they do. They make sure that you're hooked. That you're already half theirs. And then they make you pay." She pauses. A tendril of her long hair, pale and fine as a cobweb, wavers on the air between us.

"That woman who came to the Crow's Nest last week," Thea goes on. "She was one of theirs. You could tell, couldn't you? You could feel the woods on her." She waits for a beat, staring down at me. She can read the answer in my eyes. "She tried to make you sign. She would have made you theirs. And you said no." She leans even closer. I can feel her breath, just barely, on my face. "So they're not just going to take back what they gave you. They're going to take *the things you love, one by one.*"

I'm not even sure my heart is beating anymore.

"I've been watching," she says, which is such an understatement that I bray out a weird, nervous laugh. "That's what I do. I'm here to protect you." Her hands shift on the handlebars, opening and closing. "You may not believe any of this. That's why I usually hide it. But I'm not going to lose another one."

For a second we're both quiet. I'm still sitting on the cold mud, staring up at her. She's still clenching the handlebars of her bike.

The weird thing is, I should be afraid of her. The things she's said turn my skin to ice, but right now, this girl is one of the only things I *don't* fear. She's so steady.

So certain. Her forcefulness, her insistence that I believe in her, has taken the choice right out of my hands.

I can let go. I can just believe.

"Okay," I say, and a huge weight that's been balled up in my chest floats out, exhaled on that word. "Okay. So— what now?"

Thea straightens up at last. She scans the trees. "Go home," she says. "Right away. Lock yourself inside. And take the guitar with you. Leaving it here won't do any good anyway."

I rock awkwardly to my feet and scramble toward Yvonne's tree. "And then what?"

"I'll be with you. Watching," she says. "You'll be safe. At least for tonight."

Yvonne's metal case is cold. Clods of mud are stuck to the corners. I scrub them away with my thumb. Her handle fits back into my fist like somebody else's hand holding mine.

We head back to the parking lot. Thea stays right beside me, walking her powder-blue bike. I feel safer with her there, and then I feel pathetic for feeling this way. This soft, weird, long-haired girl thinks that she's protecting me. I'm letting myself think so, too.

She walks me to my car.

"Drive carefully," she says as I get behind the wheel. "I'll be right behind you."

I drive home about ten miles under the speed limit.

I keep checking the rearview mirror. There's nothing behind me, as far as I can see. Including a girl on a blue bike. Of course, even with me going only forty miles per hour, there's no way she'd be able to keep up with me. Right?

As soon as I bump into our driveway, the phone in my pocket starts to buzz. It buzzes and buzzes. *Ping ping ping.* I pull it out as I head up the walk and unlock the front door.

There are five messages from Jezz, plus one missed call.

- Where are u? Patrick and I are at my place

- Call us

- NOW

- OK just check yr email

- Check it and then call us. We can't waste any more time.

Jesus. What now?

I glance back at the road, damp and pearly with mist. There's no one there. Of course not. On her bike, it should take Thea several minutes to catch up with me.

I step into the entry and lock the front door behind

me. The stillness in the air reminds me that Mom and Dad aren't home; that I'll be alone here for hours. I bolt down the hall to my room.

It takes forever for the crappy old computer to fire up. Long enough that my head is swirling with a million confusing possibilities by the time I finally get to my email.

Jezz has sent one message with an attachment. The subject line reads: "Psycho Stalker."

I open it.

**We know what happened to Frankie,** says the note. **It was that girl. Thea. Check it out.**

There's a list of links pasted below.

I glance over my shoulder. For a second I'm sure I'm going to find her face at the window, staring straight back in at me, even though I know that's not possible yet. There's nothing through the pane but the usual view of brown-black trees, stretching away into darkness.

Still, just in case, I lunge out of the chair and pull the curtains closed. Then I switch out the lights, so only the glow of the computer tints the room. I dive back into my desk chair and click the first link.

It's the police blotter from some small town in Wisconsin, three years ago. Someone named Josiah

Malcolm was held in Beltram County Jail for disturbing the peace. The next link is another newspaper, another town, another police blotter. Josiah Malcolm, cited for public intoxication and disturbing the peace. I skim as fast as I can. The third is a slightly longer article, mentioning Josiah Malcolm, 48, who was arrested while standing knee deep in the Arapahana River, screaming about the wrath of God and the works of Satan, after making a series of threats against some local church group. I'm starting to wonder what the hell any of this has to do with Thea, but then the article mentions that Josiah Malcolm's fifteen-year-old daughter was with him at the time of the arrest.

Thea *Malcolm*.

Then there are a bunch of articles about arson. Barns, sheds, one dive bar. Unsolved. I check the locations. Beltram County. Arapahana Township. Everywhere Josiah Malcolm—and his daughter—has lived.

Okay. So Thea's father is a drunk and a wacko. Sounds like it runs in the family.

I open the attachment.

It's a screen shot—page after page after page—from someone's Facebook account.

It's some girl I don't recognize. She's pretty.

Dark-haired, small-featured. She looks a little like Frankie.

And she's dead.

I only have to skim a few messages to figure it out. *Rest in peace* notes, crying emojis, photos of the same girl with group after group of friends.

Then a conversation starts.

- Corrine, you were the nicest person in the entire world there's no way you did this to yourself I just wish you knew how much we all love you
   - She DIDN'T do this to herself
   - That's what I've been saying for like a week!!!
   - It wasn't suicide. It was that girl. Thea Malcolm.

I lean closer to the screen.

- We all knew there was something screwed up about her
   - But they moved away before it even happened
   - Yeah I know. They had to move because of what she did to Corinne.
   - Thea was totally obsessed with her. Following Corinne everywhere. Marking her window with that X in blood. Fricking MESSED UP.

A sour taste fills my mouth. I shoot another look at the curtained window.

- We don't know that was her
- It WAS. Corinne even knew.
- So why didn't she go to jail or a mental ward or something?
- Because Corinne is CORINNE. She thought Thea was just trying to "protect" her or something. That's what she told me.
- She's too nice
- She WAS too nice.

There's more. Lots more.

But I can't go on. My hands are shaking.

Jesus.

I fumble at the buttons of my phone.

Jezz picks up on the first ring.

"Hey." His voice is hushed. A little breathless. "Did you read the stuff?"

"Yeah. I read it." I swallow hard. "Where did you get it?"

"Google, dude. Plus, my cousin Noah lives up by Beltram. I texted him when Patrick and I found that thing about Thea and her dad living up there, and he told me—" Jezz pauses. There's a little crackle in the background. "Dude," says Jezz, softer now. "He told me she's done this before."

"Done what?" I say. Even though I already know.

"She kidnapped that girl. Corinne." Jezz speaks rapidly. "She kept her in some old barn for days. Then Corinne escaped, and Thea and her dad left town, and like a week later, Corinne was dead. Noah said the police called it suicide, but . . . it was something else. And everybody knew it."

"So . . ." I scrape out the next words. "You think she has Frankie somewhere?"

"Yeah," says Jezz. No hesitation. "And she's dangerous."

I get up and check the window curtains again, making sure there's not even a sliver of a gap between. I can't force myself to peek out. "Maybe we should go to the police."

"We already called them. They said they'd look into it." I hear a muffled crackling, like Jezz might be standing beside a snapping bonfire. "But that's all. They might be too late."

"Where are you?"

Jezz's voice gets even softer. "In the woods, out off County N. Near the Malcolm place."

"What?" My brain fuzzes. "Jezz. What are you *doing*?"

"We're just checking. Patrick's with me." Jezz murmurs. There's more snapping. Now I realize that it's the sound of their feet crunching on the forest floor. "And Sasha and Carson are out here somewhere. They're going to go up to the front door and pretend their car broke down, and then while the old lady's distracted, we'll check the place."

"*Sasha* and *Carson*?"

"I know. They're asses. But they're the only people we knew would definitely be in on this."

"What do you think you're going to do?" I ask. "Raid some old lady's house?"

"Dude," Jezz says, a little more loudly. "She *has* Frankie."

My thoughts won't line up. "We don't know that for sure."

I hear Patrick mutter something in the background. "Right," says Jezz. "Plus, Sasha saw stalker girl loosening your wheel."

The floor tilts under me. "What?"

"She was driving past your place that afternoon, and she saw Thea in your driveway, messing with your car."

The floor tilts in the other direction. I'm barely staying upright.

Sasha could be lying, covering up for herself or for Carson. Or not.

How would Thea have known about the wheel if she hadn't loosened it herself? Some psychic vision? Should I really believe that?

"I'll come out there and help," I say. But then I stop.

Thea is watching my house.

She said she would be. She'll be here by now. I can practically feel her out there, her eyes staring at me from somewhere I can't see.

There's no way out. The Nissan's right in the driveway, in clear view of the woods. Even if I sneak out a window or something, I can't get into the car without her seeing me. Seeing me and following me—or at least trying to.

"We're coming up behind the backyard," Jezz whispers. "I'd better go. Park way down the road and come find us."

The phone goes dead.

I lift the very edge of the curtain. The woods are there, dark and thick. It's getting close to midnight now. There's a fingernail of moon in the sky. I scan for anything moving, anything with wisps of long white hair.

And then, much closer to me, I see something else. The rusty red X that had been streaked across my windowpane is still there. But it's thicker and brighter now. It's fresh.

I'm not just being watched.

I'm marked.

And she's done all of this before.

I stagger back from the window. My heart hammers.

Okay, I tell myself. Okay. So, everything you felt—about this girl actually trying to protect you, about her being essentially good—is a lie.

And everything that you thought, in the dim, rumbling, paranoid parts of your mind—about her being some obsessed psychopath with a plan to control you, a psychopath who might actually, somehow, be behind all the other insane and terrifying things that are happening to you, and who might have kidnapped or hurt or even killed the girl you wish could be yours, just like she's apparently done before—is true.

And she's standing right outside your house.

There's an old wooden baseball bat under my bed. I reach under the box spring and grab it. I haven't used it since middle school, and the handle is fuzzy with dust.

I grip it tight. I close my keys in my other fist.

Now I can stay here, trapped, with a target painted right on me. Or I can get out and move.

I fly through the house's front door. I shove it shut behind me, moving so fast that I'm already beside the car when I hear it slam.

I yank open the car door. My hands shake as I shove the key into its slot. Damn it, why am I so afraid of a wispy-haired girl on an old blue bicycle?

I can do this. I can do this.

The Nissan roars. I surge down the driveway, into the road, hoping that it's as deserted as usual. The baseball bat rolls in the footwell beside me. I have to get away before she can catch up. I have to get to Jezz and Patrick before she has time to call her aunt, bike home, do anything else that could get in the way. I have to be fast.

Something flashes in my rearview. I glance up.

No cars behind me.

I flick on my brights and push the accelerator: Fifty. Sixty-five. Seventy-five mph. The roads are twisty, and the trees come close to the shoulders. I have to slam on the brakes at one tight curve. Centrifugal force drags the Nissan sideways, its tires shrieking. My stomach flips. Then the road straightens, and I'm back on steady ground.

I reach the straightaway that will take me to County N, where I'll turn again. I hit the gas. Seventy-five again. Eighty. There are no other cars anywhere, and no lights but mine, casting their foggy streaks on the road. From the corner of my eye, in the mirror, I see something flicker through my taillights again.

Maybe it's some big nocturnal bird, I think. But this time, when I look in the rearview, I see something else.

A girl on a bicycle.

She's only there for a second, but she's there, keeping pace with me. Her white hair is flying. The spokes of her bike are a silver blur.

We're going eighty miles per hour.

I nearly skid off the road.

I force my focus forward again, watching the painted line on the pavement. My heart is banging against my ribs so hard that it hurts.

It wasn't real. No. My imagination is messing with me.

I careen around the curve onto County Road N. My hands are freezing cold and sweaty at the same time. The wheel slips in my palms. Almost there.

This road is narrower. Rougher. The trees lean closer.

I've never been to the Malcolm house, but I know which one it is. Everybody does. It's the sagging, paint-peeling blue place up a bumpy dirt drive, just past the next bend. I need to get close, park the car, and then run, alone, into the darkness and the trees and hope that I find my friends before anything finds me.

I floor the gas pedal again. And again, I see it. The shape on the bicycle. The tendrils of her hair.

This time it doesn't disappear. I clench my teeth so hard it feels like they'll shatter. It barely keeps a scream inside.

She's there. She's right behind me.

I peel my eyes away from the mirror, back to the road. Just in time.

I've reached the last bend. In the distance, the dim light of the house prickles through the trees. And on the pavement right in front of me is a woman.

She's old, dressed in a flowered nightgown, with a crocheted sweater dangling around her shoulders. Her hair is wild. Her feet are bare. She's running straight at me, into my headlights. She's screaming something.

Her mouth is a black, open hole. A hole that I am driving straight into.

I slam on the brakes. The tires screech.

The Nissan comes to a shaking halt. The old woman is still running toward me. I grab the baseball bat, pushing the car door open at the same time. I'm ready for whatever comes.

But the old woman isn't even looking at me. She's looking just past me, at the bicycle that's rolling to a stop.

"They've got her!" the woman is screaming. Her eyes are cloudy white, like dusty chunks of ice. "Thea! They got her!"

That's when a hand like an iron cuff closes around my arm.

Aunt Mae hasn't buttoned her sweater. It's cold and damp out here. The impulse to do it for her crosses my mind, but there's not time. And I've got to keep my grip on Anders's arm, too.

He gapes at both of us, his mouth shifting, wordless, as I reach out and take the baseball bat from his fist. He's gripping it as hard as he can, but I don't have to struggle to pull it away. I toss it into the ditch without looking. My focus is on Aunt Mae. Her terrified face.

"What happened?" I ask her.

"It wasn't—the dark ones." Aunt Mae is short of breath and shivering. She presses one veiny hand to her heart, like she's pushing a bird back through its cage door. "Two kids. About your age. They came to the door. Said they'd broken down out here—and their phones were dead. . . ." Aunt Mae takes another gasping breath. Anders is fighting against my grip, but I barely notice.

"And then they grabbed me and pulled me out the front door and locked me outside."

I glance down at Aunt Mae's knees. They're muddy. So are her hands. Her nightdress is grass stained. I can see a scrape on her ankle, bloody and broad.

They knocked her to the ground. Two teenagers against an old woman. Anger pulses inside me.

"Ow," says Anders.

I guess I'm gripping his arm a little too tight.

"I went all around the house—trying to get back in," Aunt Mae gasps. "But everything was locked tight. Then I thought to check the shed. And she was gone." She crumples. "Everything. Everything . . ."

My heart starts to hammer. Hard and steady.

No. I won't lose her. Not this time.

"You *did* have her." Anders's voice cuts through the pounding in my blood. "You had Frankie." He's staring at me. Steel eyed.

He knows.

And he's seen. He's seen me move. He's felt the strength in my arms. He can feel it right now.

He looks at me, so stunned that his face is a perfect blank. "What *are* you?"

And then I move.

I race into the woods, with him beside me.

He stumbles at first, then tries to run, then falls. I drag him through the trees like a purse on a broken strap. We rush up to the shed, Aunt Mae padding as quick as she can behind us.

The shed door is hanging open. Even by the moonlight, I can see that the root cellar door is open, too, the barrels and bags shoved messily aside. The cross drawn in my blood, the circle of river stones; they don't matter against a bunch of clumsy human hands. Their power means nothing to the powerless. I pull Anders, who has clambered to his feet again, toward the gaping cellar.

"I'll be right back," I tell him. And then I shove him as gently and quickly as I can down the cellar stairs. I swing the door shut and bolt it.

I turn to Aunt Mae, who is staggering up to the shed. "Are they still in the house?"

"I believe so." Her voice is raspy now. Painful to hear.

"Will you stay with him?" I point to the root cellar. "I'll be back."

Aunt Mae nods.

With my key, I open the back door and slip inside. I can already hear them, thumping upstairs, two loud voices. They're in my room.

I'm up the stairs, standing in my bedroom door-way, before they can even turn toward the sound of my steps. They've switched on the bedside lamp. Frankie is nowhere to be seen. Sasha is digging through the dresser drawers. Her head is down. Carson is standing nearer the door, looking up at the picture of Anders onstage, the one I printed at the library, posted above the row of candles.

" . . . sure we'll find proof. Because this is seriously sick," he's saying just as his eyes float toward me.

I keep still.

I can see the thoughts flash through Carson's mind. Weighing the risks. Guessing my next move. Then he lunges. He's aiming for my shoulders, his big hands out and open, ready to knock me down.

It's only once he touches me that I move.

My hands strike his chest. He flies into the air, lands, slides backward across the hardwood floor. The back of his head strikes the wall. Hard. He slumps, his chin nuzzling his own shoulder.

Sasha gapes at me. Her face is flat with horror. She drops the thing she's holding—I think it's pair of my socks—and takes a small step backward.

I could throw her through the window. The image of glass shattering in a wide, blossoming burst and Sasha flying through it, out into the woods, is satisfying for a second. Like scratching an already-raw rash.

But I just grab her by the arm ("No—no—no," she's sobbing) and throw her into my closet.

"Where is Frankie?" I demand.

Sasha gapes at me. "I don't—*you're* the one that had her!"

I block the doorway with one arm. "You didn't let her out?"

"Let her out from . . ." I see hope and horror mashing on her face. "No. The others must have—"

I slam the closet door and bolt it from the outside. I bolt my bedroom from the outside, too. I was prepared. Sasha's beating at the closet door, sobbing and screaming, as I run back down the stairs.

But there's no time for this. Not even to think about it.

I'm back inside the shed in a heartbeat.

"You go inside, Aunt Mae," I tell her. "They're secure."

"Are you sure?" She reaches up and puts a cold hand on my cheek.

"Yes. I'll find her. It's all right."

With a last look at me, Aunt Mae shuffles out into the darkness.

I unlatch the root cellar door. A waft of sour, stale air breathes over me.

Anders, inside, is quiet. He's standing on the steps, staring up at me. His eyes glitter in the dimness. His face is tight. His words come fast.

"You kept Frankie here," he says.

"Yes."

"You kidnapped her."

"Yes."

"You've kidnapped people before."

"Yes."

"Did you loosen the wheel on my car?" he asks. He isn't even trying to climb out. He's just watching me now. "Did you take my cat?"

"I found your cat," I tell him. "I checked your wheel. I told your friends."

"But you could have let Goblin die," he says. "You could have let *me* die." His voice is calm, all the panic and anger washed away. He's blank faced, wondering, not quite believing the things he's seen with his own eyes. "You've killed other people. Haven't you?"

I don't answer. My silence is an answer anyway.

I want the truth in the open. I want him to see it. To see me. Before the end.

Anders goes on staring at me. I see him putting the fragments together, looking down at the reflection that starts to form. "That woman," he says. "The music executive. The one in the river. You did that."

"She wasn't a woman," I tell him. "Not anymore."

The line of his jaw flickers as it clenches. His body is shaking, but he's trying to hide it. He doesn't break his gaze.

"And that girl," he says. "Corrine somebody."

"No," I say quickly. He knows. He found out somehow. No wonder everything is falling apart. "Not her. I tried to save her."

His eyes narrow slightly. "Then . . . what happened?"

I hesitate. I still feel the need to keep Corrine's secrets. I promised her I would, more than a year ago, on one long night in that old blue barn.

"She wanted things," I tell him. "That's all it takes. She wanted things too much." I tilt my head toward the woods, toward the whispering darkness. "That's how they get in."

Anders stares at me, unblinking. "What did she want?"

We can't keep wasting time. And I need him to believe me. I want him to believe me.

I want it too much.

"It was her stepfather." I let it fly out. "He'd molested

her for years. When Corrine told her mother, she wouldn't believe it." Anders's face shifts. I see sympathy. Anger. "Corrine wanted him gone," I continue. "She would have done anything. And they knew it."

"What happened?"

"Car accident. Slippery road. He was dead before help arrived." Anders almost smiles. I understand. I might smile, too, but I know what came next. "Of course, then they came back for their payment." This part still hurts. It hurts like a broken branch between my ribs, like something jagged, healed over, buried inside. "At the end, I wasn't there. We'd had to move. Things went wrong. Just like this." I gesture down the steps, to the empty root cellar. "I couldn't save her. But *they* didn't get her, either." I add. "When they came for her . . . she took another way out."

Anders is silent for a second. Then he asks, in a thick voice, "Why Frankie?" He glances down, into the cellar where Frankie has been trapped for days. He's sick and horrified by it; the darkness and smallness and the smell. "Is she one of them?" he asks. "Or were they using something she wanted against her?"

"Neither. Anders." I lean closer, making sure that he can see my face as well as I can see his. "They are taking everything you love. They will destroy everything you love. Do you understand?" He doesn't answer, but he doesn't look away. "I was keeping her safe."

"You were?" He wants to believe me. I can hear it seep into his voice now, a rivulet of water cracking through ice.

"This was the one place where they couldn't touch her. And now she's out *there*."

His breath catches.

"How did you know she was here?" I ask him. "Who told you? *Who is she with?*" Anders keeps mute. Shadows flicker on his cheeks as his teeth clench. "I know it isn't Sasha and Carson. They're still inside the house. Is it Will and Gwynn?" Anders looks away. "Who is it, Anders?" I push on. "You need to tell me. Whoever took her— they're in serious danger."

I bend closer. The smell of the cellar is strong, but I can still catch the distracting scent of him, carried on the warmth rising from his skin.

*No.* I snap my mind away. *This is not for you. This will never, never be for you.*

"Anders," I say. "Please. I know you don't trust me. But please. Please believe this."

His eyes move over my face, like he's reading something written there in small print.

"It was Jezz and Patrick," he says at last.

Of course. The fragments fall into place.

All of them at once.

Everything he loves.

"Come on." I reach down and grab his hand.

# ANDERS

I haven't ridden on the back of someone else's bike like this since I was ten. My feet are balanced on the little pegs that stick out on either side of each rear wheel, and I'm stuck in a half squat, with my arms wrapped tight around the shoulders of Thea Malcolm.

That would be messed up enough. But we're also moving so fast, faster than any car I've ever been in, and we're weaving through thick, pitch-dark woods, and I have to keep closing my eyes so I won't completely freak out, and it all seems like one huge, horrible, ridiculous dream.

With my eyes closed, I feel everything even more clearly. Branches *whish* over my head. Damp leaves scrape my skin. Clearest of all is the feeling of the girl in my arms. Not that she's *in my arms,* not in any normal way. But I can feel her, soft and solid at the same time. I have to hold on tight. I've got no choice.

"We could have taken my car," I say again, over the roar of the air.

"Not through the woods," Thea answers. "And I can't drive a car this fast, anyway."

"Oh," I say. "Is—is this bike magical or something? Or is it just . . . you?"

She doesn't answer.

Her hair whips around my face. It brushes my cheek, slides into my collar.

It doesn't have a scent. Not like Frankie's. Not flowers or spice. It just smells clean.

"Where are we going?" I ask her.

"To the gap."

At least that's what I think she says. For a second I picture a store at the mall, racks of sweaters and slacks. Then I realize this isn't what she means. It almost makes me want to laugh. But the question of what could be happening to Frankie and Jezz and Patrick—the question I'm trying so hard not to ask, not even to myself—rears up in my brain, and I have to swallow a wave of bile instead.

We roll up and down a ridge of earth. I close my eyes tight again.

"You think this is where Jezz and Patrick have taken Frankie?" I ask her, when I can talk again.

"No."

"No?"

She doesn't go on. I open my eyes to see that we're starting down a steep, wooded hill. Thea leans lower over the handlebars, and I lean with her, my arms still clenched around her shoulders. My face presses against her back. Her shirt is soft and warm.

She veers right, then left, zigzagging sharply around trunks and rocks and roots. When the ground finally levels again, I pull myself backward. My knees ache from holding this pose. My hands and arms are freezing.

"You said no?" I push. "This isn't where Jezz and Patrick took her?"

"It's where the darkness will take them all," she says softly. "A crack. Where the world is thin."

We hit a bump, and for a second we're airborne. I brace for the landing. We strike the ground, still flying forward. Thea's body barely jolts.

"We're getting close," she says.

"How do you know?"

"I feel it."

I try to feel it, too. I don't know what I'm waiting for. The air is cold and black and nothing feels real.

The bike tilts down another slope.

"Hold on," says Thea.

So I do.

We plunge downward. The tick of the wheels is one continuous hiss, mixing with the shush of air in my ears. I clench my eyes and teeth and hands. Thea's hair whips around me. I'm holding her tighter, even though I'm not sure I should. But I can't force myself to loosen my arms.

And then, at last, the bike slows down.

The ground flattens. Thea sits upright, pushing me upright, too.

I look around.

We're in some part of the woods that I don't recognize. It's old growth, though. Huge, thick trunks with huge, thick branches spear upward into the canopy. Just a little moonlight slips through. There's a riverbed ahead of us. It's dry, but deep, with jagged, jutting edges that make it look like a crack in stone.

It's dark. Really dark. But I can still see that we're the only ones here.

Thea has stopped the bike. She's waiting with one foot braced on the ground.

"Why are we stopping here?" I drop down off the pegs. My legs are stiff, and now that I'm away from the steady warmth of Thea, I realize just how cold the night has gotten. "I don't see anything."

"You don't?"

Thea climbs off the bike. She props it against the trunk of a big oak and scans the branches above us. Then, suddenly, she freezes. Her body doesn't stiffen, but it goes perfectly still. Only her eyes keep flickering in the dark.

"What is it?" I'm whispering and I don't know why.

"I think we're too late," she says.

"Why?" Now I'm scanning the branches above us, too, desperate, but I can't see anything. Nothing but swaying branches and rustling leaves. "What is it?" I turn back to her. She's still staring up, and all at once I'm terrified. My whole body vibrates with it. *"What?"* I scream.

Thea finally looks down. Her eyes meet mine. She looks at me for a long, steady second.

"Do you want to see how I see?" she asks.

"Yes," I say, without even thinking. Because I need to know, and I have no idea what she's going to say or do anyway, and everything is just a black, murky, horrible blank.

She steps toward me, fast. She puts her hands over my face.

"Close your eyes," she says.

So I do. Her thumbs rest lightly on my eyelids.

And then everything explodes.

Actually, it's just everything inside my head, but because my eyes are closed, it's like everything has been seared apart by a blast of light.

I stagger backward. Even with my eyes open again, for a second I can't see anything. The flash strobes in my vision. There's only light.

Fragments come back slowly, gray and red. Trees around me, the riverbed, a tendril of Thea's hair.

The fragments solidify, and I can see in a way I've never seen before.

Every tree pulses softly with a cloud of light. The moss on the ground is a sort of luminous fog. I look down at myself. I'm glowing, too. The light burns through my shirt, like a bulb inside a lampshade. I move my fingers in front of my face. Streaks of light.

Thea's voice comes from over my shoulder. "Look up."

I stare up into the canopy.

Dangling above us, slowly twisting on thick black boughs, are five bodies. Their limbs are limp. Their heads are slumped. The thick branches that hold them also half hide them, and I can only see them now because of the glow that nests inside them all. Some glow more dimly than the others, but the one in the middle, the smallest one, seems to be the brightest.

The branches creak. The bodies sway limply, pushed by the wind. The face of the small one shifts into view.

It's Frankie.

And the others. Jezz. Patrick. Mom and Dad, slightly higher, to one side. Mom is wearing her pink sweater and the gray pearl necklace she puts on for special occasions. I can see the scuffed toes of Patrick's work boots.

All hanging there.

Their eyes are closed.

I can't tell if they're alive. Or if they're—

Jesus. A wave crashes through me. I'm sick and frozen and I think I'm screaming, but I can't hear anything, just a low, thumping hum that fills my entire mind.

I'm about to grab Thea, to start climbing tree trunks, to do something, anything, when I see what else is hanging above me in the trees.

Darkness. Not shadows, but living, solid darkness. They fill the trees: twisted shapes with long limbs and big, staring, milky eyes. I can hear them, or what I think is them; a deep, gurgling, clicking sound.

They crouch in the branches. They hide behind the trunks. They're everywhere. Everywhere.

"Oh my God." I'm not sure if I say this out loud.

"Hold on," Thea says softly. "They'll come for me first. Just hold on."

But I don't know what I can do against a mass of animate darkness. Demons. Monsters. Whatever they are. I don't know if this is real, even now, when I'm staring straight at it. I don't know anything.

"What do we—" I say, turning toward Thea.

And she's only a flare of light.

It's so bright I stagger back. I shield my face with my hands, and still I can see her, searing and golden, like the center of a fire multiplied by a thousand.

She is light. Solid light. So bright it makes me want to fall to my knees. If the dark things are demons, if they're pure, hungry evil, then she is their opposite.

The afterimage burns in my eyes. The outline of a girl made of light.

"They'll still trying to claim you." Her voice comes to me through the glowing blur. "They'll use tricks. They'll use everything they have. Just don't—"

Something dives out of a tree a few steps ahead of us. Something with long, clawlike feet and a bent, bony back and a bald black head full of teeth. It opens its mouth— too, too wide—and hisses.

Then it lunges.

So does Thea.

She's faster. She strikes the creature in midair, and even though it's far, far bigger than she is, she sends it streaking backward. The course of her motion slashes across my vision like the tail of a comet. The two of them land on the wet ground, near the riverbed, many feet away. The dark thing disintegrates into wisps, like floating ash, and then into nothing.

But more are already coming.

They're falling from the trees all around her. They hit the ground without any noise. The silence is eerie. Thea whirls around, burning hair, burning face, burning eyes. She's a blur smashing into a knot of crawling shadows.

The creatures fall backward. Their bodies collapse. But this time I see them pulling themselves together again. Black scraps knitting with other black scraps. They crouch and slither back toward the light.

And I'm just standing here like an idiot.

My body makes a jerky move to the right, like it's actually going to do something. Be part of this. But what am I going to do? Pick up a rock? Swing a big stick? This is so much larger and stranger than anything I expected, back when I silently agreed to let this girl protect me. And now here I am, watching her take on an entire throng.

The creatures must know I'm no threat. They're only focused on her. For all the attention they've given me, I might as well not be here at all. I don't have time to think about *why* before Thea charges forward. Her palms are open, her arms straight out in front. They smash through a knot of creatures like a battering ram.

But the things keep coming back, more and more of them. They scuttle out of the trees. They crawl up out of the muddy riverbed.

I glance up into the trees again. Mom and Dad, Jezz and Patrick and Frankie are all still dangling there, the glow coming from them faint, but steady. I have to do something. I lurch toward a nearby tree. Maybe I can climb high enough. But before I can even touch the trunk, a black silhouette drops in front of me. Its cold, slick hair brushes my skin. I shudder, leaping back. But the thing doesn't even glance at me. It springs toward Thea instead, joining the swarm.

They're closing in. Their bodies writhe between me and Thea's blinding light. There are too many of them.

She's fast, but soon they've got her surrounded. She can't gain enough ground to pick up speed. I see one of them reach up and grab her throat. A dark limb lashes out from somewhere in the crowd and reaches down into her gasping mouth. The light raging from inside of her dims.

My heart stutters.

Then Thea whips around, and for a split second, the grasping demons fly back. Thea throws a look at me. I think she does, anyway. Her face is only a blazing blur. I can't tell if she's speaking. I can't see her expression. If she's desperate. Furious. Smiling. Her hand flashes out.

Then she lowers her head. She bursts through the ring of darkness. The creatures regroup in an instant, but Thea is already streaking away into the woods. The dark things shriek and hiss. They scramble after her.

And I'm left alone.

On the ground, in the clutter of dead leaves a few feet away, something glimmers.

I stumble closer.

It's a pocketknife. Thea didn't just raise her hand toward me. She was throwing something.

I pick it up. The handle is red enamel. The blade, when I unfold it, looks sharp and clean.

I glance back up into the trees, at the bodies slowly turning. If I can reach them, if I can just get out to those smaller branches, maybe I can cut them free.

There's a sturdy pine with plenty of branches just to my right. I shove the knife into my pocket and rush toward it. Maybe I can climb high enough. Maybe I can creep out onto just the right limbs.

I have to.

Of course, if I cut them loose, there's a drop of two or three dozen feet, all the way down to the hard forest floor. But I'll think about that when I get up there.

My hands are shaking so hard they seem electrified. I grab the jagged bark of the trunk, but I can't even feel it. I don't have nerves anymore. There's nothing in me but fear and fury and flickering light.

I've just pulled myself onto the first branch when someone steps out from behind the tree.

"Anders," says a voice.

I know that voice. Warm. Calm.

Flynn.

I'm so startled I almost fall off the branch. I jump back to the ground a few feet below and stumble backward. "Flynn?" I choke out. "What are—"

"Anders." Flynn moves farther into the clearing. A guitar case swings from his hand. With the dark things gone, just enough light falls through the canopy for me to see him perfectly. There's no glow or flare or shadow coming from him. He's just Flynn. Thank God. "So glad I found you," he says.

"We—" I make a jerky motion toward the canopy. The swinging bodies. "Flynn. You've got to help me."

"I know," says Flynn. "That's why I'm here."

Everything I felt about Flynn, all the confusion and distrust, melts away before his words even sink in. It's Flynn. My mentor, my idol, my almost-family for half my life. I could practically throw myself into his arms.

"Okay." I speak fast. "I'll climb up there and cut or break the branches. If you can—maybe—catch them when they fall, or—"

"That's not going to work." Flynn shakes his head. He's as cool as ever. Like he could be leaning back on his folding chair in the middle of the studio. "They're too high."

"Then—what?" I'm hanging on to the tree again, because until there's another plan in place, I need to get up there. "Should we call for help? Do you have a phone?"

"Anders." Flynn lets out a breath. "You're too late. It's too late for all of this."

He steps closer to me. Dim light from the sky coats the guitar case. I recognize it now. I know every tiny scratch on its hard silver surface. It's Yvonne.

Wait. How did he get her? Has he been in my house?

The questions fly away when Flynn speaks again.

"You've only got one chance now," he says.

"What?" My heart is screaming. I'll do anything. *"What?"*

"You have to give in to them," he says very clearly. "Anders. It's over. You have to let them in."

It's like he's punched me in the gut.

I told myself that Flynn kicking me out of the studio was my own stupid fault. That it was one more loss meant to punish me.

But maybe it was something else.

I stare at him. This close, I can make out a flickering darkness around his edges, like a knot of shadows that's stuck to his skin.

It must've always been there. I just couldn't see.

For a second I can't breathe.

I reach into my pocket and pull out the knife. It's solid in my fist. I don't know how I'll use it, and it's so small and childish looking, I might as well be fighting a monster with a toothbrush. But holding it makes me the tiniest bit stronger.

Maybe this is why Thea threw it to me. Maybe I wasn't supposed to saw off branches with a pocketknife. Maybe I was supposed to fight.

"Really, kid?" Flynn glances at the knife, then gives me a half grin. I can't tell if he's laughing at the knife or at me. "They're stronger than you are. They're faster. There are more of them. Besides, the things they can give you . . ." He sets Yvonne's case on the ground. The silver lid shines. "You *know* what they can do, kid. Just accept it. Like you should have done forever ago. Then you wouldn't have had to risk losing everything first."

"Why?" I burst out. "Why are they doing this to me?"

"Doing this to you?" Flynn frown-smiles, shaking his head. "They *chose* you, Anders. You're special. You're exactly what they want. You're going to be a rock star, adored by millions. What's more powerful than that?"

For a second the words *rock star,* the image of myself onstage in front of a massive, screaming crowd, actually makes my heart lift. Then I hate myself for it.

"I don't care about that," I say. Lie. "But if—if I give in—" I look up. Frankie sways from the bony black twigs. Mom's unconscious face tilts toward me. "Will they be all right?"

Flynn gives a little shrug. "Sure. Of course." He gestures down at Yvonne, lying on the dirt. "Plus, the songs will come back. The ones you were writing. You'll be able to play again. As well as you did before, maybe even

JACQUELINE WEST

366

better." He meets my eyes. "Don't tell me you haven't missed that."

He knows me too well.

The branches creak above me. When I listen, I can't hear anything else. No crackling steps racing through the woods. Thea isn't coming back. I'm alone.

"That's how this started," Flynn goes on, in his calm, cool way. He might as well be telling me about the history of Fender guitars. "You wanted this. You asked for it. You got it. Now you've got to give something in return."

I'm gulping air, but I feel like I'm drowning. "How do you know all this?"

Flynn holds up both hands in an innocent shrug. Then he wiggles the fingers of his strumming hand. The finger that's just a stump. "You take something from them," he says, "you've got to give something up."

My mouth fills with sourness. I can hear my heartbeat. I've got all the answers now, loud and clear.

So Flynn was like me once. He made the bargain. He let them in.

"What did you get out of it?" I spit. Flynn tilts his head, mildly puzzled. I plunge on. "You made a deal with the devil, and for *what*? You teach guitar in a *basement*."

Flynn's eyes narrow to glinting slits. "I had exactly

the life I wanted," he says. "I've seen the world. Played for millions. Made a living with music. You should be so lucky, kid."

He sounds angry. I can't tell if it's at me, or at them, or at something else. I can't tell whether it's a lie or whether he believes it.

It doesn't matter anyway. I can save my family and friends plus have everything I've always wanted, and in exchange, I give up myself. There's not even a choice.

"So—what?" I croak out. "What do I have to do? I need to make some kind of flesh sacrifice?"

Flynn nods once. "But that's just a gesture, really. It's their way in."

"And then . . . they have me?" My mouth can barely form words. "They have my *soul,* or whatever?"

Flynn grins. "'Or whatever.' Yeah." He steps toward me. "You'll be theirs. You'll share in their power. And that's a pretty amazing thing." Flynn reaches out and grabs the knife. I'm so numb, it slides right out of my fingers. He holds it up, squinting at it in the faint moonlight. "This should work," he says.

Flynn reaches into his pocket and pulls out something small and square. When he flips it open, I see that it's a silver Zippo lighter. He crouches on the ground, a few feet from Yvonne's case, and starts scraping together a pile of dry leaves and twigs. In a minute he grazes the tinder with the lighter's flame. It sparks to life. The twigs catch. Flynn looks around for some larger sticks, adding them to the fire one by one until a bright, steady blaze is burning.

"What are you doing?" I ask. "Why do we need a fire?"

Flynn looks up at me. "Got to get rid of what you cut off, don't we?" he says. He's wearing a smile that makes my stomach churn. "Can't have you taking it to the hospital, trying to have it reattached, either. You're giving it up. For good."

I stare down into the curling flames. My guitar teacher is building a fire to burn my own severed finger. It's so unbelievable, so sick and ridiculous, I almost let out a laugh. But the force heaving up inside my chest might just as easily be puke.

This can't be real.

But it's real.

"We'll give it a couple of minutes." Flynn adds a snapped pine branch to the flames. "Make sure it's nice and hot."

I squint upward. Light and smoke from the fire rises

up into the canopy, touching the hanging bodies. The bodies of everyone I love. I can see the color of Jezz's Converse shoes, the glint of the beads on Mom's necklace. The firelight makes all of them look more detailed. Warmer. More alive.

It feeds my hope. It makes me desperate.

Flynn has found a small, flat rock. He balances the pocketknife on it. Its blade reaches into the flames.

"There," he says. "We'll make sure it's clean." He gives a casual wave of his missing-fingered hand. "The blade's pretty small, but you have to show that you mean it. You've got to open yourself up. Give them a way in. So no half-assed little nicks, got it?"

"Flynn." I swallow. He's been here, where I am. I wonder who he was back then. If he was another small-town, metalhead teenager, too floored by the gifts all around to see past them, into the dark. "Afterward—will I be myself anymore?"

He looks at me, hard. "Who do you think you are?" he asks. "You're the kid who writes the songs. You're the guitarist. That's what you are. You'll be those things again."

His answer falls through me like rocks falling through water.

That's not what I am. Not *all* I am.

That's not me, deep down, at the very core.

Flynn puts a hand on my shoulder. A second later he pushes me down. I'm so wobbly, I don't even resist. I drop onto my knees next to Yvonne's case. Firelight turns the surface to a sheet of liquid gold.

Heat from the fire washes over my face. My head swims.

Flynn adds another snapped branch to the flames. In the distance, somewhere behind his back, I think I spot a patch of light glowing between the trees. But I might just be wishing.

Flynn crouches there, watching the leaping flames for a while. Then he takes the knife by the handle and lifts it up. I can see the blade glowing, red-orange color fading away as it leaves the fire for the cold night air.

Flynn touches its edge with one calloused fingertip. "Should be sterile," he says. "Seems pretty sharp, too."

He hands me the knife. So casual. He might as well be passing me a guitar pick.

The instant I have it in my hand, the darkness around us shifts.

The creatures are coming back. They're drawn in. I see their long fingers wrapping around nearby trunks, their milky eyes staring.

I take a breath, and for a second, I think I'm going to black out.

Flynn casts a look at the bodies above us. Patrick has shifted so that his face is staring straight down at me. His eyes are closed. Frankie dangles beside him, her profile hidden in the shadows of her hair.

There's no way out.

I have to do this. I will do this. Because any one of them is worth more than I'm worth to myself.

I spread my hand out on the case's cool, firm surface.

"Hang on," says Flynn. "You'll want to do it to your strumming hand."

Of course.

I switch the knife to my left. I place my right hand, palm down, on the case. With any luck, I'll miss the major nerves and tendons. I'll sever some veins, sure, but not enough to kill me.

I can live with this. If I'll still be myself at all.

Out of the corner of my eye, I see another burning flash. It could just be a sputter from the fire, but it could also be something in the woods, moving closer.

The dark things are drawing closer, too. They surround us, creeping inward, gurgling, waiting. I can practically feel their hunger.

Cold and heat clash on my skin. The light is burning out. I'm ash inside. A lump of dead coal.

"It's okay, kid," says Flynn, and I hate him for the kindness in his voice. "Focus on all the songs you're going to write. The shows you're going to play. It's all going to be worth it." He squeezes my shoulder. "Just get it over with."

I'm done fighting.

All right. Let's get this over with.

Before Flynn can move, before I can rethink, I drop the knife. I lunge forward on my knees. I thrust my hand—my left hand, the hand I use to create chords, the hand that needs every finger—into the fire. My hand closes around a piece of smoldering wood. I grip it tight.

They want the guitarist. But they can't have him. Nobody can.

I'm going to destroy him myself.

My. Self.

At first, the pain can't even break through. There are too many other things. The molten texture of the burning wood against my palm. The smoke and heat stinging my eyes. The darkness and the light. Everything feels like a dream, and none of it can possibly be real.

And then the pain hits in a first giant wave. My arm

shakes. My hand sears. My skin shrieks. Every cell of me is trying to get away. To drop the burning branch. But I hold on. I can't let go yet, not until I know the damage is done. Until I know that I'll never play a guitar again.

Flynn is shouting something. I can't even hear him. Because all around us, the warped, dark things are roaring.

Their fury is like a tidal wave. It wants to drag me away. But I hold on. I clench my teeth and close my eyes.

The roaring gets louder. The demons hiss like they're the ones being burned.

But there's nothing left for them to take. Nothing for them to want.

At last, when the pain has gone so deep that it's only a throb at the top of my shaking arm, I let go. At least, I try to let go. My hand is locked in place like a claw. The smoldering wood tumbles out of my grip and rolls across the muddy ground.

The skin of my hand is black and wet and cracked. I can't stand to look at it. I'm going to be sick. But even out of the corner of my eye, along with the bloody fluid oozing out of the cracks, I notice something else.

Light.

Pure white light. The light Thea passed into me when

she put her hands over my face. It's pulsing out of me, filling the gray air.

Flynn staggers backward.

And then another streak of light, a thousand times brighter, strides through the shadows. It stops right beside me.

Thea is even brighter than before. She's like staring into the sun. She erases everything else. The light pulsing out of me adds to the light that flares from her, until every shadow is burned away.

There's a scream so loud that it makes the ground tremble.

In one thick, writhing mass, the black creatures disintegrate.

The air fills with ash. Fragments of darkness float and slither toward the crack in the ground, sliding through, disappearing.

Thea rounds on Flynn.

I see him trying to scramble away, blinded by her brightness, squinting and stumbling. Thea grabs him by the shoulders.

Flynn screams.

I've never heard a grown man scream like that, not in real life. It's a scream of fear, I think. But I can barely think at all.

Thea takes off, dragging Flynn with her.

My head is sloshing, and my stomach is heaving. For a second everything around me shudders. The air has dimmed again. Blood and water drip from my hand onto Yvonne's silver case.

From somewhere far away, there's another scream. Flynn again. This time, it's a scream of pain.

It's awful. So awful it almost eclipses the pain roaring through me.

Then the screaming stops.

There's silence.

Silence.

Only silence.

**They will all wake up in their own beds.**

Tomorrow, late in the morning, a few blocks apart, Jezz and Patrick will roll over and stretch and rub their eyes with the heels of their hands, wondering why their heads feel so heavy and their bodies so sore, with their memories full of black fog and not much else.

Anders's parents will doze until nearly noon, not even able to hear the ringing phone when the hospital calls again and again. They'll shake their heads at themselves, thinking they had too much to drink at that retirement party. Later, when they hear the nurses' messages and rush out into the driveway, his father will spend one quickly fading thought to wonder where the scratches on the truck's paint came from, as if it had driven off the road into the trees.

Sasha and Carson, bruised and sick, will wake up in

their beds. Their clothes will smell like whiskey—a slosh from Aunt Mae's bottle—and they'll both be grateful that they made it home safely. They'll think their headaches are hangovers. Nothing new.

Frankie will open her eyes in her own pale gray bedroom. She'll wake to the sound of screams. Joyful ones. Her parents and little brother will hug her and sob and pile onto her bed and ask her ten thousand questions that she won't be able to answer. She'll remember fragments. Darkness. The woods. Something wrapped tight around her neck. Police and doctors will question her next, examine and evaluate her. Teams will keep on searching the woods for her kidnapper, for clues, for an explanation.

They won't find anything. I've taken care of it all.

There are lots of benefits to moving fast.

For Flynn: the river.

For Yvonne, in her silver case: a hole in the ground. A circle of white stones.

Memories are sacred. I don't like to tamper with them, as a rule. But this time I had no choice. There were too many loose ends, too many snapped and sparking wires. Besides, I didn't have to take much. The ones who had been held in the darkness, between this world and the one below—Jezz and Patrick, Anders's parents,

Frankie—had minds that were already clouded. A quick touch. Erasing light. Nothing left but shadows that will fade away as another sunny spring morning pours through their bedroom windows.

Only Anders will wake up in a strange bed.

The darkness didn't drag him to sleep, like the others. He'll wake up with his memories intact, but impossible. He will have seen things he can't even bring himself to name.

Because I let him see.

I let him see the darkness. I let him see me.

*Blessed are those who have not seen, and yet have believed.* That's one of Aunt Mae's favorite verses.

Anders will float into consciousness. He'll try to move and find that he's in a bed with railings, with tubes and needles in his arm. He'll discover that his hand is fat with bandages and his blood is syrupy with painkillers and people in pastel scrubs are hurrying back and forth beyond the hanging curtains all around him.

Then his parents will arrive, looking stunned and rumpled and terrified, and the doctor will talk about second- and third-degree burns and grafts and permanent nerve damage and physical therapy, and everyone will absorb about a third of what she says.

They'll all ask what happened.

And Anders will remember what he saw. Darkness and light. Demons and something else. Something he's still not sure what to call. Something that looked like a girl made of light. The hanging bodies. Flynn. Fire in his fist.

And he'll say that he's not sure.

He can't remember.

Probably shock, the doctor will say. Not uncommon, perhaps another result of the injuries.

She'll tell his parents that Anders will stay in the hospital for another few days, under careful observation, making sure there's no infection, that the pain is never more than he can stand. They'll discuss a plan for the future. And Anders will drift off again in that crinkly electronic bed.

For a moment last night, I held him.

I reached an arm under his head and eased him up into my lap. I elevated his burned hand.

I touched his skin.

His eyelids fluttered. I wasn't sure if he could hear me, or even feel me. There was nothing to say anyway. But I wished that I could stay there even for a minute, holding on, while the empty woods creaked and breathed around us.

But I couldn't.

And neither could he.

I brought him to the hospital. Left him at the ER doors, making sure no one caught sight of me.

I watched from behind a row of bushes as someone in white scrubs hurried to the doors, summoned others, pushed a gurney out onto the pavement. I watched as they wheeled him inside.

It took everything I had not to follow him through the doors. To be there when he woke. Just to sit there while he slept, holding his other hand.

But the glass doors slid shut and stayed shut. And I went home to wash the blood out of my clothes.

# ANDERS

**You dress differently when you've only got one working hand.**

Pulling on your own jeans? Hard. Zipping and buttoning them? Really hard. Tying your shoelaces? Really freaking hard.

For the first couple days after I came home from the hospital, I wore sweatpants and old pullover sweaters. I barely left my bedroom anyway, so it didn't matter if I dressed like a total slob. On the second day Jezz and Patrick came over. The both stared at my big bandaged lump of a left hand while trying to look like they were staring at anything else, and then we all sat around and watched videos on YouTube. Not music videos. Just stupid comedy stuff. People doing voice-overs for their fat pets.

Finally, after we've been sitting there for almost two hours, Jezz turns so he's sort of halfway facing me, and says, "Your mom says you don't remember what happened. How"—he nods toward my hand—"how you got that."

I shrug.

I can't explain. Not yet. Not even to myself. The memory is like an open wound in my head. I don't want to look at it too closely. I don't even want to think about it. I just want to leave it alone, let it start healing, and maybe when I'm halfway back to normal, I'll feel ready to touch it again. Maybe.

"Everybody is saying that there was somebody in the woods," Jezz goes on. "Like, some psycho kidnapper. And you went out and found Frankie, and whoever was holding her tried to stop you, and that's how your hand got burned. Or something."

I nod slowly.

"So," says Jezz. "Was that it?"

He's looking straight at me now. His eyes are worried. Patrick is watching me, too.

And then, because it seems like the right thing to do, I lie.

"I don't remember much," I start. Both Jezz and Patrick keep staring at me, frozen, hanging on every word. "And I don't think there was a kidnapper. I just think it was some kind of accident, and Frankie was trapped, and I had to reach into a fire to get her out. To get both of us out. That's all I remember."

They watch me solemnly.

"That makes sense," says Patrick at last. "Maybe it was a car accident or something."

"Oh," says Jezz. "Yeah. Maybe the car caught fire, and you had to reach in to open the door and get Frankie out."

They nod at each other.

Of course, that *doesn't* really make sense. No one's found a burned car. Frankie didn't have any fire injuries. But it makes a lot more sense than what actually did happen. And right now, Jezz and Patrick are being kinder and more careful with me than they've ever been before. They'd agree with any stupid thing I said, I'm sure.

So I smile and say, "Hey. Let's watch that Swedish cooking clip again."

They smile back. And we do.

On the third day, in the middle of the afternoon, Mom taps on my bedroom door. She's been working only half time this week, even though the bills for my hospital stay and the coming physical therapy are going to be huge, which means money is going to be even tighter. I'm try-ing not to add that guilt to the pile of bad things in my head.

"Come in," I say from the bed, where I'm lying with Goblin on my stomach.

The door swings open. Frankie Lynde steps inside.

She's always slipped in through the window before. Seeing her just walk through the door, like any normal human being, makes her seem more real than she's ever been.

I sit up so fast that Goblin shoots to the floor.

*Mrrk,* he says, giving me an insulted look before duck-ing under the bed.

Frankie takes a little step closer. She's wearing dark jeans and a sweater that makes me want to rub my face on it. I'm wearing drawstring pants and an ancient hoodie with *Camp Longfellow* printed on it. But right now, I barely care. I'm not pretending to be the rock star anymore.

Mom pulls the door shut from the outside.

"Hey," says Frankie.

"Hey," I whisper back. "You all right?"

"Yeah. I'm all right. And you're"—she nods at my hand—"sort of all right?"

**LAST THINGS**

385

"Yeah. Mostly."

We look at each other for a second.

"Do you want to talk about it?" she asks. "Or do you *not* want to talk about it?"

"I don't know," I say. "Do *you* want to talk about it?"

Frankie gives me the tiniest smile. "I don't know, either. For me, it's mostly a big blank spot." Her face is a little thinner than I remember it. Her cheeks are hollow. It makes her eyes seem even larger. "I hate it. That I can't remember. It makes it so much worse." She hugs herself with both arms. "There are a zillion stories flying around, of course."

"About you?"

"About both of us. People think it's all connected. That there's some crazy kidnapper in the woods who trapped me in a burning building or something. But whoever it was . . . they didn't hurt *me*." She glances at my bandaged hand again. "Are you going to be okay?"

I shrug with one shoulder. "They're not sure. There's a lot of nerve damage. They say time and therapy might help, but I might never regain full use of it."

Frankie looks into my eyes. "And you're okay with that?"

Nobody has asked me this.

Everybody assumes that *of course* I'm not okay with it. That I'm the guitar prodigy whose rocket ship to fame has just come crashing back to earth, and it's so tragic and unfair. But it isn't; not really. Because this was my choice. And all the parts of me that aren't my hands want to remember what it was like just to be myself. Maybe, eventually, weeks or months or years from now, I'll start learning to play backward, with my right hand forming chords. Maybe I'll try writing songs again. Now it will be just me, not something occupying me, attacking me. I wonder what my own songs will sound like.

I take a breath. "Yeah. I'm okay with that." I readjust the bandaged hand on top of the blankets. It itches. "Guitar took over everything in my life. But it's *not* everything. You know? That's not all I am."

Frankie's smile widens slightly, her mouth going from one perfect shape to another. "Yeah," she says. "It isn't."

"So," I say, after a beat, "what do *you* think happened?"

Frankie takes a minute to answer. "I think . . . there *was* something strange going on out there. Something big. I'm not sure if it was just one person, or—or what, but I think it caused a bunch of crazy things lately. And I think . . ." She pauses again. "I think it's over now. I think everything feels different. Do you know what I mean?"

"Yeah." My voice is a whisper again. I look down at the carpet between us. "Hey, Frankie? I'm really sorry. Really sorry."

She doesn't answer. I can't bring myself to look her in the face.

"How I talked to you that night . . ." I force myself to go on. "I'm not even sure what I was trying to do. But it wasn't right. I'm sorry. I'm sorry."

Frankie glides closer. She sits down on the bed beside me.

One thing I told her during that stupid fight *was* true. She doesn't really know me. And now I realize that I never really knew *her,* either. I just liked the idea of her. Gorgeous, cool, confident. Loved by everybody. But I don't know if this is the truth of her. I don't know what's inside.

I could change that. I could try, anyway.

It takes all the courage I've got, but I reach out and wrap both arms around her, the normal one and the big, clumsy, mangled one.

For a second she holds still, and I swear my heart is going to stop. But then she presses her face into the nook between my shoulder and the hollow of my neck.

She smells so good, it makes me dizzy.

"So, do you finally believe I don't like you just because of the music?" she asks. Her breath brushes my neck.

I don't answer. But I hold her tighter.

We stay there, holding on, for a long time.

**I've emptied the root cellar.**

Load after load of objects traveling back to the spots where they belong. Empty jars back to the kitchen cupboards. Ropes and buckets to the basement. Blankets to the laundry, then to the closet shelves, every bit of skin and hair rinsed clean.

I've scrubbed the *X* off the door. I've put the barrels and bags and other clutter back in the corners of the shed, and I've wiped everything clean, rubbing fingerprints and traces of anything else from door frames and stairs and walls and locks.

I've tied up other loose ends, too.

I went to the Crow's Nest yesterday afternoon. The place was quiet. Only two tables occupied, and both of them out on the patio, in the warming May air.

Janos was wiping down the steamer when I walked in.

His face brightened. It's nice to have someone's face brighten when they see you.

"Hey," he said. "Long time no see."

"Yes," I told him. "Crazy times."

"Crazy times," he repeated. He poured some fresh milk into one of the little metal pitchers. "You know what I think?"

"What?"

He ground some espresso into a filter cup and latched it into the machine. "Aliens."

I smiled. "Aliens?"

"Yes. A small town. Isolated. Surrounded by woods. The perfect place for abductions. And people have been seeing strange things out there. Lights in the trees. Fast-moving objects."

I couldn't tell if Janos was joking. From the way he looked at me, he might not have been sure, either.

"But at least they brought one back. That girl." Janos poured the espresso into a cup, followed by a rush of steamed milk.

"Maybe they're good aliens," I said.

"Like E.T.," he agreed.

He pushed a cappuccino across the counter toward me.

"Thank you." I reached into my pocket.

"No, no." Janos shook his head. "You didn't order that. So you don't pay for it."

I watched him for a second. He didn't relent, staring at me with one eyebrow up and both palms flat on the counter.

"Fine," I said at last. "Then thank you again."

I waited until he turned away. Then I put all the cash I had with me into the tip jar.

I sat at one of the small tables near the edge of the stage. Up close, bare and quiet, it looked strangely small. Just a little carpeted platform. All its fire and magic and energy gone. Anders gone.

I could never get this close to the stage when Last Things played. I had to stay on the edges, so I could keep watch over everything. Now I wished I could have been here, this close to the music, just once. I could almost bring it to life in my head: Anders, tall and sharp, standing right above me. The sound of his voice in my ears, reaching me a fraction of an instant before it rang out to the rest of the room.

I left my empty cup on the table and stepped back outside.

Flowers were just beginning to pop up in the dirt-filled

bathtub. There was sun in the pale blue sky. The grass was green and fresh, and the trees rustled with peaceful whispers.

Ike Lawrence strode across the parking lot, carrying a load of supplies from the back of his truck. He spotted me from a distance. Nodded.

I nodded back.

"Nice day," he said.

I smiled. Because it was.

Then he stepped through the kitchen door, and it swung shut behind him.

I'm going to miss that place.

"All packed?" Aunt Mae calls as I come down the stairs from the bedroom, my backpack over my arm.

Aunt Mae has been helpful, as much as I'll let her. But last week wore her out. I'd rather keep her on the couch, wrapped up in blankets, sipping her whiskey-tinted coffee.

I worry about how she'll do without me.

But she's lived without me before.

"All packed," I tell her, moving down the hall and into the living room. "Just one more outdoor job to do."

Aunt Mae holds out her arms. I go to her. She hugs me tight. She smells like talcum powder and whiskey and coffee and leaves.

"Bless you, sweet girl," she says, close to my ear. "You come back. Anytime."

"I will," I promise. "Whenever you call me. I will."

I step out the back door.

Anders's photo is in my hand, the one that hung on my bedroom wall. A box of matches waits in my pocket.

I burn the picture in the firepit.

I can't help but think of Anders himself burning. Anders holding his own hand in the fire, until all of the darkness was gone.

He's safe.

*Thank you,* I think. I let the thought rise up with the smoke, toward the gray-white sky high above. *Thank you. Thank you.*

"Hey," says a voice.

I turn.

And it's him.

He's standing at the edge of Aunt Mae's backyard. Just a few steps away.

I stand up. Slowly. As slowly as I can.

I would like this moment to last.

"Hello," I say.

Anders looks around. He's wearing jeans and a light black jacket. His bandaged hand sticks out of one sleeve.

"I can't talk to anyone," he says. He's speaking slowly. Deliberately. "I can't tell anyone about what happened. Nobody else remembers anything. No one would believe it. I can't really believe it myself."

"I know."

"Yeah. You know. You were there. You know it was real." He looks at me. "It was, wasn't it?"

I take a breath. "It was real."

He nods for a few seconds, like he's letting the words sink down and down. "There are demons in the world. They're real. There is darkness. And then—there's you."

I watch him. One scrap of hair flutters across his forehead, sweeping back and forth above his eyes.

"You said angels don't exist," he says. "But I saw you."

I don't answer.

He's seen me. Just like I've seen him. Like I've always been able to see him.

For a little while we both stand there, looking into each other.

"You told the truth," he says. "You really were just trying to protect me."

My heart moves. Lightens. "Yes."

He steps closer. I hear his boots crunch. "You saved me."

I shake my head at this, pointing at his hand. "You saved yourself."

He's quiet for a moment. So am I.

"Do they think you'll be able to play again someday?" I ask.

"The doctors?" He shrugs. "Maybe. Probably not. I'm not sure if I want to."

"You should," I say, without hesitating. "You're wonderful. Without anything from them."

He takes another step. He's looking at me in a strange way, like he's spotted something he recognizes but can't quite name down at the bottom of my eyes.

"I was wrong about you," he says softly. "I've been wrong about a lot. But with you—I don't know how I couldn't see it."

He's so close, I can smell him. I can feel his voice on my skin.

*This is not for you.*

But I want him to go on.

"See what?" I ask.

"What you really are."

He looks at me for another long moment.

Then, before I know what's about to happen, he leans forward and kisses me.

I'm almost as tall as he is, so I don't have to move, and he doesn't have to stoop. He just leans in until his lips meet mine. His eyes are partly closed. His eyelashes are so close I could count them. His skin brushes my skin. His cheek. His chin. His lips are warm and soft, with the roughness of shaved stubble surrounding them, making them seem even softer.

No one has ever kissed me before.

Maybe my mother, when I was small.

No one since.

I'm not ready for the way it shifts everything inside me. The thunder of my heart.

He hasn't put his hands on me. There's something shy, or polite, about the way he stands, like he doesn't feel like he should hold on. It's only our lips that touch. One bright, warm, living spot, with everything around it dissolving into nothing.

My eyes slide shut. In darkness, I feel everything. Every twitch of motion, every strand of his hair brushing softly against the side of my face. The way he catches his breath, like he's surprised by this, too. The warmth. The light.

And I know this isn't about attraction, or even about love. Not really. It's another thank-you, another apology, another question. It's him wondering what else could be real.

But this time, it can't be.

I pull back.

Anders's eyes flick open. He blinks at me, startled. And an instant later, ashamed. "Oh. God. I'm sorry."

"No," I blurt. "Don't be sorry. I—"

I want to tell him. I want to explain. I want to thank him for this moment of pretending that I am anything like him. But I am not. I am not meant for this.

Loving everyone means you can't love just one.

"I'm not supposed to," I finally say. "I'm not supposed to get too close to the ones I'm protecting. Or anyone else. It would get too . . . complicated."

"Oh," he says again. He takes a step backward. "I didn't even—I didn't know I was going to do that."

I smile. "So it was a surprise to both of us."

He smiles back. Grateful that I broke the tension. "Yeah."

We're quiet for a minute.

"Well," he says. "I should go. I just wanted to thank you."

"You're welcome."

He turns. His steps crackle in the leaves. "See you around."

"See you."

I watch him walk away. Around the house, back down the drive. I hear his car start. The sound of the engine drones and fades away into the woods.

I make one last check of the circle of stones, ringing Aunt Mae's house with protection. The circle is unbroken. Moss grows around the white rocks, soft and green. Here and there are tiny, starry flowers.

I slide my arms through the straps of the backpack. My father is down the river, a few days' ride away. I'll find him, or I'll find the next one who needs me. There's more to do. Always.

I climb onto the old blue bike.

And I'm gone.

# Acknowledgments

Last Things and I owe huge thanks to:

Universal Music Center of Red Wing, Minnesota, including founder Mike Arturi, instructor Mark Woerpel, and all the guitar students who let me lurk around their lessons and ask a thousand questions.

Phil Hansen, librarian/guitarist/metalhead/all-around awesome person, for giving this book an early and careful read.

My critique group: Anne Greenwood Brown, Lauren Peck, Connie Kingrey Anderson, Li Boyd, and Heather Anastasiu, for just the right mix of encouragement and evisceration.

My brother Dan, for being my go-to source for answers to odd medical questions.

The amazing Danielle Chiotti and the rest of the team at Upstart Crow Literary, for supporting this book from the very start.

My editor, Martha Mihalick, and everyone at Greenwillow, especially Lois Adams, Anne Dunn, Virginia Duncan, Bess Braswell, Audrey Diestelkamp, Gina Rizzo, and Haley George. This book and I are so unbelievably lucky to have you on our side.

Leo Nickolls and Paul Zakris, for this gorgeous cover.

A whole lot of bands: Opeth, In Flames, Trivium, DragonForce (Anders plays an Ibanez because of Herman Li), Chelsea Wolfe, Killswitch Engage, Mastodon, Type O Negative, Tool, Alaya, and Source. In my daydreams, Last Things sounds like a mixture of all of you.

My family, for the endless support and for all the babysitting.

And to Ryan—who, like this book, is all of my favorite things in one place.